Believer's Crossfire

Defending God's People

Stephen L. Thompson

Believer's Crossfire

Books by Stephen L. Thompson

The Crossfire Series

Colorado Crossfire
International Crossfire
Israeli Crossfire
Believer's Crossfire
Spirit Crossfire
Faith Crossfire
Chinese Crossfire
Texas Crossfire
Dark Crossfire
Island Crossfire
Jagged Crossfire
Violent Crossfire
Russian Crossfire
Nuclear Crossfire
End Times Crossfire
Revelation Crossfire
Gates of Hell Crossfire
Assassin's Crossfire
Albatross Crossfire
Global Crossfire
Far East Crossfire

The SFO Series

Station Force One - Onset

Believer's Crossfire

A fast growing "Temple" is dedicated to the total takeover of the United States. To rule they are threatening to destroy the world. The enemy of all mankind wants to use their threat for his purposes. The Crossfire Team is anointed by God to lead a global effort to prevent them from succeeding.

- Stephen L. Thompson

Believer's Crossfire

Published by
Stephen L. Thompson
Facebook.com/CrossfireNovelSeries

ISBN- 978-0-9850758-8-0

Published in the United States of America

Foreword

To my Christian readers –
The Crossfire series of action/adventure stories include depictions of violence which are unusual in Christian literature. It would be nice if there were no conflict or violence in our world. But we live in a time when evil is increasing instead of diminishing, when some men seem to be controlled by selfishness, madness, or evil forces. When the enemies of decent mankind are bent on subjugation of other men and women, righteous men and women must stand against evil. Please remember that the yoke of oppression is not lifted by prayer alone. God is our shepherd and we are his sheep. As long as there are wolves about, God will use some of us as sheep dogs to defend the rest of us. These stories are about people like that and the forces they fight against. The stories describe violence because it occurs in the real world and it is active in the lives of all people whether they recognize it or not.

To my non-Christian readers –
The Crossfire series include depictions of spiritual warfare and spiritual activity with which the non-Christian may not be familiar. These stories describe the realms and activities of both God and Satan because they are real and active in the lives of all people whether they recognize it or not.

Steve Thompson

CHAPTER ONE

Jack Malone thought it was nice to be home. He looked out the windows lining the airline terminal on both sides. The summer breezes blew down from the Rocky Mountains and across the runways at Denver International Airport as he and his wife, Laura, had exited the passenger ramp from their first class flight, a little after noon on Tuesday. The air conditioning in the terminal was pleasant and almost unnoticeable. The gusty breezes outside didn't affect them at all.

They were met near the baggage claim area by a young man in livery with a sign with the name of Jack's Company on it. Jack stopped by the man and asked, "I'm with Technology Alternatives. Who ordered your vehicle?"

Careful not to hit any of the people flooding by into the terminal, the driver lowered the sign and turned it over. Looking at the tag on the back of the sign he read off, "Bob Wexler, Technology Alternatives, and Littleton, Colorado". That was the correct answer.

They allowed the driver to retrieve their luggage and then walked out to the reserved parking place for the limousine. Under the airport canopy the shade was restful and pleasant even with the heat of the day. Jack noticed a slight smell and feel to the noon day atmosphere that triggered an old memory in his mind.

He had grown up and gone to college in the Rocky Mountains and knew the feel of the seasons. Although it was late summer and the air was still very warm, there was that subtle sensory feel that told of the coming winter that a long-time resident of the area could detect, mostly on a subconscious level. It was going to be cold at night soon. Jack stood at the open back door of the long white car while Laura waited patiently for him in the back seat. The sounds of the arrivals and departures and frequent jet engine noises vibrated around him. The view of the mountains and the expanse of the land east of Denver spread out all around. He didn't sense any trouble as he slowly looked around. "Yeah", he thought. "It was going to be an early winter this year". He ducked into the large plush compartment and the driver shut the massive door. Jack picked the middle rear seat in the spacious interior and settled back with Laura for a quiet ride to his plant in Southeast Denver.

Jack had left his car at his company several weeks earlier for a weekend flight to Chicago. He recalled that he and Laura had then embarked on a series of adventures that led up to their return today from Israel.

The driver looked at them in the mirror and Jack returned the look. The driver respectfully averted his eyes.

Jack's mind recalled that Laura said that he had intense gray-green eyes which dominated his face. He didn't know about that. He did know that at 175 pounds his six-foot, four-inch height gave him a slender and contemporary look. Jack ran his hand through his blondish hair.

The activities of the last few months had hardened his body, but he sat quietly relaxed, comfortably at peace with himself and the world around him.

He looked over at his wife. She was an attractive young woman who radiated both energy and class. Her honey-blonde hair was cut short to hide the damage a bullet had done to her hair style during their recent visit to Tel Aviv. For the flight home she had picked a simple, light blue-green outfit. Jack thought that the outfit was pretty and the color was very complimentary to her skin tone. Her jade-green eyes, normally full of humor had taken on a more mature and calculating quality, but her impish outlook on life hadn't been completely erased. Today she looked relaxed and her attitude sparkled with an inner joy. Jack could tell that she was glad to be getting home, thankfully with both of them still alive and intact.

As the limousine glided from the airport, the driver took the on-ramp that led to I-270 and then to I-225 southbound. Laura held Jack's hand and as she relaxed into the plush leather upholstery of the Cadillac stretch limo. As they exited I-225 to I-25 Southbound they crossed over to the middle lane and headed south towards Arapahoe Road. The traffic volume increased in the flood of people headed south out of downtown towards the southern suburbs and Colorado Springs.

Jack's attention snapped back to the road when a sudden lurch of the limo sent it into the right hand lane of the four-lane freeway. An older Chevrolet Monte Carlo with a smiling devil's face on a sun foil across the rear window had cut the limo off when the smaller car suddenly changed lanes. The limo driver took it all in stride, slowed down and smoothed out the ride again.

Jack hadn't liked the looks of the passenger in the car. He had his hair frozen in an ugly wave that resembled horns. He had at least six earrings in his right ear and the arm he had hanging down the outside of the passenger side of the car was covered in tattoos. He had glared at the limo driver from behind his black sunglasses and flipped him the one-finger salute as the Monte Carlo accelerated past and then away from the bigger vehicle.

Jack also noticed that the Monte Carlo had obscene markings on the car and hanging from the mirror. He studied the car and noticed it had tan and white Utah plates that stood out among the Colorado green and white Mountain motif on most of the cars on the highway. He watched the Chevrolet literally ride up on the rear bumper of the Toyota in front of them. The Toyota was a smaller sedan and couldn't stand up to the bumping of the bigger vehicle. There were three young people in the Toyota and the driver signaled and pulled over to the right lane to let the car full of obnoxious jerks get by. As the Toyota pulled over Jack noticed the sign of the fish on their trunk with the name of Jesus in it.

The Monte Carlo accelerated past the other car and then the driver suddenly slammed on the brakes and swerved to the right. The smaller sedan was forced up onto the shoulder and to a tire-smoking stop just behind the Monte Carlo.

Five black-clad teenage boys piled out of the Monte Carlo and surrounded the Toyota. Their intent was obvious. Jack picked up the intercom phone and told the driver to stop. Although it would not have been his first choice, the driver did as requested, bringing the big stretch to a stop a hundred and fifty feet from the other two cars. He immediately backed up and came to a halt a car length in front of the Monte Carlo. Jack had the back door open and by the time the car stopped, he was out of the door.

As Jack exited the limo he was praying. He prayed silently for the strength and ability to help the kids in the little car. As he tensed his muscles in preparation for battle he sensed a confidence concerning the coming action that went way beyond his normal confident feelings. Prayer made, prayer answered. "Thank you, Lord", he thought.

Jack raced past the Monte Carlo on the driver's side with only inches between his right arm and the traffic flying by in the right hand lane of the Southbound I-25 Interstate. He arrived at the rear end of the driver's side of the Monte Carlo so quickly no one had taken notice, so intent were they on their mayhem. The five punks had been smashing at the Toyota with a bat and some tire irons. They had smashed the windshield and broken out two of the side windows. They had gotten the doors open on both sides and were trying to pull the three kids out of the car.

Pulling on the driver, the closest punk had greasy hair in some form of dreadlocks with a bone tied into his topknot. He was skinny and had a terrible complexion with a case of acne that made his face look like it had been used as a dart board. He definitely identified himself as a Satan-worshiper by the symbols on his forehead and bare chest. Jack wondered what types of demons controlled this lost child. The punk with the dreadlocks, while surprised by Jack's unannounced appearance, let go of the driver and came toward the front of the Toyota. He grabbed for his back pocket and whipped out a switchblade. Slamming the Toyota's driver-side door to clear the way, he fisted the blade in his right hand and brought it up in a savage arc towards Jack's stomach.

To Jack, the punk's face suddenly changed into a horrible, dark-skinned mask with red, glaring eyes, a hooked nose, and a thin-lipped mouth with jagged teeth and definite fangs. The grimace on the excited face was cruel and menacing. Jack's mind was suddenly attacked by feelings of doubt, failure, and worthlessness.

A few months ago this would have been unexpected and hard to handle. But after the path the Lord had opened for Jack to walk since then, he was able to take it in stride. While he let his highly trained reflexes handle the physical warfare he used his mind to do the spiritual combat.

Because, that was exactly what was happening, the demon controlling the youth was attacking Jack on the spiritual plane while the youth was moving in the physical world. Jack rejected the feelings being impressed on him and stated clearly and aloud, "I rebuke you, spawn of Satan, in the name of Yahshua. You are bound on Earth and in Heaven by the name of Yahshua." The demon visibly shrank back and faded from view while vainly attempting to escape from the name of the Lord.

Knowing that these violent punks weren't going to listen to reason or common sense, Jack had come into the physical melee on the offensive. While he was renouncing the demon he used a Jui Jitsu front-hand block with the heel of his left hand and knocked the blade away to his right. His left front-hand block was strong enough that the switchblade flew out of the punk's right hand and imbedded itself in the side of a Mercedes Benz that was flying by at seventy miles an hour two feet away.

While he was completing the block he drove a crossover, full power palm-heel strike to the kid's chest with his right hand. Since he was moving forward Jack was able to use the entire force of his body in the palm-heel strike. The blow drove the punk backwards so hard his feet came up waist high. When his head slammed into the pavement, he hurried off into unconsciousness.

Everything had happened so quickly the other four attackers simply registered the fact that their friend dropped out of view and this tall stranger was among them before they could quit beating on the car in front of them. The four remaining teens were also dressed all in black and had a variety of body piercings and numerous vulgar tattoos everywhere one could see on their bodies. Jack wryly noticed that while they were violently anti-social in their behavior, they all dressed alike, sort of like a uniform.

The second of the attackers scurried around the front end of the little car swinging a tire iron to attack Jack. Jack made an X of his arms and caught the wrist swinging the bar as it described a downward arc. Rotating his body to the left, out of the way of the bar, he brought the tire iron down to the right with the punk's wrist trapped between his hands. Twisting the wrist with his right hand he took the tire iron away from the punk with his left hand. Jack then rapped the surprised kid in the forehead with his own tire iron. Semi-unconscious, the kid grabbed his head in both hands and slumped to the ground. Unfortunately he was too close to the front of the Toyota and slammed his chin on the hood. This additional assault to his head caused him to lose all interest in the fight.

As Jack rotated back towards the far side of the car the largest of the offenders pulled a handgun out of his belt. Stepping around the front end of the Toyota he pointed the gun at Jack's head and pulled the trigger.

Jack had a great deal of recent, well-reinforced, familiarity with handguns being pointed at him. Dropping quickly by flexing his knees caused the gun to go off above him. As he surged forward, he rose up, caught the barrel of the gun with his left hand, and twisted it back to the punk's right. The gun rotated neatly at the handle but the gunman's trigger finger shattered at the third knuckle as the trigger guard caught it and wouldn't let go. Jack yanked the gun away from the idiot not caring if the finger was still with it. Who knew where that first bullet went, it was fired directly into the traffic lanes of the Interstate highway just behind Jack. The punk ignored the damage to his hand and rushed Jack like he was going to push him into the traffic behind him.

Mad at this sudden introduction of deadly force, Jack didn't have a qualm as he stepped to his left and slammed the butt of the pistol into the right side of the punk's face, hard enough to shatter his cheek, break his jaw, and knock out a handful of teeth. The force of the blow caused the punk to stagger past Jack into the traffic lane. The muscular thug's shoulder got clipped by the mirror assembly on an eighteen-wheeler passing closely by in the right lane. The impact launched the kid over the Toyota's hood and slammed him headfirst into the back window of the Monte Carlo. Jack had a brief impression of cold hatred brushing his spirit as another demon detached itself as the body flew past him through the air.

Jack thought that it looked like the grinning devil's head on the rear window swallowed the top half of the teenager as he slammed through the glass.

Seeing the impact in his rear view mirror the driver of the eighteen-wheeler locked up his brakes. Smoke rolled from the tires as the truck lost speed, shuddering down from seventy miles per hour. The box of the eighteen wheeler started jack-knifing in a slide shutting down the two lanes to the left. This set off a chain reaction of tire-burning, braking, metal-smashing, and horn honking as the traffic in all three lanes suddenly attempted to avoid the slowing truck and each other.

Jack watched as an older pickup truck in the right hand lane locked up his brakes and slid onto the shoulder coming right at the back end of the Toyota. This all happened in a split second not leaving any time to react. Even though the pickup's speed was dropping, there was no way for him to stop before he hit the little car, which would then pin Jack between it and the Monte Carlo.

Twenty feet from the car, the pickup truck was broadsided by the back end of a Buick, which shot out backwards from between two trucks. It literally flew out of the mess to slam into the pickup truck. Both vehicles impacted the guard rail and the whole mess slid to a halt ten feet from where Jack was standing watching the impending collision. There had been nowhere to go so he just prayed quietly and waited to see what the Lord had in store for him.

After this last collision, the other two attackers figured out that they had more than they could handle in the guy in front of the Toyota let alone the sudden addition of dozens of other people exiting their vehicles all around them. They turned together and jumped the guard rail. Running to the barbed wire fence next to the roadside, they tried to jump it. They must have been rattled by the fight and the excitement. They finally got over the fence but left numerous pieces of clothing and themselves on the fence. Nursing their wounds, they glared back at the scene and took off limping away leaving a bloody trail behind them.

Jack turned and grabbed the sobbing punk with the bleeding head and his sleeping partner and dragged them over to the safe side of the Monte Carlo. He carefully dropped them and went back to the Toyota. As he walked back he scanned the cars involved in the accident. He didn't see anyone who needed help. Maybe the new accident victims were not in the best of moods, but physically, they didn't look seriously injured. They were all capable of climbing or crawling out of their cars and seeing if anyone else needed help.

Looking north he could see the traffic backing up from the accident as far as the eye could see. Between the eighteen-wheeler and all the other vehicles involved, all four lanes of the Southbound Interstate 25 were blocked like a cork in a bottle. Fortunately there hadn't been any fires that he could see.

Turning to the Toyota, he could see that there were two girls and a boy in the smashed little car, all teenagers. Jack looked in where the passenger window had been and asked, "Is everyone all right?"

Even though they were obviously very scared and each one had a myriad of small glass cuts, the girls nodded and opened the passenger door. They had managed to get it closed again as the attackers on their side lost interest while watching Jack eliminate their buddies. The young man got out of the driver's side and came around to where Jack and the girls were. He was also cut in a dozen places but didn't look seriously injured. He was very agitated and nervous, but he still managed to shake Jack's hand and say, "Thank God you showed up when you did". He looked at the crumpled attackers, in and around their car and shook his head. "They were going to kill us, you know."

Jack noticed that Laura had gotten out of the limo and was coming back to where he was. He looked at the young man, "What is your name?" he asked.

"Josh Doling," the young man answered.

As Laura reached Jack she gave him a hug. Putting his arm around his wife, Jack asked Josh, "Why were they attacking you and what makes you sure they were out to kill you?"

One of the girls entered the conversation. "Because we are Christians and they are Satanists." Answering both questions with one statement, she frowned and looked directly at Laura. "In our world that's all-out war on the spiritual level. This is the first time I've seen it turn physical."

Jack noticed a half a dozen helicopters circling above them and there were sirens coming from both directions, indicating that someone had called the police, "Probably more than one someone", he thought.

Laura looked at the young girl. "They definitely are made out like Satanists. Rather open about it aren't they?"

The young girl shook her head, "You're not that old but you really don't know what is going on, do you? The law allows them all kinds of freedom while labeling Christians RICO mobsters. These sleaze bags get away with almost anything they want to do in our world without being stopped by the law. If we complain at school or home we are labeled as troublemakers."

Laura asked, "What does RICO mean?"

Josh Doling spoke up. "It refers to the "Racketeer-Influenced and Corrupt Organizations Act of 1970." A previous U.S. Attorney General labeled Christians in general as a RICO organization."

Josh then looked at his battered car and shook his head. "They taunted us while they were beating on the car. They told us that they worshipped Satan and that he had called for our lives." The young man looked at Jack and Laura. "If you hadn't shown up when you did, they said that they were going to sacrifice all three of us to their god right here by the roadside." He walked over to the grass at the side of the road and kicked at a knife that was half-hidden by the grass. Jack walked over and looked at it. He felt the check in his spirit that told him the thing was connected to evil. He had no urge to touch it, much less pick it up.

It was an ugly thing with a blade that snaked back and forth with arcane markings on it. It also looked to have old dried blood on the blade. George continued, "That's their sacrificial knife. Their group is going to be really ticked when they find that they've lost it." He stared at the two girls and a silent message passed between them.

Jack saw that a Colorado Highway patrol cruiser had managed to work its way through the pileup and pulled up behind the combination Buick/Truck, behind the Toyota. It was one of the new high-speed pursuit Dodge Chargers with ground-effects foils. The trooper that got out, stood by the side of the cruiser with its flashing lights and talked on the radio for a minute and then threw the microphone into the cruiser and came over to the group standing by the Toyota. Jack wasn't sure that he had met a man with a flintier expression in his life. He silently sized up the people lying on the ground, stuck through the rear window, and arrayed around the Toyota. The trooper then decided to speak to the most involved adult. He stepped over and addressed Jack.

Later, Jack and Laura watched as the dozens of emergency vehicles performed their functions. Some of the EMS personnel extracted the cursing body out of the back window of the Chevrolet, patched up and transported all three of the wounded crazies with a police escort. After that the EMS had attended to the glass cuts on the girls and Josh

Doling. Jack saw the trooper finish his report, bag the bat, tire irons, and the knife as evidence.

Earlier, he had also officially arrested the three attackers for assault and battery with intent to commit grave bodily harm. The Toyota was towed off to a repair shop and the Monte Carlo to the impound lot. An APB had been issued for the two teens that had fled the scene. Jack offered to give the three bandaged kids a ride to one of their homes in the limousine.

After dropping the kids off and finally getting to his company, Jack had lost interest in working anymore that day. He checked in with the security officer and then he and Laura took his car and drove home to their almost new house in the southeast suburbs of Denver.

CHAPTER TWO

The second evening after their return, Laura had finally caught up on her backlog of mail, telephone messages, and house cleaning. In her mind the nesting was complete and she was entitled to a long bath and a good night's sleep. Jack was working late at the plant on the LifeCape project and thought that he'd be home around 1 to 2 a.m.

After she had finished her bath and dried off, she stopped and looked at her body in the full-length mirror by the tub. She could see nothing that needed immediate help or replacement. She smiled at herself when she thought, "All this action has gotten me into great shape. Oh well. If I am to be a warrior for God, I might as well look good doing it." She got dressed for bed and turned out the bathroom lights. She could hear the Bathbot in the bathroom doing what Jack invented it to do, automatically cleaning the tub and tile, in the dark.

Laying down she realized it was already after eleven p.m. She was too tired to read much tonight. She put the financial trade books she had been reading recently on the floor and took out her Bible. After reading for a while she prayed her thanks to the Lord for His Grace and His Love that protected both Jack and her. She continued to praise Yahshua and God's Holy Spirit as she drifted off to sleep.

Laura soon found herself in an extremely vivid dream. She was walking along a garden path through a beautiful and colorful flower garden. She could smell the flowers and feel the sun on her back and the push of the breeze on her hair and face. She was dressed in her nightgown and the smooth rocks of the walk felt good on her bare feet. She continued to move slowly and peacefully through the garden for what seemed like a long time when she sensed a presence behind her. She turned and beheld a wondrously beautiful image.

She saw a woman, or perhaps a man, it was hard to tell. The being floated above the ground about two feet, and seemed to be made of flowing light, mainly a fierce white with a tint of gold.

Knowing that Lucifer often masquerades as an angel of light, Laura knew she had to test the spirits as she had learned. "Spirit, who do you confess as your Lord and Master?" Laura heard herself ask.

The voice that came back to her in her dream was feminine yet powerful. "I confess The Lord Yahshua as my Lord and Master and as God on high." The being drew closer and a wave of peace with purpose enveloped Laura like a curler of surf at the beach. It was wonderful. Laura felt no fear or trepidation about this vision. Not all of her dreams had been so pleasant lately.

The being smiled and happiness sprung to life in Laura's spirit, which confirmed that this was an angel of God. The angel spoke. "Laura, God wants you to know that you will be the mother of great warriors for the Lord." Laura's heart rejoiced to hear those words as she had always wondered if she would have children and what they would be like.

"What is your name?" Laura asked the angel.

"I am called Rose." The angel answered in the dream. Laura smiled, "You are a woman then." The angel considered for a moment and then replied to her statement. "I am a creation of the Lord God. For us, sex has no fundamental meaning like it does here on Earth." This was not delivered in a condescending or superior way. The angel spoke. "I am filled with a sense of awe that a person could live in the flesh in a world cursed by Satan and still stand for God and His Will."

Rose continued, "We are all as God has made us and we glory in our service to Him alone." "But, I am more feminine in character than some others. My makeup seems to be more of the maternal and that is why I am glad to have been given the task to bring this message to you."

Laura nodded silently and answered the beautiful angel, "I thank you for the message. Can you tell me how long before I have children?"

The angel seemed to look right through her for a few seconds. Laura noticed that 'Rose' had darkened somewhat in color, with the gold overshadowing the fierce whiteness of the light that made up her being. Rose seemed to focus on her again and spoke. "Soon, but that's still years in your time frame. But that is not the entire message."

Rose seemed to draw closer in the dream and carefully studied Laura. Effortlessly floating around her she completed an inspection and smiled. The angel radiated a power that ebbed and flowed around her and within her. She held out her arms toward Laura and the power seemed to flow silently from the angel and surround Laura. Laura felt joy and the emotion flooded her entire being. She didn't know how long she stood there in heartfelt rapture. She certainly didn't want it to stop when it did.

The angel smiled at Laura and then her expression sobered. "God wants you to know that soon you will be involved in crucial spiritual warfare for His Kingdom."

Laura had doubts about her actual warrior capabilities. The angel sensed her doubt and seemed to grow larger and fiercer. The voice grew in volume and timbre. "Do not think that a woman cannot be a warrior. Yes, you are smaller in muscle, mass, and frame than a man, but your spirit embodies strength of purpose many men would envy. Remember, the battle is not won with your might or strength but by your faith and the spirit of the Lord. You will be fierce in battle, this I know. The Lord wants to assure you that you are more than capable of fulfilling His will in this matter if you will let your faith flare up like a strong flame within you." Laura felt those words burned within her heart and silently agreed with them.

The angel said, "All of God's saints are engaged in a spiritual battle. You find yourselves subject to Satan's attacks because you are no longer on Satan's side. Because you and your husband have humbled yourselves and surrendered your wills to the Lord, you have found favor in His sight. He has ordered your steps and will continue to use you as His hand on Earth. Because you have shown yourselves capable of doing His will in little things, He is giving you greater tasks. Very soon, the two of you together will face the enemy under the sternest of tests and each of you must stand firm in your faith in God and in each other if you are to win the battle."

Rose moved her hand and Laura felt a pressure on her body and looked down. She was encased in a flaming golden armor from her toes to the top of her head. She felt a weight on both arms and she saw a round, golden shield on her left arm. In her right hand was a solid metal sword that shone like polished chrome with a golden hilt. The sword blade gleamed and reflected light in all directions. She looked up in amazement at the angel. "Is this to be my armor for battle?"

"Yes, Laura, this is a special anointment of the armor of God that your life in Christ allows the Lord to supply to you".

Rose pointed at Laura's body. "This is the "Breastplate of Righteousness" because Satan often attacks your heart, which is the seat of your emotions, your self-worth, and your trust. God justifies all His children as righteous when they accept Yahshua as their Lord.

The angel pointed at Laura's waist. "The Belt of Truth is your knowledge of God's truth which you can use to defeat the lies of Satan. You stand firm in the truth and don't allow the evil one to make you believe his lies. God has given you all authority over the devil and his legions, to trample on them."

The shining hand then pointed downward. "This is the Footgear of readiness to spread the Good News of the Gospel". Then it pointed upward, "The Helmet of Salvation protects your mind when Satan attempts to make you doubt God.

Rose continued, "The Shield of Faith protects you from Satan's flaming arrows of insults, offenses, setbacks, and temptations. You know the truth as you pray, read His word, and listen to God."

"Lastly, the Sword of the Spirit, the Word of God. This is your only offensive weapon of God's armor in your spiritual war against Satan. Trust in the truth of God's Word."

"When the enemy approaches and the Holy Spirit within you rises to do battle, pray in the spirit and this armor will appear as a symbol of God's power to the righteous and unrighteous as you do battle with the forces of evil."

Rose seemed to refocus her attention to something Laura couldn't see. The angel nodded slowly, Rose seemed to almost lament as she reached a hand out to Laura, "And you are going to need it. The trials you face are going to be impossible to bear on your own. Look to God in all things."

As the angel and the garden began to fade away, Rose made a last statement. "Remember the armor, Laura, call on the Lord and never forget that He will never leave you or forsake you."

Laura woke up and sat up straight in bed. Looking at the clock she saw that it was only a few minutes after she had fallen asleep. She glanced down, checking to see if she was still in her armor and she wasn't. She quickly grabbed a pen and a pad and wrote down the whole dream in detail." She lay back down and thought about the dream.

"WOW! I'm going to be a mother. Wait until I tell Jack." She decided not to wait. Picking up the phone she called the digital phone her husband always carried with him.

By the time Jack answered she had reconsidered her words and realized that to blurt out that she was going to have children could be a little confusing and possibly embarrassing for him, depending on who he was with at the time. She heard him say "Hi honey." Then she told him that she had heard from God and wanted to tell him about it when he got home. He said that he was about wrapped up there anyway and would be home in about thirty minutes. She hung up the phone and smiling, she lay back in her bed and basked in the glow of her encounter with God in the form of one beautiful angel named Rose.

A half an hour later, when Jack got home, it was quiet around the house they had decided to call their own after losing their original home in a gangster's drive-by bombing attack, several weeks earlier.

As Jack left the detached garage and approached the house a floodlight came on and illuminated the entire area around him. At the same time a sign lit up in a niche in the stone wall on the right hand side of the path. The lettering on the sign read "Please identify yourself at this station. You are approaching a building defended by a NovaStar Defense System. This will be your only warning."

Jack spoke into the small microphone set into the panel. "Jack Malone". He had modified the programming so that his, or Laura's name, when spoken by them, gave them unlimited access to the active defense system. This system didn't just sound an alarm or call the authorities. It fought intruders very effectively, as he had seen it do not too long ago.

There was no appreciable delay. As he finished speaking, the floodlight went out, the path to the door was softly illuminated, and with a soft 'click' the door unlatched ahead of him. The panel lit up with the words, "Welcome home Jack Malone. Unlimited access is granted."

He walked to the front door and opened it. The front entry hall was elegantly styled and softly lit by indirect lighting that came on when he entered the hall. As he closed the door it locked automatically and the NovaStar system rearmed itself.

The soft blue-green carpeting was plush and the room smelled of furniture polish and flowers. It gave one a sense of security, which it was designed to do.

As he walked into the main living area the lighting there automatically came on and a small waterfall next to the ornate stone fireplace began to splash and gurgle. The light in the hall faded out after he left. The main living room was done in fine woods and textures.

Jack saw Laura sitting in the kitchen. The lighting in there was still indirect and gentle but when Jack went to use a counter, a cabinet, or the stove, more direct overhead lighting came on which allowed him to see exactly what he was doing in that area.

It was obvious that the interior design of the home had been done by someone with class and taste. Jack remembered thinking before that these were two qualities that seldom seemed to be applied at the same time. Everything from the furniture and fixtures to the tile and toilet paper was excellent quality and pleasing to the senses. Jack was pleased that a curious or careful person would notice that a great deal of attention had been paid to the scent of each area. There was a fruity/grainy smell in the kitchen and a floral scent in the bathrooms.

There was even a pleasant fresh air smell created by ion-generators in the main rooms. Jack had installed smaller ion generators in the master bedroom and three guest bedrooms but gave the room's occupant the choice to have them running or not. The ion generator added negative ions to the air of the room and provided a wonderful uplifting sense like one gets when smelling the air in the country, right after a summer rainstorm. The effect was subtle but it encouraged a positive frame of mind.

Over coffee, Laura told Jack about her vivid dream. And prophesy concerning their children. Jack sat there amazed. He was truly impressed and felt a whisper of jealousy or envy try to assert itself. He mentally burned that spirit up in the fire of the Holy Spirit and felt it replaced by a feeling of happiness for Laura. Jack asked her for details and together they speculated what the warnings meant in light of their recent activities. While Jack pondered her vision, he saw the kitchen time readout. This was a light blue-green digital readout about eight inches high in the wall above the sink. The numbers said 1:46 AM.

But, the urgency he felt in his spirit wouldn't be denied. He clasped hands with Laura and he prayed. "Dear most precious Yahveh, cleanse us with the blood of the lamb, Father. Forgive us our sins, for we are sinners and repent of our transgressions and sins against you. Father Yahveh, you created the universe and everything in it. We hold your Name above all names. You are a faithful and awesome God. Father, grant us wisdom to understand the vision you gave your daughter. Explain the meaning of the vision and what we should do with the knowledge." They both fell silent and listened with their hearts, resting before the Lord.

As Jack focused his mind on his metal image of Yahshua, he cleared his active thinking and went into a deep receive mode. He had learned to do this as a training exercise in his martial arts and found it crystallized his focus during his Kamete sessions, and before he competed. Since his born-again conversion he had found that it was helpful in focusing his mind to listen for the voice of the Lord. That still, small voice of truth. Most times he was led to read the word of God to determine the answer to his questions.

This time his mind formed a picture of Alan Throman, the elderly minister that had led them into the kingdom and baptized them in a dramatic sequence of events. Alan faded from his thoughts and it was replaced by a view of the home they were in. Suddenly, a giant spear flew through the air and penetrated the house and came out the other side. That was the extent of the images that he received.

As he thought about their old friend who had led them to Christ, Jack realized that there was nothing 'coincidental' in their being present at the attempted outrage on the highway. God doesn't bring you to events, nor have events come to you, without a reason. As he kept on praying, he concentrated on that incident, seeking God's direction. All he understood was that there was more to this "meeting" than met the normal, earthly eye and he needed to look into it more thoroughly than he had so far. Realizing he had placed his work on the LifeCape project before seeking the will of God was a form of idolatry, he felt a real remorse and mentally sought forgiveness for the error from a forgiving God.

Jack pulled his cell phone out of his shirt pocket and found the numbers for the Minister and the State Trooper that had investigated the fight scene. Bringing both numbers onto his "Tasks" list made sure he would remember to call them both in the morning.

He then turned to the idea of this house as a piñata. "Hon, the Lord gave me a warning about our vulnerability in this house. I know it has the view systems and the NovaStar system, but I don't know that it could withstand a serious attack. This place is like most homes with nothing but two-by-fours and siding between us and the world out there."

Laura prayed about the possibility of an attack against them inside the house. She was rewarded with an image of a giant spear going through the house. She looked up startled and said, "I just asked the Lord if we were vulnerable here and I saw a picture of a giant spear being run through the house. That is scary."

Jack smiled, "That was the same image I saw. Tell you what, I will get a team together and have them design a more secure home for us. Somehow I think we'll need it fairly soon." Laura nodded her agreement.

Standing, he suggested that they both try to get some sleep. Laura said that she was so keyed up that she might not be able to. Jack went and put his arms around her like a protective hen. "Honey, you've got to take care of yourself as a future pregnant woman."

Laura punched him in the stomach. "You watch your tongue, mister." She took his hand and headed out of the kitchen. "I'm not pregnant, yet, so stop acting like a father-to-be and start thinking about the other half of Rose's message. Considering what we just went through in Libya and Israel, I'm concerned about the "having done well with little", the Lord is going to give us more. I would think that a nuclear bomb and global poisoning was rather significant. What are we getting into now?"

Jack shook his head as they went up the stairs, "I don't know, but I'm going to trust the Lord to enlighten me."

In Heaven, Rose was praying for them. Seeing some of the future events facing them concerned her. The things they were heading into would make human leaders quail and want to hide their heads. These two people had to be up to the test. They just had to be. "Father, strengthen them now in their time of trial."

CHAPTER THREE

Jack walked down the corridor of the jail and looked at the inmates on the left and the right as they approached the cell holding two of the three young Satanists that had attacked the Christian teenagers on I-25 the day that he had returned from Israel.

Reaching the cell, the guard struck the bars with a nightstick, causing one of the two young men in the cell to jerk to his feet. "You've got a visitor." He then stepped away from the cell and stood in the middle of the corridor with his arms crossed, keeping an eye on the Satanists in the cell.

The standing boy had a bandage over a swelling on his forehead where Jack had applied the tire iron and a smaller one on his chin where he had hit the hood of the car. He looked at Jack without recognition for a few seconds and then fear flooded his eyes. He backed up against the wall of the cell as far away as he could from the tall man standing outside the door to the cell.

The other youth was still lying on his stomach on his cot. He glanced at Jack and grimaced. The shaved portion of the back of his head showed the swelling and stitches from his impact with the pavement. He almost growled as he said, "Get the *@!** away from us!" He then turned away from the cell door and ignored Jack. Jack said, "I just want to ask you a couple of questions and then I'll leave."

The one youth ignored him and the other one put his hand in front of his face and shook his head. Jack looked at the guard. The guard shook his head, "That's all you'll get from these dirt-bags. I can't let you in to have more of a heart-to-heart without losing my job and I don't think they want to talk."

Jack looked back at the two youths and silently prayed, "Father God in Heaven. These boys know what I need to understand and I pray that you will assign your angels to help them talk to me."

For a while the two in the cell didn't move or say anything and the guard was about to end the session when the punk against the wall seemed to change his mind and said, "I'm

Earl and if answering your questions will get rid of you, I'll do it."

At this point the other punk was pushing himself up by his arms to basically strangle Earl so he would not say anything. His left hand slipped and he fell back to the cot. Now, visibly upset and angry he threw himself up and back to get off the cot. He must have overdone it because he seemed to accelerate himself backwards against the cell wall. He slammed the back of his head against the wall, right on the welt he already had there. His eyes rolled up into his head and he fell back to the cot and was quiet.

Earl watched the antics of his cellmate as the other punk lost in his bid to attack him. He then walked several steps closer to Jack and asked in a rational and even courteous voice, "What do you want to know?"

Jack saw a rationality in Earl's eyes that was probably not there very frequently. He silently thanked the Lord for His help. He asked the most important question first. "Earl, who is the sponsor of your group in these attacks on the Christians?"

Earl looked thoughtful and glanced quickly at the unconscious youth and then at the jail guard. Looking back at Jack he whispered, "The Master Prophets."

"Who are the Prophets?" Jack knew he was learning something that was important from an extremely fragile source. He didn't want to waste any of his advantage while he had it.

Earl shook his head slowly from side to side. "I don't rightly know who they are, but I do know they have more money and power than anyone else. I also know that they have another bunch of guys that are meant to make sure we don't step out of line." He looked introspective for a few seconds and shook his head again. "Just like I'm doing right now... Man!" He looked up at Jack with a beginning of the fear showing in the whites of his eyes again. "Man, I have just killed myself." He became maudlin and started to moan slowly as he sank to the floor of the cell.

Jack squatted down to match Earl's level and spoke quietly. "Thank you for the information Earl. Remember. Jesus loves you and he can keep you safe from anything."

Earl looked up with something like hope, "Anything?"

Jack smiled, "Anything, all you have to do is ask Him."

The guard's radio beeped and he answered it. He then looked up at Jack. "Time's up." He took Jack's arm and hurried him on through the cell block and out the far door from the one they entered. After he shut the door, he put his finger to his lips in a signal for Jack to be silent and he gestured with his thumb for Jack to look back into the cell block through the small barred window in the door.

Jack looked and saw two young men coming down the corridor from the other end. They were dressed almost identically in dark suits with power ties and with white handkerchiefs positioned carefully in their breast pockets. Both were Caucasian and slender. They stopped at the same cell Jack had been at and spoke unheard words to the two people in the cell. Then they stood there until another guard came down with some paperwork. They signed the papers and the guard opened the cell door and Earl came out helping the other youth to walk down the corridor.

As they left Jack turned to the guard with a questioning look.

The guard checked the cell block and motioned Jack to come with him. He entered a small room and shut the door behind Jack. He switched off his radio and sat on the table. "Did you mean what you said to that kid, that Jesus can keep you safe from anything?"

When Jack nodded in the affirmative the guard continued, "Well, that boy had better make a friend of Jesus in a hurry, because he is going to need it."

"Why?"

The guard looked sincere as he said, "I'm risking my career to tell you this, but you're rubbing up against an ugly group that seems to have inside information on just about everything. They're not playing around and they will probably squish that boy like a bug now that they have him out of our custody. These guys are connected at all levels and have all sorts of politicians and judges in their pocket. They literally run many small city governments and they are rapidly becoming THE power in cities as big as Denver."

Jack was intrigued by this information. "Just who are we talking about here, the Communists?"

The guard smiled, "No, somebody much more organized than the Reds. You are interfering with the Omniscience

Temple, their enforcement arm, the Master Prophets, and their nationwide organization."

Jack thought for a few seconds. "Why are they interested in those satanic punks if they are a religious group?"

The guard looked incredulously at Jack. "You really don't know what's going on do you?" Jack realized that was the same comment the teenage girl had made at the fight on the highway. Maybe he didn't know what was going on.

The guard shook his head. "You look like a smart man and move like you can handle yourself, so I'll give you a little free advice. Those two "young men" in suits you saw are just the tiniest tip of the iceberg. They have an organization that has its claws into a lot of people in government around here and it's even worse to the west of Denver. The reason they were bailing out those punks is because they use the punks to do their dirty work. Plausible deniability is a wonderful thing if you're the one pulling the strings. The other guy takes the fall and you just find someone else to take their place."

Jack sat on the edge of the table in the little room and quizzed the guard. "Why don't the punks just blow them off and not deal with them?"

The guard softly laughed, "Because the Master Prophets own them after they make a deal and there is no going back on your agreement with them. The prophets will hunt them down and then no one hears from them again. It's the fear of death that keeps the punks in line. We don't have a clue how they do what they are doing and even if we, the police, did know how, some judge would make sure we lost our jobs for interfering with the prophets."

Jack knew he was out of his element here. He rose to his feet and thanked the guard. Pulling two hundred dollar bills out of his pocket, he handed them to the guard. Noticing the look on the guard's face Jack said, "Relax, this isn't a bribe, its payment for doing something for me. I want you to keep your eyes open for me on this specific issue." Jack took a business card out of his wallet and handed that to the guard. "Here is my phone number. If you discover anything that could give me more information on this "subject", give me a call. The picture you've given me is worth a lot more than you can realize. But, I'm going to need all the input I can get to stay ahead of these characters."

The guard pocketed the money but looked sideward at Jack for a minute. "You wouldn't be a reporter or anything are you? I sure don't want my name connected to anything about an expose of this matter."

Jack smiled a cold smile that made the guard start. "No, I'm not a reporter and I will keep where I got this information strictly to myself. You're safe but, you could still help me discover why the Master Prophets are having the Satanists attacking Christians in Denver."

Taking Jack's measure, the guard realized he was telling the truth. "Okay, you have a deal. Now I really have to get back to the job before someone starts to wonder what I'm doing."

Jack accompanied the guard back to the front of the jail and left quietly.

CHAPTER FOUR

The next day was clear and warm. The early fall warmth hadn't started to be absorbed and reflected by the miles of concrete and buildings that make up the extended community of Denver and its suburbs. Jack breathed deeply through his nose, sucking in the clean air of the region and letting it clear the semi-fog of exercise he had drifted into during his five-mile run. The run had started naturally enough but he had taken his stress out by pushing the envelope of his exercise regime in terms of time and distance covered.

He had been running flat out for the last six minutes and had covered the last mile and two hundred feet in near world-class time. He was in excellent physical condition and it showed in the ability to extend his normal exercise routine and reach for new heights of ability without being either completely worn out or totally out of breath.

As he was almost finished with his accelerated run he flew by a young woman and an older man fast enough to cause their clothes to flutter about them as he passed. He slowed to a trot to prevent sudden heart failure from a lack of need during a high supply period. He trotted about two blocks, one out and one back to where the two people stood watching him.

Jack greeted them cordially and shook hands with the older man. "How are you today, Alan?"

The Minister, Alan Throman, nodded his head as he greeted the athletic young man. "I'm fine, Jack. I'd like to introduce you to a nice lady that could help you with your interest." He motioned to the woman to his right. "This is Sheryl Cantor and she has a tremendous amount of education and experience related to comparative religions and specializes in the areas which with you are dealing.

Jack looked at a woman who was about forty years old but looked thirty, five foot, five inches tall, wearing color-coordinated slacks and a blazer outfit. She had obviously once been very blonde, but her hair had darkened as she had gotten older. Some blonde highlights from the sun mixed with a few gray hairs. She had an infectious smile and an upbeat attitude which was evident as she shook his hand.

Sheryl explained that she had been born and raised in Texas. Grew up in a small town and lived in the same house all her life, until recently.

As they walked towards his house, Jack asked her about herself. She explained that she had never had desire for wealth, power, or status. She smiled at the handsome young man walking beside her, "I'm perfectly satisfied buying used cars and shopping at a discount center."

As they entered the kitchen area of Jack's house, she took in the luxurious accommodations and continued with her description of her life. "When I'm not out researching religions, I teach at a Christian Elementary School. As a teacher I'm much more open with my students than a lot of teachers. I balance this with an expectation of mutual respect, cooperation, and order from my classes.

They respond very well, at least, the majority of them do. The kids tell me they appreciate being seen as a person and having someone really care about them. I get a lot of daily hugs, which surprised me at first, but little kids need love and support just like at home. I have lots of the older students talk to me about problems in their lives, and it's amazing what they deal with and more amazing that their parents don't have a clue."

Jack agreed with her and her assessment of the general chaos facing kids in all grades of school these days. He offered both her and the minister a cup of tea and had them sit at the table in the breakfast nook. He left for a short while so that he could clean up and put on dry clothing. He returned to find them happily discussing some of the children. He sat down and asked Sheryl to go on.

Sheryl continued with her general description. "I was shy as a kid, but definitely not since I've been an adult. Public speaking doesn't scare me a bit. I also like to talk to strangers at the grocery store and stuff like that. The teacher, or maybe it's the mother in me tends to pop out in public too; I've corrected other people's children when no parent was in sight, to control them when they were obviously getting out of control."

She took a drink and alluded to the information she was about to give him concerning the Believer's Temple. "I'm constantly busy. I don't even like to watch TV without something in my hands, like a crossword puzzle or some kind of needlecraft. But I'm certainly not a type-A personality or perfectionist. I'm more of a clutter queen, so many irons in the fire that I jump from one thing to another. But I know where everything is. I can go to the appropriate pile and find it when it's needed. At school, though, everyone thinks I'm amazingly organized." She gazed into the distance for a few seconds. "I guess I can be organized when it's needed. I like having my school binder, grade book, etc. organized so I can find anything immediately when I want it. This year I'm teaching challenged first-graders. They want to do so much and have such big hurtles to climb. It's a change from teenagers and I like the special attention you can give them."

She smiled a big smile as she touched on the things that she had a special interest in. "I'm much more careful with my yard than my house. I guess because yard work is like therapy for me. I love having everything beautifully trimmed and lots of flowers. I like your garden back there." She pointed out the back doors. "God comes through in the natural themes of nature so much easier than through the complications of mankind."

She finished up her description with, "I also eat when I'm stressed, Carbohydrates and sweets. A piece of pie and cup of coffee can cure just about anything. But, if it's really serious, you have to bring out the big guns: a hot fudge brownie sundae." She laughed and the men laughed with her.

Her honest revelation of her life and habits made the group feel like old friends. Jack responded with a more guarded version of his recent life.

"I don't know what Alan has told you about us. My wife, Laura, and I have been through some curious events lately. Some of these have been so different from our previous lives I'm not sure anyone could believe, let alone understand them. But I assure you that I am not the architect of my life, Christ is." He shook his head with a wry smile as he thought back over his recent history.

"Six months ago I was as far from doing God's work or even acknowledging Him or his involvement in our lives as anyone who is lost. It all seemed like foolishness to me then." He looked intently at Sheryl. "I want you to know that I am very serious about our commitment to the Lord and His plan for our lives. He has led my wife and I through things that would cause most people to simply curl up and withdraw from life. There is no doubt that the world here is in the hands of the enemy and his efforts are destroying people right and left."

Sheryl was nodding her agreement with Jack's assessment. "Minister Throman has given me some details of the events in Houston, Israel, and here in Denver and I have to admit they could only be understandable in terms of God's plan for us."

Jack nodded and looked at Alan. Alan stood up and said, "I think we need to pray for understanding and protection before we discuss the on-going problems both of you are researching."

Both Sheryl and Jack agreed and bowed their heads as Alan began praying.

CHAPTER FIVE

As Sheryl prepared her materials, Jack realized he had always liked this room. It was cool and quiet, lit by the morning sun streaming through windows that ran down one wall of the study. Outside the windows the garden was ablaze with early fall colors. The breeze moved the plants softly from side to side and the grass ruffled like waves on the sea. The entire garden area was tastefully decorated and provided a couple of park benches at strategic locations so that one could sit and enjoy the restful environment.

Inside the house the temperature was a cool 72 degrees Fahrenheit with just the right amount of humidly and a soft movement of air through the room. The sound proofing was sufficient to keep the outside noises from interfering in normal conversation.

Sheryl got out some books she had brought with her and set out to enlighten Jack about the ten-year old Omniscience Temple and their unique ruling class called the Master Prophets.

She looked at him for a few seconds and then smiled. "First, understand that we are just a couple of amateur investigators out of a loose knit organization based out of Omaha, Nebraska. We pool our findings with the others and they provide us with data gleaned from across the country concerning the Omniscience Temple. Out of the, approximately, three hundred thousand church members and hierarchy of the Omniscience Temple, the Master Prophets comprise only, again approximately, two thousand members. Three-fourths of these are called High Saints and do the majority of the church and daily work as directed by the Master Prophets."

She took a drink of her tea and set the cup down. "The Omniscience Temple itself is patterned after another well-known church, the Mormon Church. When I say "patterned after" I mean the founders of the Believer's Omniscience Temple studied the workings of the Mormon Church because they are very profitable in their operations. There is no connection or even the slightest relationship with anyone in the Mormon Church. The Believers feel that the Mormons are

29

as lost and decadent as the Christian churches. That dislike, nay, hatred of anything Christian alienates them from everyone else including anyone in the Mormon Church.

While the majority of the Omniscience Temple follows the dictates of the Master Prophets, they have no idea what they are doing. Alan Roswell used demon-powered magic, deception of the highest order, and standard cult rituals to create the temple itself and especially to form the Master Prophets. The top level of the Master Prophets are a dedicated group, and quite aggressive in recruiting members.

Roswell awed, embarrassed, intimidated, threatened, or eliminated everyone involved in the original temple to get the "authority" he needed to be "anointed" as the true founding father of the Omniscience Temple."

She got up and started pacing as she pulled her information together. Jack told her that she only needed to hit the highlights here, not do an in-depth study at this time. She looked up and smiled at them.

"Okay, I'll begin this overview of the "Omniscience Temple" by stating the obvious. Without a doubt, in the real world, the Omniscience Temple is a financial success and growing. They are very wealthy and demand a tithe from their parishioners that carries the penalty of ex-communication and quite possibly an early death, for failure to pay."

Sheryl sat down again. "The basis for their membership is their covering by the Omniscience Temple and promises that if you are a really good Temple believer and do everything the Temple tells you to do, you will get to go to heaven. Of course, this requires essentially worshiping the Temple and its leaders and especially their occasional prophets, at all levels, as well as that "other guy", you know, God."

"Jesus comes into their theology as a person of scorn. The whole theology of the Omniscience Temple has strong anti-Jewish, anti-Muslim, anti-Mormon, anti-Asian religions but, it is violently anti-Christian. I believe that is because they see Jesus as competition and they have to be better than he is in the eyes of their followers.

They are very good at plausible deniability, but are known, or thought to be behind the great majority of attacks on Christians, Christian Churches, hundreds of abductions, and ritual mutilation slayings. Even though they are acting as the power of Satan on earth, they put up a good smoke screen. If you don't study them closely you won't see that they are doing everything they can to discredit Jesus and at the same time blame it all on the Christians. The disgusting thing is that they are swaying the people who are weak in faith and are looking for a quick "fix" to solve their dilemma of how to get to heaven and still go on sinning. They are also infiltrating themselves into every level of American government to get legislation passed to ban Christians and their activities everywhere around the world. I don't have to tell you what legal group supports them, do I?" Jack shook his head, the four-letter acronym of the leading advocates of anything against God was well known.

"They demand that their youth proselytize locally for five years and require each good member to bring in at least five new members in a five-year period. If they don't, then they have to pay an equivalent in tithe money for their missing members. Each member is "responsible" for the financial income of the new members they are recruiting. If they go two years without persuading some people to join the "Temple", or if existing members they have recruited leave the temple for any reason except death, they have to pay that person's tithe for the next five years. I guess it is fortunate for their recruiters that almost nobody leaves the temple except by the way of death."

She smiled at the two men. "And they are diligent workers, these Jesus-haters. Oh yes, very diligent and well trained to recruit new members. Of course their arguments fall apart if you know the Scriptures, but they counter the truth by referring to their own books, the 'Omniscience Bible' and other contrived literature. I've read them and they closely imitate real Scripture, but twist and warp it to favor the Omniscience Temple heresy."

Shaking her head she plowed on. "The Omniscience Bible" was handed to Alan Roswell by an angel. This event was seen by hundreds of people and videotaped. I've seen the tape. It's obvious that he set the whole thing up. He was holding a 'special' service on a Monday at noon. There is a clap of thunder which makes most of the congregation duck and cover. The air in the middle of the church sort of splits open and a bright light floods out of it. This angel appears out of the light and floats down to the podium. The only one still on it is Alan Roswell. An acolyte tries to come onto the platform and the 'angel' puts out a hand and the kid falls backwards off the platform to be caught by the crowd. The angel then announces in a very loud voice that Alan Roswell is the founder of the true Omniscience Temple and their purpose is to punish the lies of Jesus and the Christians. It then hands him the book and floats back up into the split and disappears. The rift in the air closes with a bang and everybody stands there in shock looking at their high Prophet Alan Roswell. The last words on the tape are his asking the congregation, "You know what you need to do, are you willing to do it?"

Jack wrinkled his brow. "That sounds like a supernatural event. Was it an angel or not?"

Sheryl laughed. "Oh, it was an angel all right, but, whose angel? Remember, Satan can appear as an angel of light if he wants to. He was the brightest one in heaven at one time." Sheryl shook her head. "If you want to test a spirit, you judge it by the fruits its appearance generates."

Alan Throman concurred with her. "Over time, all false as well as true spirits can be identified by the results of their visits. Remember, even though Satan can appear as a bright angel, his beautiful offers and apparent miracles always have the seed of death in them. He is the father of lies and he always destroys all those that serve him when they are no longer useful. Also, keep in mind that spiritual beings, such as angels, don't appear on video tape or are captured by cameras."

Jack thought back to the basement in Castle Rock, Colorado and could still hear the pitiful screams of Don Miland as the demon took him. An involuntary shiver went down his back. "What were the observable fruits of this visit?"

Sheryl made a frown and consulted her book. "The young man who tried to get onto the platform died. The Temple the angel's visit founded has systematically attacked and destroyed Christians wherever they can. It isn't a personal thing. The Believer's Church demands "signs" of their faith in the acts they do against Christians. The Omniscience Bible, supposedly came directly from the hand of God, right? Kind of strange when it is supposed to be the inerrant word of God, that they've made wholesale changes in the last five years. Add to that the fact that this "angel" denounced Jesus. It also inspired believers to attack anything Christian as an antithesis to their basic beliefs. This "fruit" sounds absolutely demonic to me."

Even though he was convinced that this "Temple" was based on Satan, Jack asked her, "What did you mean when you said that they were also based on cult rituals?"

She opened one of her books and read him a passage. "Alan Roswell's father was a senior Workman's Lodge member and I believe they conspired to use the "secret" lodge rites and rituals as "secret" temple rituals. Do you know that the top levels of the Workman's lodge directly worship Satan? The other, lower, members think they are just in a good ole' boys club with secret passwords and rituals. They don't realize they are bonding themselves to demons every time they swear allegiance to the lodge."

Jack shook his head at that. The Minister sat quietly listening to the discourse, nodding his head, but without comment.

Sheryl brought out another book and detailed some of the ways that the Omniscience Temple enticed and lured naive or unsuspecting people into their organization. They held elaborate friendship parties at member's houses. Now, if you decided not to join the church or refused to revile Jesus, at that point the party ended and the invitations ceased. Unlike Christians who are instructed to "love thy neighbor as thyself", the Omniscience Temple congregants love everyone that they can turn against Jesus or that join the Omniscience Temple. Of course apostates or non-Believers are not going to be allowed into heaven and therefore should not be associated with, if they weren't being cooperative."

Sheryl took another sip of tea. "Once the initiate has accepted membership in the Omniscience Temple, they are indoctrinated in anti-Christian thought and behavior. Any acts against Christians or the Christian Church are seen as a holy act, similar to the terrorist attacks on Jews in Israel. The more damaging and lethal the act the more blessed the member will be in the Omniscience Temple's heaven. Oh, they feel the same way about Hindus, Buddhist, Jews, Muslims, and Mormons, too. We believe that once they've achieved their diabolical designs concerning the Christians, they'll start the same treatment of the other religions."

Sheryl opened the first book again and read Jack a short passage about the true goal of the Master Prophets. The goal was complete authority over the world, but first, the United States and the induction of everyone into the Temple. They would then run the world the right way, "With their Master's viewpoint". They use all the good words and look very pious but the main tenet they are taught is hatred of anybody that is not them, especially Christians. This is one of their main reasons for attempting to bring in new members. They don't want them to remain "ignorant" of their chance to be saved to the "new" Lord of the Omniscience Temple."

Sheryl added a great deal of detail to her description of the Temple and the Master Prophet's efforts in its five years of existence to control larger and larger portions of the population. Jack realized that many of the things she related sounded just like the tactics employed by the Mob or terrorists anywhere."

Sheryl got up and stretched. Pacing back and forth she concentrated on her next comments as they were the most critical. "The majority of the Omniscience Temple is made up of members who, "honesty believe", that they are on the right path and that we, not they, are the ones being misled. But, they are only a minor part of your problem."

She looked grim, "The Master Prophets started as an action committee that grew slowly and simply issued mandates and called for action for the first three years. This had little or no effect on temple members or the Christians. Then, Alan Roswell assumed the control of the Master Prophets and their activities. Within two years the number of the Temple members sworn to faithfully obey and serve only the Master Prophets tripled."

She looked questioningly at Jack. "The working faithful of the Master Prophets at the higher levels have attitudes similar to the zealots of Hitler's SS troops, 'Extreme Dislike', for anybody not agreeing with them or their take on life. The rising levels of cruelty and violence which originally drove off the moderate and conservative members, allowed Roswell to isolate the group from the main body which, by the way, actively pray to Roswell as a god. We've discovered that the membership of the Master Prophets use their solutions on their own members. Two years ago, Randall Altman disappeared and Alan Roswell assumed his place as the head of the Master Prophets. Since then they've been working on a massive secret project. We're not sure what he has in mind but we have heard a rumor that he promised the membership of the temple that by the end of this year, everyone in the world would be clamoring to become members of the Omniscience Temple." She sat down, fussed with her books and got up to pace again.

"Forget about the majority of the Omniscience Temple. They have been deceived and misguided by an end-times false Messiah. Altman had arranged an unlimited amount of financing, not all of it from the Temple either, before he disappeared. Roswell has been consolidating his control on both domestic and even some international governments while the Master Prophets do ... something."

She raised her hands in confusion. "What he is doing doesn't seem to make sense. Our national group has amassed a great deal of evidence and proof that he has personally directed efforts having people kidnapped and, we think, tortured and probably killed, both within and outside the temple. They tolerate no interference in their affairs and have no compulsion in beating people to death that stick their noses in where they don't belong. I personally know of three people, not in their temple, but normal Christians that crossed swords with the Master Prophets and disappeared. One of them turned up dead and mutilated. Her heart had been cut out of her body. It is so inhumanly evil."

She was getting upset and to give her a break, Jack got up and offered to make her some more tea.

After drinking the tea she composed herself and finished her lecture for the two men. "We've heard from frightened Omniscience Temple members that nobody messes with the Master Prophets. On the surface it is because they are about God's work and should not be bothered. Actually, most people are afraid of them, and for good reason. We know that Alan Roswell has spent over two billion dollars overseas in the last six months. Apparently, to complete the financing of the secret project that he started two years ago. "

She looked concerned for Jack. "Be wary of these people. Their general membership is violently anti-Christian and they don't even hold a candle to the Master Prophets, especially their higher-ups. Beyond the "angel" sighting, they exhibit almost supernatural knowledge and power. It is reported that one of the men, a Joseph Malen, actually walked through a solid wall when he was blocked from leaving through the door.

They have healings in their churches, 'Wonderful, Miraculous Healings'. But, if the person doesn't live up to the Omniscience Temple's creed they lose their healings." She looked directly at Jack. "Things like that require power from the supernatural and there are only two sources of that type of power. I personally don't believe it was from the loving God I know.

Then she sat back and asked if there were any questions she could try to answer.

The Minister asked her how she had managed to do all the local research when she taught school and had such a busy schedule herself. Sheryl shook her head, "No, I could never have done all this by myself. I've relied on the information in some of these books and, to be honest, I've relied even more heavily on the work of Jenny Samuels. She is a bright young woman, a friend of mine for the last nine years. Because of my schedule she has done most of the leg-work and local investigation for me concerning the Master Prophets and, this disturbing new use of the young Satanists in the Western U.S." She stopped and looked at her watch. "I expected Jenny to call me here by now. I don't have any voice mails either.

After Jack said goodbye, and the two people left, he sat down and mentally reviewed the information that he had been given. In summation, he now knew that the cult that made up the Omniscience Temple was violently aggressive and a major problem for all Christians, Jews, and Muslims. He was quite sure that the majority of their members were just trying to fill that 'God-shaped' hole in their soul and had been deceived. They mistakenly thought they were doing God's work and living for Him. It wasn't the first time in history that people had been deceived into believing they were serving God while in truth they were serving a different master. The Master Prophets on the other hand sounded like a cancerous entity that needed to be eliminated. The leading Jack felt was that God wanted him to focus on the worst case.

Laura came home and they made dinner together. After discussing the events of the day Jack described his efforts on their new home. "I have assembled a great team which includes two of the designers of the Abrams tank. They have some radical ideas and have taken to the view system and the

NovaStar defense system with glee. I think this house is going to be very expensive."

Laura said that all the money was God's anyway and He had told them to do this. She smiled, "It'll be worth it, I'm sure."

Jack decided to read his Bible and seek the Lord on the meaning of the partnership between the Satanists and the Prophets. He was reading a few minutes later when the phone rang and he picked up the receiver on the desk next to him.

Sheryl Cantor's concerned voice was audible in the background as Alan Throman told Jack that Jenny Samuels, the assistant to Sheryl, was missing and Sheryl believed that there was foul play involved.

Jenny had left Sheryl a voice message that she was going to meet with an Omniscience Temple inside informant to get some direct news concerning the recent Satanists operations in the Denver area. She had not been heard from for the last six hours and her house was dark. Sheryl drove by the address Jenny was supposed to be at and saw her car being towed away by some people she knew to be part of the Master Prophets.

As they were talking, Jack felt the familiar tugging of the Holy Spirit's leading. He responded to the elderly Minister. "I think I agree with her, something has happened to her friend and somehow I doubt that the police are going to help much." He was presuming a great deal when someone's life might be on the line but Jack knew the urgings of God fairly well by now. "Finding her is something we will have to do by ourselves in the strength of Christ."

After he had hung up, Jack told Laura what was happening and they pondered what to do. Laura asked, "What do you think Mark and Sarah would do?" Laura looked at her husband, "Do you think we could ask them to break away from their trip to Russia to help us?"

Jack shrugged. He felt inadequate to the job at hand and realized just how much he had relied on Mark's experience and knowledge in the past. "We'll give it a try. We can do whatever we can until Mark and Sarah can get here, if they can get away. It would sure be good to have them with us." Jack and Laura prayed an earnest but short prayer to the God of the Universe that He would help get their friends to Denver.

Jack consulted his cell phone for an international telephone number for Mark Connelly, working somewhere in Russia as an anti-terrorist consultant, with his new wife of less than a week, Sarah Connelly nee Cohen. As he waited for the connection to be made he smiled over the phone at his wife. "I'm sure he will try to break off the job to help us, but I'm not sure he'll want to shorten their honeymoon."

Laura laughed at that. "How long would it take them to get here?"

Jack said, "I don't know, they aren't answering... the?" He broke off as the front door bell interrupted him.

Laura went to the door and opened it. There, standing on their front porch were their friends, Mark and Sarah Connelly.

CHAPTER SIX

After hugs and handshakes, everyone gathered in the kitchen. Mark was smiling a large smile and had his arm around Sarah. She was quietly grinning, too.

Laura looked at the two people who had become their best friends over the last several months and asked, "Okay, what are you two "honeymooners" doing here at our house instead of hard at work in cold Russia?"

Sarah smiled, stepped away from her husband and bent at the waist and held her hand out to Mark, indicating that he got the opportunity to explain their sudden appearance in Denver.

Mark shook his head. "Well, it seems our Russian friends weren't as forthright with their information concerning their need for my company's security capabilities as we hoped they would be. Anyway, by the time we got there the political situation had changed hands three times and the new "managers" did not want our services. They told us to leave Russia immediately, and stubbornly would not talk about any money changing hands regardless how I tried to bring it up. They said the people who signed it were no longer in charge and the contract was null and void. They insisted that money not be mentioned and that we were to leave immediately. They then escorted us to the airport and sent us back to Israel."

Sarah shook her head. "The newly installed idiots didn't take the time to learn that Mark doesn't work for unstable governments without his full fee up front. The hard currency they weren't going to pay us was already in the bank here in the U.S. So we got a one hundred and fifty-thousand dollar, all-expenses paid honeymoon, courtesy of the bankrupt Russian economy."

Jack wrinkled his forehead with concern. "If they shipped you right back, how come it took you five days to get here?"

Mark grabbed his wife and pulled her to him. He kissed Sarah on the back of the neck. "We're newlyweds remember?"

Laura smiled at that. Then she got serious. "Well, we all know that there are no coincidences with God and you could not have showed up at a better time."

Mark smiled and rubbed his hands together. "That's what I like about you guys, always a crisis. What is it this time? Aliens taking over the citizens or has Godzilla decided to eat Denver?"

Jack smiled back at his friend. "Well, how about a radical sub-group, within a three hundred thousand member church-like Temple. The sub-group, at least one of which has demonstrated supernatural abilities, has in their employ a group of teenage Satanists. We suspect this group may have kidnapped a young Christian woman and she could be in great danger."

Sarah tipped her head to one side. "That sounds like a challenge. What do we know about this?" As usual she reverted back to her Mossad training and characteristics, straight to the point and lethal while she was at it.

Jack and Laura brought their friends up to speed on the little that they did know and then called Alan Throman for any additional help he could provide. While he did not have a great deal of more information he did have a gem. The address of the appointment that Jenny had gone off to that morning, and the name of the person she was going to see.

Jack relayed the information to the others. Mark went out to the porch and brought in their luggage. He opened up the travel case and pulled out some dark clothes and a pair of Para-ordinance P10-45 automatics. Laura looked at that and said, "Here we go again." Then she walked over to the front closet and brought back a matching set of guns and black clothes to the table for Jack and herself. She looked around at her house and realized that if the truth be known, she no longer wanted to be just a housewife anyway.

Mark commented as they were gearing up, "At least this time we don't need to involve the President."

Laura looked at Jack and said, "If what Rose said is happening, I'm not so sure that is a valid statement."

Using Jack's new SUV, the team headed for the local headquarters building of the Master Prophets. As they rode along with Jack and Mark up front, the women were in the back seats bringing each other up to speed on the happenings in their lives, since they had parted eight days, ago in Israel, after Sarah and Mark's wedding.

Mark looked at the various systems that Jack had in his new vehicle and then turned to stare at Jack for a moment. "You're sort of getting into this stuff aren't you?"

Jack looked at Mark after he maneuvered around a corner, "What do you mean?"

Mark indicated the heads-up night vision system displayed on the windshield. "I don't think the normal Cadillac has auto-ranging indicators or distance to target call outs. I also don't think the computer detection of incoming objects with range finders and chaff dispensers is in the normal parts brochure either. I especially like the multi-band, police, and satellite communications equipment with the hands free feature and the NOS emergency power system."

Jack laughed. "Okay, so this nitrous-oxide powered wagon was ordered by the CIA. The president thought it was a good idea and a small compensation for our efforts in Israel."

Mark smiled. "It's a good thing I'm not a jealous guy. I thought I was the only one with one of these."

Sarah piped up from the back, "What, they got one too?" Everybody laughed at that.

They sobered up as they approached the target building. Well lit, obviously guarded, and rather imposing. Leaving the SUV several blocks away, they carefully worked their way to the bushes just outside the back of the main tower.

Surveying the building in the darkness, Jack prayed that God's Holy Spirit would lead them to the right place and protect them in the process. Being led by an intuition he was just beginning to fully trust, Jack made the decision to keep the team together on the raid rather than leave someone on guard outside where they might be seen. As they avoided the floodlit parts of the grass and raced to the wall of the building, they heard voices. Sliding down to a sitting position behind the bushes at the base of the building to minimize their profiles, the two men and two women watched two guards with automatic weapons walk past them on the sidewalk not four feet away.

After the guards were gone, they crept carefully over to a doorway set into the side of the building. On a hunch, Mark reached up and turned the door handle. It smoothly rotated and the door opened with a soft 'click'. Waiting a few seconds to see if there was any alarm the team slid through the door and into the building. They found themselves on a concrete stairwell leading up the inside of the building for six floors. Jack saw something attached to the wall and examined it. It was a small monitor screen for service personnel. It was illuminated with a simple directory of the building. It took only a second to find the name and room number of the person Jenny was supposed to see, "Fourth floor, room 408, Mary Kimball".

As the four of them silently climbed the stairs, Sarah giggled and whispered to Mark, "Honey, do you think when we have kids that we can take them with us on these little excursions?"

Jack could see Mark slowly shaking his head side to side as if to say, "What have I started here?"

After they reached the fourth floor, Jack moved to open the hall door. Mark suddenly stopped him. The stairwell was cool, dark, and dry. The cinder-block construction reflected little sounds like a sounding board. Jack could feel the cool air on his neck as the hair there stood up with the tension of their endeavors. He had been mentally prepared to fight or flee as he began to open the metal door. Mark's hissed words had stopped him in his tracks.

Jack slowly removed his hand from the door handle and in the dim light of his small flashlight he gave Mark a questioning look.

The resident expert in breaking and entering hostile buildings, moved closer to Jack and the women. He whispered, "I saw the logo of the electronics group that installed the automated systems in this building. I've come up against them before. If they are still doing the same thing, then all of the light systems in this building are keyed to automatic infrared sensors in all the rooms and hallways. If you open the door it will cause the detector to turn on the hall lights. I suspect that it will also trigger an alert in their security center, since no one is supposed to be here at this time of night." His quiet words softly echoed back and forth in the stairwell

Jack whispered back, "Great. What do we do to get around it?"

Reviewing his experiences and his training, Mark thought for a few seconds. "If we disable the power, they probably have backups and will know something is up. If we cause a distraction, again, they will know something is up. We don't have the time to cause a pattern of false alarms before a roving guard finds us." He had no more than spoken the words then they heard a door open into the landing above them. Light flowed into the stairwell from the floor above, and someone started descending the stairs.

Silently in the dark all four of the team moved fluidly down to the next floor and waited to see if the person coming down the stairs would keep coming. The steps stopped at the landing they had been on and they heard the door to the hall being opened. More light entered the stairwell. The light faded somewhat as the door closed and they swarmed back up the stairs as quietly as possible and looked through the, now brightly lit, window in the door. The back of a security guard was disappearing down the hall to their left.

Mark looked at Jack with a crooked grin and eased the door open as the guard went around the corner of the building to his right. Jack sent a wordless prayer of thanks to God for making a way and all three of them followed Mark into the hall and to their right.

The soft carpeting in the hall was a big change from the concrete of the stairwell. Silent footfalls disappeared from the senses like ripples in the water. Finding the door they wanted to room 408, Mark took a blank piece of paper and shoved it halfway under the door. Then, they all retreated to the stairs and waited. A few minutes later the guard appeared to their right having completed his round of the floor. As he walked by the target office he noticed the paper. Keying his radio he talked to the security office and then pulled the piece of paper out and looked at it. Not finding anything on it he used his passkey and opened the office door. After looking around he relocked the office and went back to the stairs. He keyed his radio again as he descended to the next floor and disappeared through the door to the next lower hall.

Jack, Mark, Sarah, and Laura quietly stepped back down the stairs from the upstairs landing and into the hall that had just been checked. Moving to the door they defeated the lock and entered quickly. Mark looked at Jack and held up four fingers. Four minutes before the lights were supposed to cycle off. The security office would probably notice the office lights if they stayed on for longer than normal since they had already had a call on that office tonight. Also, the lights in the hall would go out and when they left they would be detected again.

Mark was an expert at tossing offices for incriminating information and knew what to look for in this one, automatically. He ignored the fancy desk and the large desktop computer system sitting on it. After quickly scanning the office he moved to the credenza behind the desk and carefully checked the surfaces of the imitation wood veneer on the drawers. Finding the one with the most wear he used a small meter to check for currents or live switches connected to the drawer. Getting down on his knees he checked the drawer from below and the rear of the credenza. Satisfied that they weren't about to announce their presence to the entire world, he carefully slid the drawer open. Inside he found a small ZIP-brand disk drive and four removable media. Picking the discs up, he slid them into a pocket of his night suit and closed the drawer. Everyone quickly exited the office and Mark relocked the door. Quietly racing back to the stairwell they shut the door to the hall and waited. About a minute later the lights went out in the hall. Looking back into the hall they could see that the lights in that office were already out.

Carefully working their way down the stairwell, watching for the roving guard they reached the door that they had originally gained access to the stairwell. Trying the door Mark found it locked. Taking out his meter and checking, he found live currents at the top and lock sections of the door. Turning to Jack he shook his head. They were in the bottom of the stairwell and couldn't get out. They heard a door open above them and then the stairwell was flooded with light from the recessed lighting fixtures.

Knowing they had been detected somehow, Mark took his Cold Steel Tanto combat knife and pried the lock open on the door to the outside. Opening the door a crack he saw three more guards outside waiting for them. They were trapped between the guards coming down the stairs and the ones waiting outside.

While they were all armed, Jack was against shooting or killing the guards to affect their escape. Looking up he saw the metal beams supporting the floor of the landing above them. He looked at Mark and pointed. He then braced himself between the outside wall and the other wall of the small landing they were in and using his feet and shoulders he 'walked' himself up to the beams. Grabbing two beams he swung his legs up and caught the beams with his feet. He then pulled himself up into the darkness between the beams.

Catching onto Jack's strategy, Mark quickly made a cup out of his hands and Sarah stepped up into them and he did a dead lift. This effectively raised Sarah up far enough for Jack to grab her wrists and pull her up to the beams. She quickly faded from view and they repeated the operation for Laura. Mark then followed Jack's example. Bracing himself with his feet and one arm he reached out and caught the top of the exterior door and pulled on it. As it opened the bright light from the outside poured in and lit up the landing. The area the four were in stayed dark because the top of the door limited the spread of the light upward.

Suddenly, one of the guards on the landing above saw the light. "They're going out!" A sudden pounding of feet on the stairs heralded the arrival of four armed guards. Partially blinded by the light from the outside, three of the guards, not seeing anyone in the landing, rushed outside and looked around. The fourth guard moved the door and looked behind it. Finding nothing he looked around and finally looked up. Everyone froze in position. Jack's Ninja training told him that the guard, not expecting to find them there, did not see them there. The combination of the light from outside and the black nylon night suits blending into the dark between the beams, fooled the guard into seeing what he assumed he would see, "nothing". He stepped to the door and watched the guards from the outside loudly denying that anyone had come out of the door until the guards themselves came out.

Knowing they would eventually be discovered, Mark swung down from the beams and used his feet and legs to slam the fourth guard outside the door. Dropping to the floor he slammed the door and pulled up on the handle violently, breaking the lock mechanism. Jack dropped down to the floor, and then caught Laura and Sarah as they dropped. Together they ran back up the stairs to the next level. They could hear the sirens going off inside the building and the guards banging on the locked door below them. Jack had an idea. First. he opened the door to the second floor and jumped into the hall. The lights flared on just as he jumped back and re-entered the stairwell. He then took off running up the stairs with the other three people following closely.

During their recon of the building earlier, Jack had noticed that the second floor had a covered bridge to the parking structure next door. He then ran up to the third floor and yanked open the door to the hallway. The lights flared into life as they all ran down the hall to the South side of the building. Looking out the window he spotted the walkway below them. Stepping over to a desk he took the chair from the desk and threw it through the window. Using another chair to clean the shards of glass from the frame he jumped out of the window turned to help the others out. They then ran across the curved glass and frame cover of the walkway over to the parking structure. Climbing up the short wall they dropped over into the darkness of the third parking level.

Jack pointed and everyone ran flat out to the other side of the parking structure. Jack knew this would test the endurance of each person. No one lagged behind in the entire foot race, a testimony to their physical training.

Jack looked out and found the coast clear below. He grabbed a cable conduit and let himself down to the ground hand-over-hand quickly. Each of the others copied his movements and in less than a minute they were running into the trees that covered the field beyond the grounds of the Prophet's Administration building.

Going to ground briefly while they recovered their wind, they watched for air or ground pursuit. When nothing appeared they worked their way around through the wooded area several blocks in back of the building to where the SUV was parked. Checking the area for ten minutes they saw nothing to indicate that the vehicle had been discovered. Still, Mark checked for tampering before they got in and drove quickly but carefully away from the area.

When they were sure that they were clear, they relaxed and went over their mission. Jack blew out a big breath and shook his head. "What do you think tipped them to our presence?"

Checking his rearview mirror before turning left at the next light, Mark thought for a bit before answering. "I'm not sure. There could have been sensors in the stairwell, but I think that they would have detected us before we were leaving. Let's see, they didn't seem to know we were there until we reentered the stairwell to leave. Wait a minute. When we came in the door down there, wasn't locked was it?"

Jack shook his head, "No, but it was when we tried to leave."

Mark continued with his thought pattern. "It's possible that they hadn't activated the stairway locks and sensors until after the roving guard finished his patrol. Then they turned on the stairwell sensors and we walked right into them."

Remembering the confusion on the guard's faces, it seemed plausible that their sudden appearance coming out of the building had thrown them for a loop.

By this time they had reached their house and parked the car. Checking to see that no one followed them, they entered their house and cleaned up. Dressed in normal clothing they sat down in Jack's study to look at the fruits of their labors. The ZIP drive disks didn't look impressive but they could hold 2 gigabytes of information each.

Mark got up and brought one of his bags of tricks over to the table. Taking out a powerful microscope he slid one of the disks under the light and lens of the microscope. Slowly scanning the surface he found something that made him sit back with a frown. Jack raised an eyebrow. He knew Mark was a trained counter intelligence agent and an ex-Navy SEAL. He also had the resources of the U.S. government behind him. Whatever he had been looking for was obviously very well hidden and very serious.

Noting the look on Jack's face Mark explained. "In the last six months we have had some serious injuries to NSA personnel who have been attempting to decode disks, particularly ZIP drive type disks. It seems that there is a very explosive compound impregnated into the surface of the protective cover of the disk that the owner wants to secure. They pack a serious wallop in explosive power, equivalent to about quarter of a normal hand grenade. Unless you enter the correct password before you attempt to interrogate the disk, the disk explodes, destroying the evidence and usually the person attempting to get the information. I just checked the surface of these disks and they have the distinctive signature of the explosive impregnation."

Jack looked at the disks with a new respect. "Can they be set off remotely?"

"Not without power from a drive or some other source." Mark answered. Then he thought for a while and came to a conclusion. "You might have a point there." He got up and took out a metallic package he normally used to hide weapons in during inspections. Emptying it, he carefully wrapped each of the disks in a cloth and then inserted them into the package. Locking the package tightly closed he sat down and surveyed his work.

Pointing at the package he told Jack, "Your comment caused me to think of a way that I could set one of these off remotely without a disk drive to power them. All you would need is a correct 'triggering' password and a source of radiated power. Sort of like the power from a radar or counter weapons array. Not something you could do over a wide area, but if you knew approximately where the disks were, you could arrange for portable radar or microwave beam to bathe the area of interest and send a modulation of the password to the disk." He threw his hands into the air, "BOOM!"

"But, this case will prevent any power from reaching them by causing the power wave to go around the disks and not into them, like your watch case keeps magnetic waves away from the works by guiding the magnetic waves around the watch.

Jack nodded, "Okay then, how do we get whatever is on the disks off without losing a technician along the way?

Mark smiled, "I can't tell you that or then I'd have to kill you." They all laughed with the release of the strain of the evening's activities. Mark got up and picked up the case. "Come on, I know a guy who can work miracles with things like this."

As he got up, Jack smiled, "If he screws up he will meet someone who is able to do real miracles."

CHAPTER SEVEN

Jack and Mark drove through the light traffic in the early morning in Southeast Denver, each one lost in their own thoughts about the evening's activities. Mark had made a call before they left Jack's and had convinced the person on the other end to roll out of bed and meet them at his lab.

They pulled into a technology park and drove to the back of the low, single-story buildings advertising all forms of services and products. There was only a single vehicle in the whole parking lot so it wasn't hard to figure out where they were headed. The only front area lit up was under a sign that read "Dpower Investigations". Going to the door and ringing the bell resulted in the appearance of a tall, lean individual to unlock the door.

Mark thanked him for his efforts so early and introduced him to Jack. Jack studied the man for a few seconds trying to place him in a familiar category and decided that he was a new breed in Jack's experience.

Arthur Wagner was sloppy in his dress, but then the hour and unusual notice could be the cause of that. But his mannerisms were careful and very effective. He didn't seem to waste any motion. When he moved, he left where he was and moved into the exact position he wanted to be in with no readjustments, very machine-like in a sense. His hands were like instruments in their extreme delicacy and motion. It was like his mind worked everything out before he made a move. Considering the disks he was about to work on it, was reassuring.

Art took the package from Mark and took the disks out of it and sat there for a minute and then asked why the packaging. Mark pointed at Jack and explained the theory that they had developed, concerning possible detonation at a distance, through focused energy, with the password embedded in the broadcast. In a flash Art had the disks back in the protective package and slammed his fist onto the desk surface with a bang.

He jumped up and went to a computer at the next desk and sat down. He typed rapidly for several minutes on an email and then sent it. He came back and stared at the package. He then looked over his glasses at the two of them. "We had an explosion in our other lab last week and your theory matches exactly with the circumstances. There was a rash of theories that it was a timed sequence or that there was a mistake made, or the wrong conditions. None of that made sense." He pointed at the package and nodded. "But that makes sense." He stopped, asked if they wanted any coffee or something to drink. They both took a bottle of water as did Art.

He sat down at his desk again and said, "Thank you very much for that information. That has been nagging at me for several days. In return, I'll extract the information off these disks for free."

Jack smiled, "The information is for free and we're willing to pay whatever your fees are to find out if these disks can help save a young woman who we think has been kidnapped by these people."

Art stared over his glasses and smiled," I take it that these disks were not acquired in a completely legal sense?"

Mark smiled back, "They were acquired in a criminal investigation of the kidnapping and we'll take responsibility for them."

Nodding his head, Art took the disks and had the two men follow him to another part of the lab. He opened a door into a small room and they all went in. Closing the door he said, "This is a radio frequency screen room. No radio frequency energy can get in or go out." Having said that, he then took the disks out and repeated Mark's examination of the surfaces. He then placed them into a ZIP disk drive and powered it up. He watched the analysis on his screen for a few minutes and then typed in a quick series of commands. He then sat back and waited.

Looking over at Mark he tipped his head at the drive. "These disks are marked with a caution that the information is only for the Omniscience Temple's "Master Prophets" eyes. Anyone else that sees it is supposed to receive a curse." He then used several profanities and said, "Kiss my arse!" He typed again and then got up and walked back and forth for a minute.

"What I've done is to circumvent their protection by invoking a 'back-door' maintenance routine that the great

Master Prophets' probably don't know exists with these disks. In the event someone messes up the file allocation table, this will allow them, which in this case, is us, to recover the information. It does a complete data dump and never accesses the security coding."

After ten minutes he had the first disk finished and started on the next one. Each one went faster as he gained familiarity with their coding. After thirty minutes he had all four disks back in their package and they returned to his main computer terminal. He displayed the names of all the files off the disks on his screen. There were hundreds of files represented. Jack asked, "See if there is any labeled "Jenny" or "investigator". I would think that they would keep track of what happens to their victims."

Nothing like that appeared. Jack looked at Mark. "You think that this person didn't know what they did with her? That's a possibility and I don't think they are going to let us 'investigate' any further there." He was disappointed in the failure of the long shot snatch and grab.

Mark looked at Art. "See what files were made in the last ten hours."

Art sorted the files and came up with sixteen. Eight were spreadsheets of numbers and seven more were schedules. They hit pay dirt with the last file, labeled "Dispositions" and containing several entries. The latest entry indicated that subject JS was turned over to group 126 for a TP on yesterday's date.

Art ran a search for group numbers and came up with a match for 126 under a spread sheet for payments. It seemed that 126 indicated a Satanist group labeled "TDTH" and charged with 'miscellaneous' jobs. It also seemed that they had been heavily used in the last ten months for many jobs.

More searching revealed that this particular group was a 'coven' that held meetings on every Wednesday night in their auditorium. That would be tonight. Art ran several programs and then typed in a special piece of his own code. That resulted in a nicely rendered map of the location of this auditorium. When Art matched it to a local map it turned out to be in a heavily wooded area deep in rural Arapahoe County.

Thanking him for his efforts they left armed with a map and a timetable as to where Jenny was probably going to be if the disks weren't discovered missing.

Jack called Laura and woke her up. Apologizing, he told her they had a solid lead on Jenny and would be home in a few hours. They stopped for an early breakfast and brainstormed an assault on the "coven" for that evening.

They were just getting up to leave when the whole diner shook and everything rattled for a few seconds. Jack frowned as he looked at Mark. Mark said, "That was a bomb, 'A big one'."

They rushed out of the restaurant and looked southwest at the rising cloud of debris and smoke a mile away. Mark headed for the car, "What's down there?"

Jack shook his head, "I'm not sure, no factories, just homes, churches, and schools."

They got blocked off by a Denver policeman before getting to the site of the explosion but it appeared to be an elementary school. There wasn't much fire or smoke but they could see the broken school bus from where they were. As more and more emergency personnel rushed into the area they parked the car and moved closer. The police had already taped the area off with bright yellow tape saying "POLICE LINE - DO NOT CROSS".

CHAPTER EIGHT

The night that Jenny Samuels was kidnapped, Claire Moncrief was in seventh heaven. She had made her bi-weekly trek to her Omniscience Temple service and had actually seen Alan Roswell in person on the platform. His oratory against Christ and the miserable Christians was eloquent and forceful. It fired her up and made her excited like never before.

Claire's life had not been the dream of the average high school student and young adult. Being born into a constantly unemployed family she had no aspirations to begin with. Then to be straddled with a heavy, thick, non-athletic body, unmanageable hair, and serious acne that she had just conquered as she turned twenty-six. That and every dimension that was just slightly off crushed her self-image. She didn't fit in at school, nobody liked her, and after she graduated she found men weren't interested in her at all. She had tried churches but she felt shunned there and she didn't have the nerve to talk to anybody. The people that tried to talk to her made her feel so dumpy. She didn't listen to their words but just imagined loathing in their eyes. Who wouldn't hate her?

The fact that she didn't know how to make herself look better and that she felt a diet was an unfair burden didn't help either. Her mother was an alcoholic that slept all day, usually not alone either. Her father was either out of work or always working two or three minimum wage jobs to just keep a roof over their heads. He loved his kids, hated his wife, and never had time to do either one well.

Claire had dropped into a permanent blue funk where nothing was ever going to go right for her. She knew it beyond a shadow of a doubt.

She had a surge of hope when a woman she was talking to about the lousy treatment she'd had at the Christian Church told her that she wasn't alone and there were people that thought just like her. Would she like to meet them? Sure.

Her first six months at the Omniscience Temple were uplifting and she even started caring what clothes she wore. She started taking regular showers and even tried to make her hair behave. She was a little confused that the 'Temple' acted more like a rally than a religious meeting but she heard the hateful words against the miserable Christians and she knew she fit in. And tonight was the climax of a wonderful new adventure, "to actually see the great man himself". She couldn't have been more than fifty feet away from him. She was still glowing as she made her way through the lobby and someone laid their hand on her shoulder. She stopped and turned around. Her heart jumped into her throat as she found herself standing next to Alan Roswell. He smiled and asked her if she would spend a few minutes talking to him. She nodded yes because with her heart in her throat she couldn't get any words out. The stars in her eyes were so bright she never saw the looks of envy and hatred other men and women gave her as she walked away with the great man, his arm around her shoulders.

He opened the door to an office and ushered her in. He had her sit on the couch and sat down near her. He smiled again. "My you are a pretty one aren't you?"

Claire almost lost it because she knew he was making fun of her. Her face clouded up and he said, "You don't believe me?" He got up and went to the wall and took down the mirror that hung there. Bringing it back to her he let her look at her reflection. Now the heart in her throat quit beating.

She was beautiful. Her hair was long and soft, and her face was as beautiful as any fashion model. She just stared not knowing what to say.

He put the mirror back and came back to the couch. "Claire, in my Temple you can have anything you want and be anything you want. You've always wanted to be pretty, so now you are. Enjoy it." He made to rise and she was filled with sadness at the thought of his going.

Claire reached out and grabbed his hand. Her voice was even lower and more throaty than normal. "Don't go. I want to thank you for making me beautiful." She got up and kissed him on the cheek. He smiled and returned the kiss, right on her mouth. She wasn't used to being kissed at all and this was so exciting. He pulled her closer to him and kissed her again. She abandoned herself to the passion she had never known before.

Later she was trying to express her adoration, and yes, even her love for him when he asked her if she would do him a special favor. There wasn't even a hint of refusal.

He got up and straightened his shirt. He looked at her for a minute and said, "There is a Christian woman who is spreading lies about me because she hates us. I want to send her a message that I am not pleased. Would you take this message to her for me?"

Take an insult to the miserable Christian woman that was defaming the man she loved, absolutely.

He smiled, "it's an ugly present that will tell her that she is wrong. It could even blow up in her face if she opens it too quickly, if you know what I mean."

Claire could guess but didn't care what happened to the woman that was making her man unhappy.

He went over and got the present. It was a cardboard box about one foot square with a string holding it closed. He handed it to her. It was quite heavy but she could manage it. "Where do I take it?"

He gave her an address and said that she was corrupting children with her evil thoughts and words at a Christian school on the south side of Denver. He told her which one and she knew the place. He said to look for a school bus with the number 59 on it. Tomorrow at ten a.m. she was going to take the bus and go pick up some children. If Claire could get the present on the bus before she took it, then she'd find it when she got on. He took Claire's hand and pulled her to her feet and kissed her passionately again. "You will do this for me, without fail, right?"

She nodded, "I won't fail you, I promise." She turned and sat the box on the bed. She did the best she could to rearrange her clothes and picked up the box. When she turned to ask him if she could watch the woman open the box from a distance she found him gone. He hadn't gone out the door but that didn't matter. Oh. He was so wonderful and he loved HER." She picked up the heavy box and left knowing that she would be too excited to sleep tonight. She never noticed, as she left, that the reflection in the mirror on the wall was the same one she had seen all her life.

Alan Roswell watched Claire leave the church and chuckled.

The next morning at the school was a rough one for Sheryl, after an almost sleepless night worrying about Jenny. She wondered what Jack Malone and Mark Connelly found out about the disks they had taken somewhere earlier this morning. She couldn't concentrate on her students because of her concern about what might be happening to Jenny. She made too many mistakes. Some of her students were even laughing at her.

She wanted to break down and have a good cry. But she knew that she had too many people counting on her for that. She looked at the clock and saw that it was ten minutes before the field trip to the Denver Zoo. The kids were getting excited and a bit antsy. One of the school assistants asked if Sheryl wanted her to load the kids on the bus for her, thinking about that she felt a major catch in her spirit. She shook her head and the assistant left.

Sheryl started putting her books into her bag. That was when little Timmy Clark started having convulsions. The sudden uproar caused her to rush to the middle of the classroom where Timmy was having what looked like a Gran Mal seizure. He was shaking, convulsing, and thrashing around like he was trying to hit everything in the classroom with his head, hands, or feet. This wasn't the first seizure victim that Sheryl had attended to, she knew what to do. She ordered all the rest of the kids away from him and grabbed a wooden ruler from a desk. Kneeling next to the shaking child she pried open his mouth and placed the ruler in it for him to bite on. She tried to keep him from trashing about but wasn't having too much success. She told two of her students to get Mr. Simmons, the teacher in the next classroom, and to go for the school nurse. Timmy began to arch his back and she held him down so that he didn't break anything. The teacher arrived and didn't know what to do so Sheryl told him and then the nurse rushed in and they kept Timmy from injuring himself. In a few minutes he started settling down and relaxing. The nurse took Timmy to her office to watch him for a while.

Sheryl looked at the clock. "Oh no" she thought, "I'm already eight minutes late for the trip." Going to her desk she grabbed her bag and told the kids in the room to get in line and to be ready to get on the bus. She was just heading for the door to walk them out of the building when there was a bright flash of light outside the doors they were headed for, and a horrible noise in the yard next to the school building. Glass flew everywhere and the doors at the end of the hall were blown off their hinges. Sheryl got knocked down and grabbed as many children as she could and had every one crawl under a desk back in the classroom.

When things quit falling and flying around she got to her feet and checked her students. There was a lot of crying and glass cuts but no serious injuries. Sheryl herself was bleeding from several cuts but none of them was serious.

She told the children to stay in the room and she stumbled through the debris and people lying in the hall to a gaping hole in the building where the doors to the school yard had been. There was a huge crater in the school yard and the back end of a yellow school bus was lying on the ground near the crater. She could see people from all over running towards the school and heard sirens. But her heart froze in place. That was her bus. If not for the delay to care for Timmy, the bus would have been full of her children. She thought of the closeness of the danger and it made her ill. She sat down on the ground crying out to God. "Thank you Lord, thank you, but why, why, why?"

A half a block away from the school and the crater Claire lay dying in the street with a steel shaft from the school bus through her chest. She had waited too closely to see the surprise on the teacher's face. Claire had been upset because the teacher wasn't getting on the empty bus. The teacher still hadn't shown up when the timer in the box reached zero and the bus blew up. The last thing Claire thought she heard as she died was Alan Roswell laughing.

The news reports were serious that evening. Forty-seven children and three adults hospitalized, one woman killed. All the reports noted how much more damaging it would have been if the explosion had occurred even a few minutes later. Besides the bus being full, the school yard would have been full of kids on lunch break and recess. The FBI theorized a terrorist bombing because they had already determined the explosion that shattered the bus was caused by plastic explosives.

Sheryl sat in the hospital at the bedside of one of the young kids hurt by the explosion and stroked his hand as he lay there without moving. She prayed to a loving God that he would be all right. She was so grateful that God didn't allow so many little lives to be snuffed out, but she wondered why God would even allow anybody to threaten innocent lives like that. Of course, she very rarely knew why God did anything.

While she couldn't even find room in her heart to hate the people who did this, she thought she knew who was responsible. It was eating at her because if she was right, then they were trying to kill her. The kids would have been killed just so they could have gotten to her. It was like the children's lives didn't even matter to the perpetrators.

She thought of the 'coincidental' timing of Timmy's convulsions that prevented her and her class from being on the bus. As she thought of all the hurt and destruction caused by the explosion and how close it really was for the children in her class, the tears started running again.

A little voice said "Don't Cry Ms. Cantor, Mikey will be all right."

As Sheryl dried her eyes on a tissue, a little hand took her other hand and she saw Mikey's three-year old sister standing on a step stool next to her looking at her brother. Sheryl had to smile at the innocent assurance the little girl had about her brother. "What makes you so sure, honey?"

The little girl smiled up at her, "Because God told me he would be fine." She turned back to wait for her brother to be fine.

Sheryl nodded as she saw Mikey start to move and open his eyes, "Nurse." Sheryl yelled. As the nurse came in and tended to the child Sheryl bent over and kissed the little girl on the forehead. "And God's always right honey." She had other kids to see.

An hour later, Mark and Jack were at Jack's house talking to Laura and Sarah when the phone rang. Jack answered it and listened, and then he hung up. "That was Minister Throman. The school that was bombed this morning was the school that Sheryl teaches at. He can't reach her anywhere."

Amid the prayers for Sheryl's safety, Jack had an idea. Not his, at least it wasn't along the lines he was thinking at the time it appeared in his mind. "I'm going to call the hospitals where they took the wounded and see if she is among them.

At the third hospital he tried, he was told that she was there helping but not as one of the injured. The four of them left the house and found the hospital very busy with the injured kids and their parents. There were adults and children on stretchers in the halls and in every available room. Triage was being performed in the hall. There were a lot of medical personnel there in a human response to a tragedy like this. It reminded Jack of the response in New York after the September 11th terrorist strikes on the World Trade Centers in 2001. There didn't seem to be any hysteria, just a lot of hard work being handled quickly and professionally. This bombing could have been much worse than the Columbine shootings simply because of the number of victims.

Jack looked around and saw Sheryl Cantor helping a child onto a bed in a hallway. They carefully made their way to her. She saw them and gave each one a hug, even though she didn't know who Mark and Sarah were.

They found a semi-out-of-the-way spot and listened as she told them what happened and why she thought it happened. Jack felt his anger rising. But Sheryl put her hand on his arm. "Don't. Please don't get wrapped up in this. Not yet, not until you find out what happened to Jenny."

Jack covered his eyes for a second to compose himself. Looking at the distraught woman he said, "I'm fairly certain that the bombing was aimed at you. Probably because of information they got from Jenny." He then told her about their discoveries and the location of the 'coven'. He also told her the four of them would be there before things happened tonight.

Sheryl looked scared and excited and really determined. "I'm going with you." Her look dared anyone to tell her no.

CHAPTER NINE

As the five people stood by the blacked out Cadillac SUV, they surveyed their surroundings ruefully. The small dirt lane they had used to reach this spot petered out less than fifty feet from where they were. Jack had backed the black vehicle into a hidden position near the end of the road in the event they had to leave quickly. Anyway, at that point the woods took over and there was nowhere for a vehicle to go. A gust of wind blew a mixture of stenches pass them that felt cold and greasy. The late night had turned ugly. The moon was mostly covered by dirty gray clouds that moved quickly out of the east. A mist was forming in the woods as the chill of night deepened near midnight.

Although it was Fall, and the weather in the Rockies was normally pleasant at this time of year, the woods was a damp, chill place that seemed to radiate the evil that was done there. Truly, on the spiritual level that a person feels but can't see directly, the entire wood seemed sickened by the Satanic rituals. The trees were stunted and gnarled and mostly barren while the rest of the world was still in full bloom. There seemed to be a low vibration, a drumming with a heavy slow beat which could have been thought of as a labored heartbeat if one's imagination got the better of them.

The trees groaned in the wind and twisted as if they wanted to be away from that place. All in all it was as uninviting as any place they had ever seen. Jack led a last prayer for protection and guidance from the Holy Spirit. Putting on their night-vision goggles, the group started into the woods in search of the Satanist's hideaway. They hadn't gone more than ten yards into the woods before the SUV was lost to sight and the woods seemed to surround them with an evil intent. Mark commented that there were no other vehicles near the road that they had seen. He wondered if the Satanists had called off the event after the raid on the building and the disappearance of the Zip drive disks.

Shaking his head slightly Jack threw off the imaginary fears of childhood and concentrated on their progress. There were much worse things in this wood than the fears of gnarled trees looking like spooks. There was a concentration of people whose whole purpose in life was to defy God and worship the enemy. These people had reached a point of acceptance of evil that literally eliminated normal conduct. Death and murder were simply business tools and would be used as ordered by their evil master.

Jack did not plan on allowing any of the five of them to be killed ritualistically by the ghouls in the Satanist's camp. Yet, at the same time he was aware that God wanted them to save Jenny's life. The lyrics of a song they had been singing in church recently came to mind as they carefully eased through the trees. "I went to the Enemy's camp and I took back what he stole from me." He thought, no truer words could have been written about their escapade this night. He strained his earthly eyesight for a clue to the whereabouts of the camp while he kept a prayer for guidance running through his mind.

Mark was processing every bit of information about the wood he had gleaned from his years of field craft in the military and as a freelance operative. There was a lot to be learned from every tree, bush, and ground cover he could see. He had been in a similar situation in his first year as a team leader of the SEAL team. The situation was eerily similar even though the wood was hundreds of miles to the south of their present location and, in truth, was more of a jungle than this. His memories flew quickly back to that "fun" trip.

-------------------------******-------------------------

The SEALS were on a mission to rescue a single woman. A small band of rebels had kidnapped the foreign visitor, a young American Congressional Representative, to demand closure of the American plant in their South American country. Mark and his five man team had been ordered in and were on-site in less than an hour thanks to a training op that they had been running less than a hundred miles away from the kidnapping. A quick helicopter ride and even quicker refitting and the six-man team were tracking the kidnappers into the forest. Night had fallen and the woods they were filtering through were gaunt trees with little vegetation and a mat of dead leaves for a floor. A weak moon had risen as the team silently ghosted through the mist between the trees. Each man knew what to expect and what to look for. They had been training and completing these operations for three months. These were the veterans, the survivors of the original eight man team. Each man was equipped with night vision goggles, a list of weapons highlighted by a silenced K-bar M-16 with a bayonet attached. The short automatic was particularly suited to the close conditions of the woods. The bayonet indicated how close the conditions were probably going to be.

Mark was also using a new sound detection device just being introduced in the field. The advantages of the new device were that it was hands-free and used computer-modeling which eliminated normal sounds and stressed man-made noises. Mark knew it could be fooled but using it gave the SEALs an equalizer against a crew that was operating on their home ground.

The sound detector clued him to a noise to their left and about twenty yards in front of them. It did this by superimposing a symbol in the view field of his night vision goggles. The computer was able to use the same effect as a heads-up display to place the noise where it probably would be from Mark's position. Mark pushed the silent switch next to his whisper microphone. This caused every display to indicate a fist. Each man silently stopped and knelt where he was. Mark then quietly described the noise and the location. The six man team pivoted on Mark until they were aimed at the sound and they began a super-cautious advance.

In his night vision goggles Mark made out the lone sentry holding a World War II rifle. He was watching in their direction. He sensed something was out there but couldn't be sure. Mark touched the second switch. A small bow symbol appeared on the crossbow specialist's goggles. A few seconds later a crossbow quarrel appeared in the throat of the sentry. Since the quarrels were coated in a quick acting poison the man simply fell down and didn't move. The team quietly moved forward until they were at the position of the sentry.

The night vision goggles showed the camp they had been looking for. Not a light was to be seen and there didn't seem to be anybody moving around the four tents they could see. Mark dispatched two men each direction to do a slow circle around the camp looking for more sentries or other troops. He and the other man continued to watch the camp. Ten minutes later the all clear signal was given. Mark turned off the sound detection gear and pulled out a small scope from his back pouch. This was a thermal imaging scope and allowed him to literally see into the tents. There were eight bodies all in prone positions, two to a tent. The slighter form would probably be the woman. She was in the farthest tent from Mark. He quietly assigned the men to each tent. The tent with the woman in it would be the most critical. They couldn't afford to alert whoever was in the tent with her because he might kill her before they could reach her.

Knowing there was a calculated risk in assuming he really knew which one was the woman. She might be a large female and the kidnapper might be a small man. This meant that he would have to risk a reaction to visually check his targets. He was about to order a assault when the smaller form started moving in the far tent and quickly went through the wall of the tent. Switching back to his night vision goggles he was in time to see the woman exit the tent and start running directly towards two of his men. She was quick and silent. He advised them to take her quietly. He watched as the three images came together and stuck. Then they begin to work their way around the camp back to Mark's position. This was a real blessing for the SEAL team. They could withdraw without having to engage the seven men. Their mission was to rescue the woman, not kill the men who took her. Although, the mission planners wouldn't be averse to setting an example as far as American visitors were concerned.

Recalling the second two man team, Mark used the Thermal Imaging scope again to ensure the seven men had not stirred. Putting the scope into his back pack he stood quietly and greeted the freed woman. Putting his finger to his lips he started back the way they had come. The woman worked her way up to his side and urgently tugged on his combat harness. By now they were far enough away from the camp he could risk a quiet conversation.

She was a slimly-built, athletic woman in her late twenties. Her file indicated that she had light brown hair and electric blue eyes but, Mark couldn't see that in the dark. She was wearing peasant pants and a man's shirt and had her hair up in a bun behind her head. The dim light available showed her worried expression which was enough for Mark to take the time to hear what she had to say. Her name was Constance Bowin, Connie for short. She whispered quickly but intensely.

"You've got to get away from here now. They will come looking for us in a few minutes."

Mark assumed that he knew there would be a guard rotation or something like that and when they found her gone, all seven men would track her. So he whispered back to her, "It's all right. We can cover a lot of distance with our night vision gear and they won't be able to track you until morning. That's six hours from now. We'll be most of the way home by then." He didn't like the fact that her frown deepened rather than relaxed.

She shook her head emphatically no. "It's not the seven men back there we have to worry about. The second-in-command of the rebels is on his way here right now to take charge of my abduction. He's bringing about thirty more rebels with him and they have some of your night vision gear too."

Mark was still unclear as to why they had to worry about it when he heard a sound that explained her fear. The sound of chopper blades headed their way. Now they were in for it. If the aircraft had anything like a FLIR or forward looking infrared system it would find them very quickly in the cool forest.

Thinking quickly he called everyone together in a single group and they stretched an aluminum-lined poncho over them to shield their IR signature from the on-coming helicopter. Mark told Connie, "They probably don't know you're gone yet but we don't want them seeing seven people out here and seven people in the camp. They would be sure to investigate." A minute later the chopper passed over their position and they took off in a hurry to the west.

A mile later they heard the chopper lift off again and everyone pulled out their IR blankets and hid while the bird did a first pass. With thirty-seven men to work with it wouldn't take the rebels long to find a sign of their passage and then the chopper would be all over them. If the rebels had any night-vision goggles the overhead IR blankets wouldn't shield them and it would be a fire-fight with all the advantages on the rebel's side in the form of that gunship.

Checking their topographical maps of the area Mark was attempting to plot a course of action when his number two pointed out an anomaly just to the south of their present position. It looked to be a set of caves in a tall hill. Thinking quickly Mark realized their value. He got everyone headed for the caves in quick time. This was very poor field craft and would leave plenty of signs of their passage. But time, rather than stealth, was of the essence in this case.

Reaching the side of the hill where the three caves were, he had four of the men go up and check them out making sure they left a lot of footprints. When the men returned walking on only the rocks, he had everyone move into the stream running through the shallow valley at the foot of the hill and head due north. They made good time and were able to stay in the water for over a mile before the water deepened and they had to walk back into the forest. Calling a rest break Mark unloaded the satellite uplink transponder and made an urgent call to the carrier for pickup. He warned them about the helicopter gunship.

Hearing the helicopter approaching the cave site the SEALs and Connie huddled under the IR blankets again. This went on for almost thirty minutes while the chopper circled the cave area and scanned the surrounding forest. It then returned to the area of the caves and dropped two parachute flares. The whole area of the caves lit up like daytime. The rocks threw harsh shadows and the black entrances to the caves stood out like sore thumbs. The ruse had worked and the rebels thought they had the SEALs trapped in the caves. After finding the sentry killed no one was too eager to search the caves for their captive. The haggling took another fifteen minutes before the first rebels entered the first cave and searched it. It went quicker after that. Ten minutes later the entire rebel force knew that they hadn't stayed in the caves. But the time they used to figure that out was enough time for the U. S. Navy to reach the area. The chopper was back-lit by its own flares and exploded in the first pass of two F-18s from the carrier off the coast.

Mark had one of the SEALs light up a preset reflector with a handheld laser in the open area they were next to. Two minutes later a Sea King chopper set down in the opening and everyone climbed on board while the F-18s kept the rebels busy. Mark's SEAL team and the recent captive were headed out to sea before the harried rebels came out of hiding in the caves.

-----------------------------*******-----------------------------

Mark's memories faded as he looked around. "Yes", Mark thought, carefully scanning the dark woods. "This is a lot like that except I don't have most of the gear or the troops I had then, and I didn't have a wife then either."

He did have some adequate night vision goggles and it didn't take long before he was able to detect activity several hundred yards ahead of them on the side of a large hill. He held up his fist and the five of them stopped and knelt down for a quick conference.

Jack studied the activity for a minute. Then he questioned Mark. "What do you suppose they have in the way of security or roving guards?"

Mark thought for a moment. "Out here I don't think they will have anyone out roaming around because it might attract attention to their location. From what I can see from here they have an underground building or some form of buried structure. There is probably only one normal way in and out. It would be a simple matter to place one or two people at the entrance to check who comes and goes. If you look past the hill on the far left, you'll see a bunch of warm metal. I think they have another way into a parking area near their nest."

Sarah added, "I really doubt that they have any exterior alarm systems."

Laura spoke up for the first time since they had entered the wood. "I have been praying that the Lord would go before us and do the battle for us. I'd think that they already know that we are coming on the spiritual plane."

Sheryl spoke for the first time. "I doubt that they are listening to anyone but their demons right now and those demons are probably so focused on their control of the people and the ritual they might not be aware of us either."

Mark thought about that and then he laid out a plan. "Okay, assuming we don't need to worry about sneaking up on them. Let's leave the night vision gear and just walk up and knock on their door." He gazed at the slightly green image that was Jack. "You said that this battle was against the powers and authorities of the demon world, right?"

Jack agreed and added a caution. "Yes it is a spiritual battle on that plane and that is where the power and the real struggle will be carried on. But, just as God works through us to accomplish His plans in this world, Satan works through the debased people in there to thwart God's plan. Let's not neglect the physical side of things here."

Mark took out his Ruger P90 and slid the slide back and forth, chambering a .45 caliber Hydro-Shock round with an audible 'clack'. "No problem. After we get her out of here what are the 'rules of engagement'?"

Jack knew that after their various ventures and previous run-ins with Satan's demons, Mark wasn't being flippant. Mark was a professional anti-terrorist and one of the best the country had to call on. His specialty was the elimination of the 'physical' components of the enemy with which they were at war. He knew Yahshua as his savior and had given his life to the Lord (sometimes thoughtfully and sometimes again in the heat of battle). But his life and training was based on secular warfare. He was counting on the Lord to battle the supernatural forces and he would do his part with the local components.

Feeling the anointing of the Holy Spirit in his heart Jack smiled a wry smile and replied, "God will tell you what to do, just listen for his directions." "But first, I think we need to call for reinforcements.

Jack had been praying for guidance on how to handle the rabid crowd without simply killing a lot of them. He lit up when Mark's comment gave him the answer. "We are going to call the cops and explain the situation and the type of people that we are dealing with." At that he took out his cell phone and dialed 9-1-1. At Mark's questioning look he covered the mouthpiece and explained. "In cases like this the first one to call in a complaint is the good guy and the other person or persons are the suspects." He explained the situation as kidnap and attempted murder in progress to the 9-1-1 operator and told them where they would be in twenty minutes. He left the line open to the operator and handed the phone to Laura as he stood up.

Laura frowned at him and disconnected the call and pocketed the cell phone, thinking to herself, "I'm not going to stay out here "on the line" while you waltz in there by yourself."

Jack set his goggles on a sawed-off tree trunk and walked towards the entrance of the buried building. Sarah slipped out to the right side quickly to come around from behind the entrance while Mark, Sheryl, and Laura followed Jack. The cold seemed to intensify and the tension grew.

Sheryl had been running on pure outrage at what had happened at the school that morning coupled with what might be happening to Jenny. As they committed themselves to the action and walked toward the enemy's stronghold she wanted to be brave and strong, but wondered if she really had the grit to go in there. It was a great chance for first-hand documentation of the activities in such a place, but she also wanted to live to report it.

CHAPTER TEN

The anointing of the Holy Spirit seemed to grow heavier on Jack the closer he came to the building's doorway. He sensed a distant threat or light feeling of dread but it didn't bother him enough to even slow his steps.

Laura, more sensitive to the spiritual plane, also felt the dread through the covering of the Holy Spirit and it made her shiver. But again, it wasn't enough to stop her from following her husband.

Sheryl was the least experienced at this type of confrontation and she prayed that Yahshua would cover her in His blood and walk with her as they did His will. She felt an icy dread that suddenly ceased. She had a brief mental glimpse of a beautiful white and gold figure with a face of an angel that was frowning and holding a sword that had flames. Sheryl shook her head and smiled. "Thank you Yahshua."

Sarah walked in the anointing and admonition of the Lord. Since her dramatic plea to God for the poisoned people in front of the whole world, she didn't allow any fear to get between her and God. She was too far away to notice that her husband was really having a hard time.

Mark's mind felt the full impact, too many years of doing it all by himself, relying on himself and his teammates. Honing and appreciating his abilities and tactics. For Mark, the impending failure and soul-sapping hopelessness got worse with every step. Every high-strung nerve and experienced mental concept was screaming that to go in there was the worst thing they could do, quite literally suicide. All his training and combat experience, which he knew was a lot more than his companions had, told him that they were walking into a fatal trap. Warring with his feelings was his personal moral code which would not let him abandon a team under combat conditions.

The stress factor or dichotomy between what he knew he had to do and what he was sure they should not be doing was becoming intense.

Even though it was becoming extremely clear to him that their mission was about to become fatal, he rationalized that he could go on because he wasn't afraid of death. A stray thought ran through his mind that said, "Oh yes. He *was* afraid to die". The battle raging inside of him was reaching epic proportions but he kept walking forward. The only outward signs of his unease were the sweat breaking out on his forehead and the shaking side-to-side of his head as he refused to quit.

Suddenly the gut-wrenching fear and icy dread fell away from him like a sickly garment dropped to the ground. His normal professionalism and naturally optimistic enthusiasm flooded back like a sea returning to the shore. He felt a pressure and realized that Laura had put her hand on his arm. As her anointing covered him, the spiritual sickness had left him. Darkness can't remain when there is light and Laura seemed to be filling up with light.

Mark felt a peace come over him as his normal attitude returned. He smiled at Laura, even though she couldn't see him. She leaned close in the dark and he could sense her closeness. The sweet normalcy of her closeness was at terrific odds with the setting of the icy, evil woods. Moving her lips close to his ear she whispered, "Mark, you know Yahshua, pray, cover yourself in His blood and pray for his protection." It was as if his eyes were suddenly opened and he saw the enemy in the spirit world. Demons know a person's weaknesses and are quick to exploit them. Mark realized that his pride had gotten the best of him, again.

He had believed that his physical prowess and training would keep him on top. Obviously this didn't work, not in the spirit realm. His pride in his 'worldly self' had opened him up to the assault by one or more of the demons near the nest of the Satanists. It had whispered in his ear, "fear and failure" and he had bought it because he was attempting to overcome the forces of the spirit world by his physical abilities and strengths rather than by God's spirit.

Knowing what the damage negative confession can do, Mark said quietly, "I'm not being very smart". But the continual bombardment on his spirit was still trying to muddle his thoughts and confuse him. He whispered back, "How?"

Laura squeezed his arm and whispered, "Repeat after me." Mark mentally centered himself as Sheryl came up and put her hand on his other arm. Mark sensed a flash of white and gold, whatever that meant.

Sheryl faintly saw the white and gold angel standing between her and Laura and resting its hands on Mark's shoulders as they prayed.

As Laura led, he asked the Lord to cleanse him of his sins because he was a sinner. Then he asked for forgiveness for his sinful foolishness and blind pride and he admitted that the battle was the Lord's to win. He asked to be covered in the blood of the lamb and for protection from the forces of darkness and the principalities and powers of that dark realm. He committed his spirit to God regardless of the outcome of this battle or any of the ones to come, and then he praised Yahshua and thanked Him for his love and mercy. This all took about twenty-five seconds.

Standing there in the dark in the wind-blown, icy woods Mark was given a vision. Within his mind he saw a vast expanse, tree and grass covered land near to the sea under an achingly beautiful sunset in a rainbow of colors, some of which defied description. A feeling of unlimited potential and opportunity filled his soul and he felt the presence and love of the Lord effuse his whole being. Tears came to his eyes without shame and he absolutely knew he had never felt the power of God within him like this before. The feeling on his heart was one of absolute victory and the sure knowledge that this encounter was a trivial event compared to the future he saw regardless of its outcome. He straightened up his posture and patted Laura's hand. The three of them hurried quickly across the ground and caught up to Jack just as he stopped before two men outside an entryway to the underground building.

As they approached, a low-wattage bulb came to life above the doorway to the coven. The dim light only served to amplify the evil appearance of the two 'greeters'. They both were large young men and had black hair and beards. The one that seemed to be in command had eyes that had sunken back into dark hollows. The closest Jack could come to remembering a look like that was several Halloweens back. Both men had edged weapons holstered and the backup man had a large-caliber handgun in a holster at his belt.

Jack saw a flicker of motion behind the men and recognized that Sarah was making sure no one surprised them from any direction.

The first man held out his hand, palm out with the fingers upward in the universal gesture of 'stop'. He rumbled out a deep but hollow voice, "Stop right there. Your kind is not tolerated in this "church" His eyes reminded Jack of a rattlesnake's eyes, cold, and flat, unearthly in their stare.

Jack responded to the man's warning. "I have business here and I intend to complete it. You have a friend of ours in there that is being held against her will. I intend to take her home before your "church" contaminates her."

Both of the men smiled nervous small smiles and the front man responded to Jack. "What and who we have in here is our business and not yours. You need to leave now before we have to help you to leave." It was obvious that the big men wanted to "help" them leave.

The Holy Spirit led Jack to understand that there were many demons that had control of both men. Chief among them were the spirits of witchcraft, Satanism, antichrist, and lustful perversion. This sudden discernment of the enemy was a bit startling, but helpful. Jack remembered the lessons he had learned in Israel. He raised his right hand and sternly intoned, "I ask the Lord Yahshua to rebuke you demons of witchcraft, Satanism, antichrist, and lust in the Name of The Lord Yahshua, and to bind you in His Name. I bind all other demonic forces within these men in the name of Yahshua. I ask God to have His Holy angels confine these demons and if they resist then cast them into the abyss for the remainder of eternity."

The response was immediate and satisfying. The two men stopped moving and seemed to lose interest in what they had been doing. The use of the Lord's name was dramatic, and the demons were unable to direct the men to violence. This lack of normal control resulted in two somewhat startled-looking door guards. As the demons were dragged screaming away to their eternal dungeon, the men became lost as to their purpose. Jack drew his six-foot, four-inch frame to his full height and demanded, "Now move out of the way."

Like radio-controlled model planes which have lost their command link to the ground the two men immediately stepped back out of the way for the four aliens in their midst. As Laura passed them she smiled and said, "Yahshua is the Son of God and He really still loves you, you know." This left a great deal of confusion at the doorway as they stepped inside the lion's den. Mark just stared at them. Sheryl just smiled and walked by them.

Right behind her Sarah appeared, walked past the two men, and said "Shalom." At that one man sat down on the ground and started to cry. The other man stood there and just didn't know what to do.

Going down the long flight of stairs they reached a door that opened into a great underground hall. The hall was made up similar to a normal church layout in the round, except that there was a large, heavily stained sacrificial table in place of the normal altar. The lighting ran to the red end of the spectrum but brightened up near the platform with the table on it. The mood was highly charged with emotion. The emotion was lust in all its forms as well as anger and rage and a lust for death.

The satanic session had been in full swing when Jack and the others entered the main assembly area. Jack could feel the assault on his spirit and soul, but still in a remote way because God's Holy Spirit was turning away everything the enemy threw at them. The members were dressed in black robes and some cases, black cloaks with hoods that threw their faces into sharp relief against the darkness of the hoods.

As the five members entered the hall, the main speaker spotted them. It didn't take long for their spiritual protection to be noticed and it brought forth a series of screams and howls that would have normally driven fear into anyone hearing them. The people were just echoing their parasitical demon's fear and loathing in the presence of God's anointing.

Jack and Sheryl both spotted Jenny Samuels next to the table on the raised dais. She was mostly undressed and had bright red pentagrams and other occult paintings on her head and body. She was held to the platform by a large chrome chain that ran between her wrists and a shackle on the floor. She had a drugged, vacant look in her eyes and there was no sign of relief when the five of them were pointed out by the main speaker as the enemy.

The congregation parted in the middle and moved to either side of the main hall. Jack, followed in single file by Laura, Sheryl, Sarah, and then Mark walked boldly up the middle of the open space and faced the platform with its sinister markings and bloodstained sacrificial table.

The speaker was an adult in his fifties with a hollowed look to his face as if the long association with evil was sucking the humanness out of him. His face, contorted with rage and frustration, poked out of his hood far enough to see that he had a wiry crew-cut of gray hair. He pointed a bony finger at the five interlopers and demanded, "You have no right to be here. This is our house of worship and you are not welcome. How dare you intrude on our worship service?"

Jack looked the man straight in the face, "We come in the name of the Lord Yahshua. Your abomination of a worship service is simply counted as sin in heaven. Release Miss Samuels to us and we will leave this den of iniquity." Jack's voice was clear and loud enough to be heard everywhere in the building.

At the name of Yahshua a stricken look came over the face of the speaker and he made an obscure or possibly obscene gesture with his hand in an attempt to ward off the Name of the Son of God. He screwed his face up into a sneer and shouted at Jack. "Do not use that name in here. It is not wanted. Miss Samuels doesn't want to go with you." With that he turned to the young woman chained to the floor. "Do you want to go with these people my dear?"

Sheryl cried, "Jenny, honey, come with us."

Jenny neither looked at the speaker or Sheryl. She almost screamed, "Leave me alone!" It wasn't clear who she was talking to, but the speaker tried to turn it to his advantage. "See." He screamed at the five people standing in front of him. "She doesn't want you to bother her. Now leave." The entire place started yelling "Leave." and screaming "Out" and banging on things.

Laura had been praying silently in her prayer language and felt a compulsion to act. She stepped around Jack and Sheryl and walked up the three steps of the platform and moved past the speaker without even sparing him a glance. She squatted next to the captive girl. The speaker moved to grab her from behind and Laura felt the golden Armor of God appear again as she had in the dream. The speaker fell backwards with a loud squawk as he moved his hand in front of his face to block the blinding light of the armor. At this several of the men on the platform made to stop Laura. As they surged forward toward her, Laura stood up and the sword appeared in her right hand. She raised the sword to a right hand high guard position and faced them. All the attackers fell away afraid to attack her. They had to shield their faces from the intense light streaming from her armor and the sword. Demons were flying through the walls, ceiling, and the dirt of the floor in an attempt to flee the light of God almighty.

Jack and the others stared at Laura and her armor and sword. Sarah thought it was the most beautiful thing she'd ever seen. Jack had been told about it but had never seen it until now. He was impressed and could tell that Mark and Sheryl were amazed at the new dimension of their friend.

Holding her sword in a one-hand guard position, Laura reached forward and placed her left hand on Jenny's shoulder. Jenny's eyes flew wide as if she had been shocked by electricity. Awareness came into her eyes and she pulled futilely on her chain in an effort to break free. The murmuring of the crowd became a howl as the congregation saw their sacrifice trying to get away. They were on the edge of attacking all six people all at once. After all, five additional sacrifices would please their master all the more.

Sheryl kept seeing small hints of bright white and gold whirling all around them. She also discovered that her prayers had taken on an entirely new dimension of earnest intimacy with the Lord and they had an added dimension as if there were angels praying with her.

Laura did not take notice of the seesawing of tensions behind her. She kept her focus on the young girl in front of her. Smiling, she felt the anointing of God as it flowed through her and filled Jenny. She watched Jenny relax in peace as the presence of God filled her entire being. Nodding, Laura said in a strange dulcet voice, "You know the truth and the truth you know will set you free." As she spoke forth that truth, the shackles holding the chain to Jenny's wrists snapped open and the chain fell to the floor. Jenny and Laura stood up together and walked down the platform steps. The speaker was curled up on the stage, whimpering and covering his head with his cloak.

The team and the former hostage all walked back out the length of the hall without looking back. Some of the people of the congregation tried to attack them or stop them but couldn't approach within several feet due to the anointing of the Lord. On the spiritual plane there were now dozens of angels with flaming swords surrounding the hostage and the team. These angels kept the demons at bay at the same time that the weapons and alertness of the warriors kept the human part of the Satanists from physically attacking them.

The frustration and the fear caused a mixture of depraved screams that Jack felt must be what the antechamber to hell would be like. They went through and then closed the door at the bottom of the stairs and quickly climbed to the top landing and its door.

As they exited the building into the freezing night air and a stiff breeze, the two door guards were nowhere to be seen. Laura's armor faded from sight along with the sword. The six of them hurried into the woods about two hundred feet to the small opening where they had left their night vision goggles. As they stopped, Mark took off his field jacket and put it around Jenny's shoulders. She slid her arms into the sleeves of the jacket and zipped it up. She had started to become very embarrassed by her near-nakedness not to mention the cold of the outdoors. She smiled at Mark and simply blinked her thanks. It completely conveyed her heartfelt appreciation for the gesture. She then hugged Sheryl, "You didn't forget me, and you came for me." Sheryl hugged her and smiled at Jack in the dark over Jenny's shoulder.

Sarah slid her hand into Mark's and hugged him for his thoughtfulness.

Laura was listening to the voice of the Holy Spirit and announced, "We have to go. Now! The people in there are being driven to blood frenzy by their demons. They will be after us in just a minute." The six ran back the way they had come with Mark and Sarah helping Jenny. It didn't take them too long to reach the SUV.

As they exited the woods Mark remarked, "We'd bettered get her home and get that paint off of her before we're stopped by the cops. Be sort of hard to explain her condition, don't you think?"

Everyone got in the big SUV and Jack slowly drove out along the rutted road in the splotchy moonlight and gusting wind. He kept waiting for a sign of the pursuit. Mark asked him, "What are you doing? Let's get out of here."

Jack saw what he wanted in a few minutes. About fifty members of the coven came out of the woods carrying torches and clubs. They started running towards the apparently stalled vehicle. As they got closer Jack let the SUV move a little faster and spun the wheels on the sandy soil to act like they were stuck.

Mark checked out the armament being carried by the crowd and didn't see any rifles or heavy artillery, at least, not yet. He wasn't sure of what Jack was up to but he was ready in any case.

Getting closer to the car enraged the Satanists even more and consumed them with a desire to vent that rage on the people in the car. This is what Jack had hoped for, that their focus would be completely on the fleeing Christians and not on the surrounding area. He had seen the flashing lights coming up the other side of the rise they were going up. He timed out things so that the crowd got within ten feet of their rear bumper when the first cruisers topped the rise and came rushing towards all of them.

To the police it must have looked like a riot mob was chasing the Cadillac, armed with clubs, knives, and other weapons.

The Satanists came to a stop as the police cars slid to a halt. Their anger and rage was obvious and their desire to attack the police as well as the people in Jack's car overcame their better sense. They raised their weapons and charged the collection of cars screaming at the top of their lungs. Jack looked on horrified. He had hoped that they would be stopped by the sight of the police. Mark, looking back chuckled, "Nice move."

Then a bright light bathed the onrushing cult members and a windstorm tore up the ground in front of the runners. The flying debris and grass brought the mob to a halt shielding their faces and eyes from the onslaught and the eye-watering glare of the light. Throwing up their arms they broke and ran the other direction.

The police helicopter then swooped over them and stopped them from running in the other direction. An electronic speaker commanded them to throw down their weapons and lay on the ground face first or be fired upon. All but three or four complied and fell to the ground. Two rounds from an unseen automatic weapon aboard the helicopter into the ground at their feet convinced the remaining Satanists to give up. The squad car officers ran over to the captives and began frisking them and handcuffing them with riot cuffs made of plastic. All the time the helicopter continued to hover above the scene with its penetrating light pinning the captives to the dirt like a collector pins butterflies to a display board.

Jack spoke to the Commander of the police who confirmed the 9-1-1 response. He radioed in that things were well in hand. The next hour was spent with Jenny telling her story and Jack, Laura, Sheryl, Mark, and Sarah adding their roles as the story reached an end.

Two large police trucks arrived with additional officers and all the 'rioters' were loaded on board as they were arrested and charged with flight to avoid arrest, kidnapping, attempted assault on the police, and a variety of other charges. No mention was made of attempted murder as the evidence was all conjecture. This meant that all fifty of the cult members might be out on the street before noon tomorrow. Also, Mark noticed that the police weren't too eager to hunt through the woods for the coven hall.

The team decided to take Jenny and Sheryl to Sheryl's and then go on to Jack and Laura's house to regroup and get some rest.

CHAPTER ELEVEN

Minister Alan Throman and Jenny's parents met them in the driveway to Sheryl's house. Their return was greeted with shouts of joy and tears of concern for Jenny and gratitude to all of them for risking their lives to save her. Sheryl was very grateful and promised to help them in any way she could in their work. Jenny nodded her agreement. She had come to like these brave people and wanted to stay in contact with them as much as possible. Especially she wanted to know Laura. Jenny would never forget the golden armor or the shining sword that Laura held in the face of the monstrous group.

Mark talked to the police about the abduction and possible retaliation by the Satanists. The police agreed to assign two men to watch Sheryl's house for the next week or so until the Satanist's cases came to court and a better understanding was established by the court as to the aims of this particular group.

The team drove back to Jack and Laura's house. After cleaning up and getting something to eat, the four of them adjourned to the family room.

Physically spent and emotionally drained, Jack made the decision that there were no decisions to be made until everyone had a good eight hours sleep. The entire house had a unique fiber optic 'windowing' system invented by Jack's dad that could be turned off to provide darkness even during the day. Shooing the newlyweds off to their guest room, Jack put his arm around Laura and walked upstairs with her to the master suite. Fifteen minutes later everyone was fast asleep. The NovaStar home defense system had proven itself before and there was no lost sleep worrying about intrusions.

While they slept, three men in suits showed up at the Arapahoe county jail holding the Satanists. Attempting to gain their release on bond the men were told that it would require the signature of a state court judge due to the seriousness of the charges. Undeterred, the men determined which judge's signature was required and proceeded to call him at his home.

It was 6:20 a.m. on the clock when their phone call woke up Colorado State Supreme Court Justice Steven Suitland. He had been a light sleeper all of his life, especially since his two tours of Viet Nam, and he woke on the first ring. Eyeballing the red digital display on the clock-radio, Judge Suitland snagged the phone off the hook before it woke his wife.

"Judge Suitland" was his terse announcement to the obviously brain-damaged person on the other end of the line.

The inquiry came, as oily as suntan lotion over the phone. "Judge Suitland, my name is Aaron Beeman. I'm an attorney for the Sunrise Corporation. I'm dreadfully sorry to be bothering you at this early hour, but it is a matter of some urgency."

Steve Suitland knew who Aaron Beeman was and detested him and his insidious defense of the foul and evil in the State of Colorado. He also knew of the Sunrise Corporation, which was a front for the Omniscience Temple activities. While there was some possible trepidation concerning their issues and his continued role in the judiciary or maybe in this world, Judge Suitland didn't give a flying flip for their power politics and pressure tactics. But as an honest judge it was his duty to give them a chance and observe the amenities. "It had bettered be urgent at this hour."

"Oh, I assure you that it is Judge. It seems that through a mistake, the county sheriff has incarcerated thirty-four of our associates on some trumped up charges. I understand that it will require your signature to gain their freedom while we wait for a hearing." Aaron Beeman had become used to everyone jumping when he represented the Sunrise Corporation. While he hadn't dealt with this particular judge until today, he was sure it would be no different.

Judge Suitland put him on hold while he checked with the booking officer concerning the prisoners. Connecting with the right people only took a minute and learning what the charges were took even less. Hanging up from the second call, the fifty-six year old judge pondered the situation for several minutes.

First, it was irritating that these people wouldn't wait until morning. Secondly, the charges were specific and not a "mistake". The police had apprehended the whole group rioting and attacking citizens while carrying a whole variety of weapons. Then they tried to resist the police. Judge Suitland knew that there was more to this than he knew right then but he didn't feel that it was the proper course to just put off the lawyer without more information.

Clicking back onto the first line, he instructed the attorney to call him back in thirty minutes. He cut off the imperious bleating about valuable time by hanging up on the pushy man. Dialing another number he waited while another person struggled out of sleep and answered his call.

"Hullo?" was the sum total of the response to the call.

"John Dyer? This is Judge Suitland."

The response was more alert and attentive this time. "Yes, judge, what can I do for you?"

Good. No whining about the time or idle chitchat. "I have a situation that I need your advice on immediately. It seems that there was a mass arrest this morning out in Arapahoe County of a large group of religious zealots. In this particular case, the arrested are Satanists. Their lawyer is on the phone wanting me to sign a release so that they can be released on bail immediately. Two things to consider are; the attorneys are from the Sunrise Corporation, and there were requests for federal indictments at the time of the arrests. Those indictments are being sought in Federal court presently. After our conversation last week, what should I do about their release considering my position and your involvement?"

That was a bombshell and a large bunch of input for a recently aroused man. John Dyer had no problem with it apparently. "Tell the attorney to come to your court tomorrow at, say, 10 a.m. to discuss the release. Do not agree to anything this morning. Do you understand, your Honor?"

The judge acknowledged the requirements, "Certainly. I expect to see you before 10 tomorrow?"

"Count on it" the Senior Agent of the FBI in the State of Colorado replied.

An hour later, John Dyer was dressed and on the way to the office using a cell phone to alert four of his best operatives. He had them put protective surveillance on the Judge's house and vehicle. As he pulled into the underground garage for the Bureau he ran over the facts in this case.

The Satanic cult that the Sunrise Corporation was associated with had started ringing bells in Washington when one of their members was arrested last week on assault and battery charges. In one of his pockets was a slip of paper. Nothing unusual except, that the writing was in Cyrillic and turned out to be Russian. Still, nothing to be concerned about but the local police forwarded it to the FBI in Denver. The identification of the paper was routine except that it was a Russian Military access control slip for a ten megaton nuclear warhead.

There had been a lot of attention paid to odd things or seemingly inconsequential detail ever since the suicide terrorist attacks on the United States. This one rang bells all the way to the new Homeland Security Department and the White House.

Aaron Beeman walked out of the jail empty-handed as far as his superiors would be concerned. As they walked to the long black limousine he told one of his associates. "This judge is being a stumbling block that I do not want in my way. Deal with him. I'll work with his replacement. In fact, make a statement with him. Take out his whole family so that all the other judges know who they are dealing with in this state."

As they reached the car, the door opened and Alan Roswell stepped out of the back. All three men came to a stop and stared at the big man. He walked up to Aaron Beeman and said, "You've made too many bad decisions." Beeman stepped back and coughed. He coughed again and again; he couldn't clear the obstruction in his throat. He began to panic when he realized he could cough out but couldn't get any air back into his lungs. His face turned red and he flailed around with his hands. He tried to grab Alan Roswell's coat but the leader stepped away from the weakening man. His face turned purple and his eyes bulged as he ran out of air. He convulsed and fell to the dirty ground in his eight hundred dollar Armani suit and quit moving.

Alan Roswell didn't even bother to look at the newly dead lawyer. He turned his baleful stare on the henchmen. "I don't want that judge bothered, hear me?" The two men nodded vigorously. "Your late friend has already gotten us into trouble with the government with his sloppy work. See that you don't follow his example. I won't tolerate any more trouble."

With that he got back in the car and it pulled away from the three men and accelerated down the street. The two men looked at the car as it sped down the street. The taller of the two said, "He left us here without a ride." The other man turned his head in disbelief and asked, "You want to ride with *him*?" They both looked down at their ex-leader and turned and walked away from the body in different directions.

CHAPTER TWELVE

After a good six hours sleep, the crew met around eleven a.m. for a light brunch. Mark took Jack aside and asked him a question that had bugged him for a few minutes. "You're designing a new home with military assistance? Why didn't you didn't ask me for input? The smile on Mark's face took all of the sting out of his questions.

Jack answered with a laugh. "Because I thought you'd be up to your armpits in Russians and a new married life and would not be here to help."

Mark said, "Oh. Okay, tell me about what you've got so far."

Jack led Mark over to a set of arm chairs. "Our direction was from God." He told Mark about the image both he and Laura had seen with the spear. "I told the design group that I wanted a giant-spear-proof house. You know, something that will really stop any attack of less than nuclear proportions. Well, after considering that, we had to scale it back a bit because I still wanted it above ground."

Mark whistled, "That is going to stretch your budget regardless of scale."

Jack nodded, "Yeah, I know. Anyway they have decided to essentially build us a fixed position Abrams tank with a dining room."

Mark thought for a few seconds, "Okay, I can see that." Both of them laughed at the image.

Jack continued. "What we've designed is essentially a two-story, 3800 square foot house with adiabatic reflective armor at all points. Structural members of steel-alloy that will withstand a direct bomb hit on a reflective armor roof. There is still the capability of breaking through a wall with rocket-propelled grenades if they are the type that the military uses to bust tanks. It was assumed that this level of attack is unlikely. Since the construction is being done in secret, very few, if any, people will know about the walls, roof, and flooring for the new house. You'll like the doors. Each door can handle almost a four pound C4 explosion without rupture. But, the neat part is that an attack on any door causes a second door to move into place behind the first. The second door is five-feet thick Naval ship armor plate, structured to handle ten times what the first door will take. If enough force is used to breach the second door then the whole area will be reduced to shambles."

Mark looked at the drawing Jack was making. "I see that the view system eliminates the windows as weak points, what about the utilities and air in the event of a gas attack?"

Jack drew some more lines under the first ones. "All the power, utilities, water, and air is brought in at a twenty-four foot depth in armored channels which will be monitored electronically for tampering. Also, the communications are all satellite linked via optical lasers through ports in the roof. Those are backed up by a second system which is over a half a mile away in another building. We also have gotten approval for fully automatic weapons storage here. That took Presidential approval."

Mark was really impressed by the detail and well-thought out design. "I'll let you know if there is anything I could suggest as an improvement but I don't see anything now. It's almost like I would have designed it as it is."

Jack laughed, "In a way, you did." At Mark's sharp look he continued, "I took the liberty of asking your old number two in the SEALs, Bill Carroll, to give us his impression. Several of the innovations in the design are his."

Mark smiled at the memory of his service buddy. A lot of water had passed under the bridge since they had been together. "How is Bill doing?"

Jack thought for a minute and replied, "I'm not sure. He wasn't very forthcoming in details about himself or his line of work. It was still in the service though."

Laura walked over and asked what was going on. Jack and Mark told her about the house design. She grinned, "I'll bet you have a couple of suggestions, don't you Mr. Military Guy?"

Mark made a small face and added, "Well, I would have buried it in the ground and made it totally unapproachable. Other than that, I like it."

Jack looked at the crew sitting in the kitchen. "We'd better get back to figuring out this Believer's Temple thing."

Mark agreed. As they walked back to the kitchen he asked, "When will the new house be done, and where is it going to be?"

Laura looked at him with an impish grin. "You can't beat cubic money for getting things done. It will be ready to move into in the next four weeks. It's only three blocks from here, but the 24-7 construction is being concealed by tarps and painting smocks until they get the normal decor up over the armor. That should be next week. We'll take you for a tour then, okay?"

Mark nodded, "I'll bet the warranty on this baby will be iron-clad." Laughing at his own joke he rejoined the group.

They then attempted to figure out a plan of action against this strange and violent group known as the Master Prophets.

To accomplish the most in the least time, they decided to split up. Jack wanted to stake out the building they had burgled. He wanted to see if he could spot anyone that looked familiar. Mark wanted to visit the Arapahoe county government building and see what the public records had to offer. Sarah warned him to be careful in what he asked for since this group had eyes and ears everywhere and Jack added that the Believer's Temple definitely had contacts in the government.

Laura and Sarah decided to go shopping for food and supplies in the event this action would be drawn out and they would be working out of the house. Kissing Jack goodbye she told him to be careful and stay in touch. "I love you very much. See you this afternoon.

Driving down to the front of the same building Jack noticed that there was several boarded up windows above the walkway between the building and the multi-level parking garage.

He had been watching the building for over an hour when he saw three men leave the building and head for a car parked out front. Jack focused his binoculars in on the group and recognized two of the men as the ones that had released the Satanists he had been talking to in the Denver County Jail. Since there didn't seem to be any other leads he decided to follow the men and see where they went.

They drove into Aurora and parked near a popular Mexican restaurant. Jack exited his SUV and tailed them as they walked along, oblivious to him and entered the restaurant.

As Jack walked into the restaurant he watched the three men from the Temple moving towards a table at the back of the large eating room. There were at least forty or fifty people already dining or drinking at tables in the dark, heavily beamed rooms that made up the public portion of the business. Old signs, horns, wheels, and a wide variety of other objects were fastened to the ceiling and walls as decoration, giving the room an atmosphere of history and wide appeal.

Slipping by the tables he kept his vision open and not obviously focused on the trio of young men. He found a small, two-place table and settled into it as the three men returned from looking for a table at the back of the room. The leader of the three looked around at the crowded room and then walked over to an older man sitting alone at a two person table. The man was dressed in worn casual clothes and was intent on finishing his meal. The younger man spoke to him but got no response. He reached out and tapped the sitting man on the shoulder. The older man looked up at the intrusion and focused on what the younger man was telling him. He looked down for a few seconds and then looked back up and shook his head. He then went back to eating. The younger man was obviously angry with the negative response and stood there for a few seconds. Then he leaned down on the table, held up some money, and said something quite forceful to the older man.

A young hostess rushed over to the table and pointed out an empty table towards the back of the room and over to one side. The leader shook his head and pointed at the two-person table at which the older man was eating. Although he couldn't hear the words Jack could easily figure out when the hostess indicated that there were three of them and only room for two at the table.

Looking around the leader pointed at the first two-person table and indicated that the two could be put together to make enough room for his party. The hostess looked first at the older man, and then at the young couple just leaving the second table. She shook her head attempting to point out to the young man that she couldn't just force a patron to leave his table to accommodate them.

The young man's friends walked over and lent their weight to the argument. The older man continued to eat and ignore the whole thing. The young man heaved a big sigh and pulled out a cell-phone. Dialing a number he waited for a few seconds and then spoke to someone on the other end of the connection. Hanging up the phone he continued to stand there and glare at the older man. A phone started ringing behind the cashier's counter next to the manager of the restaurant.

The manager, a well-dressed older man, answered the phone and listened for a minute. He hung up, looked around and then rushed over to the group and shooed the hostess away. He talked to the young men for a minute and then turned to the older man. Leaning down, he talked to the older man for a minute and raised his hands in the universal gesture for being unable to resist forces beyond his control. Standing up he motioned for two waiters to come over and pick up the plates and food the older man had and remove them from the table. Unfortunately all the tables had filled up by now and there was nowhere to put the older man. As the young men muscled their chosen tables together and took possession of the combined tables, the manager was obviously coming to the conclusion that the older man would have to leave even though he hadn't finished his meal.

Jack stood up and motioned to the manager. When the man came over, Jack offered to share his table with the older man. Very relieved, the manager hustled his waiters along to bring the plates and the older man over to Jack's table. The older man walked over and stared at Jack for a few seconds. Jack put out his hand and said, "Hi. My name is Jack and you look like you need a place to eat. Why don't you eat with me?"

The older man took the offered hand. "Thank you very much. My name is Caleb." Jack noticed that there was an unexpected strength in his grip that belied his looks.

The manager apologized profusely about the need to move Caleb from the table and marked his bill paid in full to compensate him for the trouble. Caleb nodded his thanks and watched the manager leave.

After they were seated and the waiter had brought a menu for Jack, Caleb suggested the chicken breast sandwich as the best thing on the menu. Jack ordered that and sat there looking around the restaurant but casually keeping an eye on the table with the three men. Caleb went back to eating but Jack could feel his eyes on him.

Irritated by the rude treatment afforded Caleb, and somehow personally embarrassed by it, Jack turned to his new guest, smiled and earnestly asked, "I hope you weren't too offended by the lack of manners displayed by the young men over there."

Caleb could detect real concern in Jack's voice and he responded in kind. "No, I was a little put out that they couldn't accept another place but it all worked out, didn't it?"

Jack could detect a wry sense of humor underlying Caleb's comments so he continued the conversation. "What do you do for a living Caleb?"

Caleb thought for a bit and smiled. "I fix things." Then he went back to eating. Jack's food arrived and the chicken sandwich was delicious as described.

Caleb had finished eating and sat there, sort of lost in his thoughts. The waitress brought Jack's bill and he paid for the meal and left a generous tip. He looked at his new friend and took another stab at conversation. "Is there anything I can do to help you? If it doesn't offend you I feel I need to pray for you." Jack wondered where that came from.

Caleb thought about that for a minute and then nodded his head. "Yes, there is something you could do for me. Tell me why the actions of those young men upset you so much."

Jack thought about that for a few seconds. Caleb could be the type that let other people do whatever they wanted to because he felt they had a right to and wasn't disturbed by them. Whatever the reason for the request, Jack felt he should be truthful about the emotions he was feeling. "I was raised to believe that common courtesy is a requirement for civilized social behavior. They don't seem to care about you or if their desires put you out. I find that behavior selfish and crude. It irritates me that a gentleman, like you, should be brushed aside on a whim of theirs. I wouldn't of let them have my place. So, yes, their actions embarrassed me. I don't feel that we were designed to be so self-centered. The Lord wants us to love and care for our fellow man, not crush them for our own benefit."

Caleb gazed at Jack and said, "Ahh."

Trying again Jack leaned over and looked into the other man's face. "No, I really mean it. Is there anything I can do to help you? I don't want to offend you or insult you but wishing you well and telling you to enjoy life isn't very effective, is it? Can I give you some money? Do you need a place to stay? Can I help you find a relative? Do any of these questions seem to make sense?"

Caleb laughed at that. Then he sobered up and smiled at Jack. "You just paraphrased the second chapter of James you know. No, I do not need any of the things you just mentioned but I would like to accompany you on your journey today if that is all right with you. I'm sure we will get a chance to pray together soon."

Jack noticed that the lost, vacant state of mind had disappeared and Caleb was apparently a lot more than he seemed at first glance. In his mind Jack formed the question, "Dear Holy Spirit, is it right that I continue to work with this individual?" He got a confirmation in his spirit and he knew it was the Lord because he definitely felt peace over the decision.

Seeing the other men paying for their meal, he nodded his head and said, "Okay, if you really want to, come along." They stood up and left the restaurant and crossed the street. Jack walked into the shadows on the far side of the street and turned and waited. Caleb waited with him quietly, watching him, not asking questions.

Several minutes later the trio Jack had been following left the restaurant and started walking north on the street. Giving them a good head start Jack and Caleb began to follow them. When the trio turned into a large building's court yard, Jack closed up the distance. Watching as they entered the building he turned to Caleb, "This could get dangerous. Please wait for me here until I come back."

Caleb smiled a knowing smile. "I think I'll tag along and see what happens." Jack could tell that it would be a waste of time to argue so they quickly walked across the courtyard and quietly entered the building. They were in time to see the three men go through a doorway and shut the door behind them.

Jack thought about what he was doing and realized that the crew in front of him could have made him and were leading him on into a trap. Certainly they could be in trouble for illegal entry or trespassing. While he wondered about that, Caleb touched his shoulder and inclined his head in the direction of the doorway. He knew that they were following the three men and was unconcerned about continuing through the door. Jack took a breath, centered his mind, covered them both in the Blood of Yahshua and walked up to the door.

Opening it, he saw a larger room. Very sparse furnishings and glossy, uncovered wood flooring, most likely the exercise room for the building. The lighting wasn't very bright and there was no sound. There also was no sign of the three men. Jack moved into the larger room with Caleb right behind him.

Still moving quietly, he began to walk across the empty floor of the room for the doors on the other side. Halfway across the room the lights flared into brightness and the two men stopped. From four different doors, two in front of them and two behind them, eleven men came into the room. All of them were almost clones of the trio Jack had been following. Young, muscular, short hair and definite attitudes.

The leader of the trio they had been following asked, "Who are you, and why are you following us?"

They may have noticed him outside the headquarters building and lured him here. Regardless, they had obviously been seen and the trap was well-sprung. There would be little reason for lying or acting as if their being there was just an accident. It wouldn't have mattered anyway, these guys were looking to hurt somebody and words only got in the way. Jack knew he had a chance to take them as long as they stuck to fists, clubs, or feet. But the thought was no more than a short-lived hope as several of the men upholstered handguns from under their jackets or from behind their backs.

The leader nodded at Jack's silence. "Okay, if that's the way you want to play it." He looked at the rest of his crew, "Kill them."

Jack's silent prayer to Yahshua was more for the protection of Caleb than himself. He knew where he was going when he left this world but felt bad about dragging an innocent into a literal 'dead-end' situation. He moved in front of Caleb to try to protect him from as many of the enemy as possible.

Caleb's hand on Jack's arm moved Jack to the side as easily as you would move a small child. Caleb stepped forward even with Jack and seemed to fill with light. He waved his hand as several men fired their guns. Jack felt a shifting in what he thought of as reality as complete silence fell around him and everyone but Caleb froze into position. Jack could see the intensity of anger or glee on the faces of the men who had been aiming to kill the intruders. Then he noticed two of the bullets they had fired. The intriguing thing about these bullets was that they were suspended in air halfway between the gun and Jack. The odd thought occurred to him then that the keys at his baptism had done the same thing.

Jack turned to look at his new-found friend and found him to be far more imposing and regal than he had seemed before. His eyes displayed far greater intelligence and his movements and actions were youthful, dynamic. Taking a guess Jack asked him, "Who do you call Lord and Master?"

Caleb turned his gaze onto Jack and replied, "I serve the most Holy God and His son, The Lord Yahshua, as you do." He then turned back to the assembled would-be killers. "What shall we do with this army of the damned?"

Jack looked at the men and thought that God would see lost souls rather than revenge. "I don't know, can they yet be saved?"

Caleb shook his head, "No, they have sworn allegiance to the evil one. By their vile actions with many other people they've made their decision and the Lord has handed them over to their sinful desires. There will be no redemption for them." He spoke as one who knew without any uncertainty the path of life each of these men would follow. Jack felt the stirring of unseen depths in Caleb. Nothing physical, but deep in his spirit he could sense huge movements and unlimited spaces with dynamic energies moving in them. There was a lot more to Caleb than an old man.

Jack sought an answer from the Holy Spirit in his mind. "What are we to do with these men? If we leave they will just come after us." He turned to Caleb and asked, "Can we make them forget us?"

"That would be charitable, but not very smart. They will continue to do their father's will as long as they are on this world. He hasn't forgotten the treasure you keep or the setbacks you've caused him. Sooner or later they would be reminded of you and then you would have to deal with them again." Caleb had been contemplating what to do and came up with an idea. "Go back by the door we came in from." There was no arguing with this command. Jack went to where he had been told to go. Caleb stood there for a while and then joined him. Turning back to the frozen scene he moved his hand and suddenly everyone started moving at once and there were startled cries and curses. Suddenly there were a flurry of gunshots and very quickly all of the men fell to the floor dead or mortally wounded.

Jack shook his head, "Why did they shoot each other?"

Caleb also shook his head. "Each man thought that the others were you and I. In their eagerness to kill us they killed themselves. In many ways, some you can't yet comprehend, it is a very fitting end for their lives on earth."

Caleb left the abattoir followed by Jack. As they walked down the sidewalk away from the building Jack was bothered by the loss of his only lead to the men behind the operation he was trying to track down. Turning to Caleb, who again seemed like a quiet older man, he asked, "I was hoping to follow those three men to watch their organization in operation and attempt to discover why they are doing what they're doing."

Caleb turned south into an alley, walked a few yards into it and stopped. Turning to Jack he placed his hands on Jack's shoulders. Looking him directly in the eyes the ageless face with the intelligent eyes made his point. "You don't have to seek them out. They were looking for you. In fact, they will be coming around the corner in about ten seconds. Remember the words of our Lord, "I will never leave you, nor forsake you." With those words Caleb faded out of sight leaving a somewhat shocked Jack Malone alone in the alley.

But, he was not alone for long. Two men stopped at the mouth of the alley and studied him. Jack came to the conclusion that if this was what the Lord wanted him to do, he might as well do it. He walked back to the mouth of the alley and confronted the two men. One man stepped to the side, attempting to distract Jack with his motion. The other man was just standing there. Suddenly Jack's vision began to dim and his body felt numb. Focusing on the man in front of him he noticed a faint mist coming from the brief case the man had in his left hand. Too late Jack realized what was happening. Having already inhaled, Jack noticed that the gas tasted somewhat bitter and that it caused him to fall into a large black nothingness. He almost laughed as he heard them speaking like they were far, far away.

"Okay, so where's the other one? He came in here too. He's too old to get away. Let's stash this one and..."and the blackness swallowed Jack completely.

CHAPTER THIRTEEN

Jack came to in semi-darkness with a terrible taste in his mouth and a raging headache. Taking a quick personal inventory he felt intact physically but was tied up like a Christmas present. His hands were tied behind him at the wrists and his ankles were also bound. They hadn't blindfolded him or put a bag over his head, so he could see. But they did gag him very tightly.

Practicing his relaxation techniques he let his body fall limp so as to not waste energy. He didn't know if he would get a chance to escape, but he wanted to be able to if, and when the time came. He studied his surroundings carefully. He was bouncing around slightly which probably meant that he was in a vehicle of some type. It wasn't completely dark, like it would be in the trunk of a car. But there was a low-level, diffused light from above him.

Tiring of guessing, he stretched his legs and found he had room to move. Carefully pulling his knees all the way up to his face, he pushed his arms down until the binding on his wrists slid below his bottom and past his heels. Straightening out, he had his arms and hands in front of him. He carefully reached up and unloosened the cloth of his gag. Removing the gag he rested for a few seconds to see if anything changed. It didn't change, but the ride got rougher. He was bouncing from side to side more than before. His hands were bound with plastic 'riot-cuffs' and would take more than teeth to remove them.

He felt his pockets from the outside and found them to be empty. Again, he pulled his feet up and reached into the lining of his right shoe near the laces. Rewarded for his efforts, Jack brought out the one-inch blade. Holding the blade in his right hand he carefully sawed the plastic around his left wrist. It took several painstaking minutes but he finally cut through the plastic and his hands were free. He carefully cut the fetters off of his ankles and replaced the blade.

Testing the confines of his mobile cell he couldn't find an exit. Stumped for a minute he started praying for an answer to this dilemma. Not getting an answer, he started putting pressure on the sides of the container he was in. Slowly the side his back was against began to bow outward. Several seconds later there was an audible splintering of wood and the panel broke outward under the pressure. A roaring noise came through the opening.

Figuring he didn't have much time after all that noise, Jack scrambled to get out of his imprisonment as quickly as possible. Rotating around and putting all his energy into a snap kick to the broken panel. The bottom portion of the panel exploded outward and was followed quickly by Jack himself. As he tried to stand up in the gloom, the floor continued to shake and move back and forth under his feet.

Suddenly the roaring noise and the darkness made sense. He was in the cargo hold of a freight airliner. The plane was on a descent which he could tell from the nose-down position. The wind noise and rattling got louder and Jack knew that the wheels had been lowered for a landing. He knew he had to do something quickly or they would find him on first glance.

Seeing the hatch to the pilot's area he knew he was in a cargo plane's main hold. He made his way to the door only to find it locked tightly. Suddenly there was big lurch and he heard the squealing of the tires as they contacted a runway. There were no windows in the hold and no way out. So, Jack found a jump seat on the side of the plane and sat down to see what would happen when the plane stopped. He had been packaged for transport. No one expected him to be free and the pilots would be very surprised when they opened the door. Jack was looking forward to greeting them personally.

The plane came to a stop and the engines wound down. There were lots of noises from the outside and from the pilot's compartment. Jack got out of the seat and positioned himself to one side of the door. A few seconds elapsed and then the door was unlocked and opened.

The first man out was about five-foot, eleven and slightly built. So Jack carefully hit him in the side of the head with sufficient force to knock him out without killing him. Expecting a second pilot Jack stepped into the doorway to confront him. He turned out to be a nice-looking redhead of about the same height. She was standing there stunned by the sudden attack on the first pilot. Jack capitalized on her inability to react and grabbed her throat in his right hand and stepped by her into the cockpit. A third member of the crew was one of the burly men that had gassed Jack in the alley.

Holding the woman in an unbreakable hold, Jack snap-kicked the third man in the stomach with his left foot as he bent the woman backwards, over his right leg. The pressure on her carotid arteries cut off the flow of blood to her brain and she put up a brief but feeble fight before losing consciousness. Dropping the woman, Jack slammed an elbow into the back of the neck on the third man who had bent over with the wind kicked out of him. Jack then reached around the man's neck with his right arm and tightened the pressure until he too was unconscious. All of this action took less than twenty seconds. Jack had complete surprise on his side and had gone through the three of them like a whirlwind.

After several minutes without a reaction from the outside, Jack peered out the cockpit windows to find that the plane had been stopped in a hanger. Since the plane was facing into the hanger, he couldn't tell if the hanger doors were open or closed but it was fairly dark which either meant it was night or the doors were closed. Looking around the cockpit he spotted the briefcase the third man had been picking up when he was leaving the plane. Carefully opening it, in the event it had been booby-trapped, he found a dozen sets of the riot cuffs. Quickly cuffing and hobbling the three crew members he was about to go look for a way out of the aircraft when he heard a heavy whining sound.

Correctly surmising it was unloading ramp at the back of the airplane he hurried out of the cockpit and snuck carefully towards the opening door. It wouldn't take whoever was out there long to find out that he had escaped. Hiding behind a crate he peered out of the plane. There was only one man there. He was in a suit and held an M-16 assault rifle in his hands. From the way he held it, it was obvious he knew how to use it.

The door completed its cycle and banged against the floor of the hanger. The man with the rifle shouted into the plane. "Come on out Mr. Malone. There are six of us out here with automatic rifles and I doubt that you are armed."

Jack let the silence grow for several minutes while he tried to figure out a way to disappear and leave them guessing. But other than the crate he was hiding behind, and the one he had come in, everything else was small and unusable.

The situation changed drastically as the man at the back of the airplane fired half of his twenty-round magazine into the cargo bay. Bullets ricocheted back and forth or just smacked into the cargo. Jack realized that if the others opened up then he would quite likely be shot. It also impressed him that the people he was dealing with didn't seem to care if they hit one of their own pilots or destroyed the aircraft and the cargo. So, he stepped out from behind the crate and walked down the ramp towards the shooter.

When he was ten paces away, the man gestured with the rifle for him to stop. He did as he was told. Several other men moved in behind him and he knew he had guessed right about the man in back. He hadn't been bluffing about the others. One of the men behind Jack poked him with a rifle barrel and told him to get on his knees or he would be glad to help him get there. Kneeling down Jack prayed that God would take care of Laura. The sudden darkness came quickly and, strangely, without pain.

CHAPTER FOURTEEN

Jack's thoughts wandered from one abstract concept to another without really deciding anything. It seemed pleasant and even if there was a pattern to the wandering, it didn't matter. This seemed to go on for a long time and then it quit. It grew darker and quieter around his thoughts and that didn't seem unpleasant either.

Something was bothering him though. It was hurting his back. He tried to ignore it but it kept hurting so he tried to move away from the pain. For a brief time it helped, but then his face started hurting. Heaving a large mental sigh, he decided that he would have to attend to these pains and leave the pleasant rest he was enjoying.

It occurred to him that he wasn't in a proper position, body-wise. Normally he didn't lie on his face. He tried to open his eyes and found it very hard to do. Then it suddenly didn't matter anymore and he drifted away again.

Sometime later a nagging though began to cause him to become concerned. He tried to catch the thought so that he could examine it. But it was elusive and kept slipping away, just as he got close to it. Finally he decided to ignore the thought completely. Then he was able to remember what it was. He was a prisoner. Now that was a strange thought.

Then the full impact of what that meant burst into his mind and he really tried to open his eyes. Slowly the left one opened just a crack and he could see a dim blur. He became aware of his body and realized he was, literally, lying on his face. He commanded the muscles of his back to straighten up and get his face off the floor. The reaction wasn't quite what he expected. He did get his face off the floor only to lose what control he had and pound it right back onto the floor again.

Pain! That washed through him like a cold wave. Everything started complaining at once. It felt like he had been run over by an eighteen-wheeler truck and left by the side of the road. His muscles in his legs were screaming, as was his neck and back. His face and gut hurt. He moved his right arm and brought his hand close to his head and levered his face off the floor for the second time. This time he was able to open both eyes.

His vision was blurry and uncertain and his muscles were erratic in operation but he was able to push himself up into a sitting position with his legs under him. That was a major relief for his back and legs and his face thanked him for not lying on it anymore.

Slowly taking stock of his physical shape he realized that the pain in his back had been a wooden bench, bolted to the wall. Apparently he had been leaning back against it and when it hurt, he had moved. In whatever mental state he had been in, he peeled off from the bench and landed on his face on the floor.

Looking around slowly his vision became less blurry and he could see he was in a small room with only one door and one window. The window was very high and not very big. The little light it was letting into the room revealed that there was nothing in the room except Jack and the bench.

Carefully stretching his muscles Jack examined his body to see what shape he was in. Everything worked but it all felt cramped. He was dressed in some cheap linen slacks and a T-shirt. He felt bruises on his face and many places on his body but didn't find any substantial damage and slowly stood up. He swayed but remained standing. Something was inhibiting his normally agile mind so that he had some trouble focusing on actions.

Realizing that he had apparently been drugged he started doing a set of exercises to speed the toxins from his brain and body. It hurt, but in a good way. After ten minutes of exercise he felt much better and more like his normal self. That was except for the aches where the bruises were. He touched his face and guessed that he hadn't been overly cooperative with his captors. Even though it hurt they hadn't broken anything he could feel.

Now, where was he and what could he do about it? He tried the door, which was not only solid metal, but firmly secured in the metal doorframe. Then he tried to see out the window but couldn't see anything when he jumped up and looked through it. It was like a basement window that let in light but didn't look out on anything but the window frame was very cold. So, he sat down on the bench and waited for his captors to come to him.

After two hours, during which he had used the time to review everything he could remember that had brought him to this point, he heard footsteps and a key being placed in the door lock. Knowing that they would expect him to either be still unconscious or dangerous, he just sat there and waited while they opened the door.

Two, large men entered the room. Both were dressed in a uniform and carried batons. Seeing Jack awake and aware, they stepped away from each other to keep him from attacking them both at once. Apparently they had learned from the pilots that he was not to be taken lightly. The man to Jack's left indicated with his head that Jack was to get up and leave the room in front of them.

Jack got up and walked between them and out into the hall. He knew he could of disabled them both as he moved between them but resisted the urge because he wanted to see what else he could before they drugged him again.

Stepping out into the hall he noticed two more men waiting just out of sight beside the door. Right, they really weren't taking any chances with him this time.

He was marched down the hall and to another hall to the left. After passing nine doors he was stopped by his guards at the tenth one. One guard opened the door and again tipped his head as a sign that Jack should enter.

Entering the room Jack did a quick scan and found two people in the room which was furnished very nicely in modern leather. The man behind the desk was of indeterminate height, probably about six feet tall. He had a full head of blonde hair and a jutting jaw line. His brown eyes were so dark they were almost black. Intelligence showed in those eyes, but so did cruelty.

The other man was different. He was buff and about six-two in height. He carried himself like a fighter and his eyes were cold and calculating. He had a pistol in his right hand hanging by his side. He was probably about thirty and radiated competence and violent domination by his expression.

Jack walked into the room and, when told to, sat in the chair facing the man behind the desk. The four guards that had brought him from his cell had not entered the room but had closed the door after him.

Jack locked eyes with the man behind the desk and waited for him to talk. Recognizing the state of combat that Jack was obviously in, the man behind the desk sat forward and steepled his fingers under his chin and spoke. His voice was higher pitched than one would have expected from his demeanor and it almost came across as comical. Jack wasn't laughing.

"My name is Karl, Mr. Malone. May I call you Jack?"

Jack nodded slightly to accede to the request.

"Very good" said Karl. "Let me lay out some ground rules for this discussion." Karl nodded his head at the other man in the room without taking his eyes off of Jack's. "Jason is my bodyguard, and he is very good at protecting me. I know about your martial arts capabilities and I am not inclined to allow you the pleasure of assaulting me. Jason has orders to shoot you if you make any move I don't tell you to do. Is that understood?"

Jack inclined his head again in understanding, but said nothing.

Karl nodded again. "The other ground rule for this discussion is that we don't lie to each other. I know a great deal about you and your life so don't think you can lie to me without my knowing it is a lie. If you lie, you will be punished. Do you understand?"

Again, Jack gave a nod.

Karl smiled, "You are too intelligent to fall for a bogus offer of freedom for the information we desire. To show you that I won't lie to you, I will tell you that you will be given one chance to leave this place alive. That is if you can give me something that will make it worthwhile to keep you alive. You have already given my organization far too much trouble and interfered in matters that are not your business. You have caused the death of nine of my men, stolen our gift of the young lady to the young men that serve us, and jailed some of those same young men."

Karl gestured grandly with his right hand. "These things we can overlook if we can profit from your intrusion." He smiled again. "I want to know what you are doing in our business." He sat back and waited for Jack to comment.

Jack was fairly sure that they wouldn't let him live even if he could give them something that would satisfy them, but they might let him live a while longer. The major problem was, if they were looking for information, he didn't have anything to give them. Stalling for time while he prayed for God's help he said, "I need to know what it is that you want."

101

Karl nodded, "Okay, we want to know three things. One, who are you, really? Two, who do you represent? And three, what do you know about us?

Jack's prayer wasn't getting any real results except a peace about the whole affair, so he decided to tell the truth. "My name is Jack Malone. I own a design and development company in Denver, Colorado. I'm married and am trained in several martial arts. I don't represent anyone other than myself, and I really don't know who you are. I got involved because some of your thugs attacked some teenagers without cause. That led me to attempt to find out more about why the Omniscience Temple would be involved with Satanists. That, in turn, caused me to free the young lady they had kidnapped from your offices. I am a Christian and I am diametrically opposed to ritual sacrifice of young maidens or children."

Karl opened a folder in front of him and studied it for a minute. Closing the folder he looked at Jack for a few seconds. Making up his mind he sat back and told Jack what was running through his mind. "What you say is exactly what you said under drugs. It is very fortunate for you that you did not try to fabricate anything. You are of great interest to our leader therefore I can't say that actually being uninvolved in any action against us will save you or erase your debt to our temple."

"But, that is not for me to say anyway. Odd isn't it? I can kill you but I cannot save you completely. I am going to return you to your "room" until Prophet Roswell has seen you and made a decision in your case. If his decision is favorable, you will be released. But in any event you will not be allowed to leave until after the end of this month regardless. After that, what you know will be irrelevant. Do not attempt to escape or you will be terminated without concern. Do you understand me?"

Jack nodded, "Can you get word to my wife that I'm all right but won't be home for a while?"

Karl thought for a minute and realized he would like to have Jack's wife available. "I'll see what I can do, but I can't promise anything."

Jack rose and walked to the door. He noticed that 'Jason' hadn't moved or said a word the entire time, but his eyes watched every move Jack made, Spooky.

As he walked to the door, Jason came towards him. Jack squared up with the larger man. Jason looked at Karl for approval. Apparently getting permission Jason casually threw his handgun onto a couch next to him and took a Karate stance and waved at Jack to fight him. This didn't seem to be what Karl had indicated was to occur but Jack was more than willing to accommodate the sadist.

Karl spoke up from the desk. "Oh, I'm sorry. I forgot to tell you that you are to be punished before you meet with the Prophet. Be very good Mr. Malone if you want to limit the damages to yourself. Jason also has several black belts and he has wanted to repay you for your murdering his friends in Denver. He won't be giving you much mercy. The only stipulation is that he doesn't kill you."

Jack asked, "And if I win, do I then get to kill him?"

Karl smirked at that, "I seriously doubt that you will win. But, in the unusual event that you do, I would suggest that you don't leave him in any shape to do anything to you."

Jack didn't like being forced into a fight but it didn't seem to be his choice at the moment. He said a quick prayer for protection and wisdom as he watched Jason's technique and realized that the bodyguard was emulating the late, pretty great, Bruce Lee and his personal style of Keet Jun Do. Jack had studied the techniques thoroughly and knew that on the opening strike he had a chance. If Jason used the normal punch to the heart that opened this form of combat it would leave a serious gap in the user's defense unless he was really as good as Bruce Lee had been before his untimely death.

Jason, a man of no words, closed on him and feinted a kick and struck with a solid right punch to the chest. The heavily muscled arm came at Jack very quickly. This was exactly the opening that Jack hoped he would use. Almost faster than he thought it, he used his left hand to block the initial punch to his left, stepped towards Jason and put all his power into a right hand straight knuckle strike to the big man's throat. The crack as the larynx broke and caved in wasn't very audible.

To Karl the initial action was so fast the two blows came as one. Jack stood watching as Jason tried to breathe but instead dropped to his knees choking on his own blood. Jack turned and walked to the door as Jason fell onto his face and quit moving.

After Jack left, Karl got up and walked over to the still form of his bodyguard. Prodding him with a toe he sighed, "Prophet Roswell could bring you back Jason, but after that poor showing, I doubt that he will." Karl called for some more guards to take the body away and dispose of it.

Jack's four guards had been waiting for him and the walk back to his room was uneventful. Jack thought through the whole set up with Jason and realized that Karl had expected to use Jason to take Jack's measure. Jack got on his knees and asked God to forgive him for executing Jason. Then he sat on the bench and wondered just what God was up to with this whole turn of events. He hadn't seen any chance to escape and he was pretty sure that Karl was both armed and had more guards ready if Jack had turned on him. He had noticed that there were dozens of guards and personnel around.

He prayed that Laura would understand his failure to call or come home when he was supposed to. He had no idea how long it had been since he had been gassed in the alley. They had taken his watch and his cell phone. He was pretty sure he wasn't in Colorado any more. It didn't make sense that they would fly him somewhere else in-state. He wondered what Laura, Mark, and Sarah were doing, probably looking for him. His prayers flew heavenward that they would be successful. Something about the visit from the head prophet and the end of the month making his contribution irrelevant bothered him.

He had passed several hours when he heard footsteps and the door to his cell was unlocked and opened inward. Instead of a guard he was surprised by his visitor. She was a beautiful blonde that had to be six feet tall with a figure proportionate to that height. She asked if she could sit down. Since the only place to sit in the cell was the bunk, Jack got up and indicated with his hand that she was welcome to sit there. Sitting down revealed her long legs. Jack wasn't impressed nor fooled by her physical charms. He had just gone through a demon-powered attack of lust in Tel Aviv and had no illusions about the body she was putting on display. It quickly became obvious to her that he wasn't interested in her on the physical level. "You are quite a package." She said, "First you take over our plane and then you kill Jason with one blow, impressive."

Jack was also onto the flattery/pride ruse and said, "Not really, there wasn't much challenge in either case."

Studying him for a minute she asked, "Where is the crucifixion nail? You didn't mention it while we were interrogating you with drugs. I don't think you have the capability to resist the drugs so it must be another form of protection that keeps it safe from us."

Jack realized that this was the real reason for their capturing him. The conversation with Karl was to see if he would offer it up in return for his life. The thought hadn't even crossed Jack's mind. The words to a popular Christian song strayed through his mind about his relationship to his Savior, "Forever I'll love you, forever I'll stand". He realized that these people were only keeping him alive until they could get the nail and that could be an advantage for him. "I am sure that it is safe in the Lord's hands."

She got up and walked to the door. Jack had heard the sounds of several people just outside the door and was sure that he would not have the opportunity to use her visit to arrange an escape. They weren't that stupid after all.

She stopped at the door and looked at him. "When Prophet Roswell gets here, you'll change your mind." She smiled, "If that won't be enough incentive to get you to give us the relic, we're going to allow your wife and friends to make an attempt to rescue you. When we have her, I'm sure you'll be willing to bargain." Then she left and the door was locked.

Jack thought about that last statement. "The Master Prophets were "allowing" the team of Laura, Mark, and Sarah to make an "attempt" to rescue him?" Jack had to laugh, "Maybe they were that stupid after all."

CHAPTER FIFTEEN

Captain Stan Hargrove sat back at his desk and thought back to the day that defined his present walk with the Lord.

------------------------******------------------------

The day had been a total mess-up to that point, and the latest call was sure to cap it off properly. For Pete's sake, he was a Captain and not a beat cop. He was supposed to be commanding from his office not from every crime scene in Salt Lake City. He was working up a head of steam over three phone calls that needed his "personal" touch. First was the prostitute that wouldn't talk to anybody but him. Then the hostage negotiations that had become stalled until the bank robber said that he would only talk to Stan Hargrove. That was a dilly. The 'bad guy' turned out to be a college buddy gone bad that hoped that Stan would give him a break. Now he had a domestic dispute between a mother and daughter and the cop requested Stan's presence before they could be settled down.

Stan maneuvered his cruiser between the two other police cars with the flashing lights and pulled to a stop. Exiting the car the six-foot tall man showed a muscular shape one would not expect from a police officer manning a desk. Stan's good shape was from three trips a week to a local exercise gym. He was a dark Caucasian with a firm jaw and intelligence in his brown eyes. He owed the rest of his good health to his girlfriend's insistence that he eat proper foods and not sit on the couch and eat junk food. He also liked to mountain bike and that keep the pounds off whenever he and Debbie could find time to go.

He walked up to the front of the manufactured double-wide and knocked on the screen door. It was a really nice non-movable mobile home. He wondered what something like this would cost and how long it would take to pay off at his salary.

The beat cop that answered the door showed Stan back to the master bedroom where the two women were holed up. Both cops looked spooked and Stan questioned them about the problem. Bill Taylor, the cop that had come to the door answered first.

Captain, I haven't seen anything like this in all my days.

The Captain's first question addressed the composure of the officers on the scene. "What is going on Bill? You're a professional policeman with five years of experience on the streets. What has you so rattled on this call?"

Bill Taylor grimaced and looked embarrassed, "Captain, I've seen a lot of strange things but this is the weirdest thing I've ever run into."

Stan considered that statement in light of the 'odd' things he'd run into as a beat cop and as a detective sergeant. This kid wasn't naive or untried. He'd been in two shootouts and one hostage situation that turned bad. He'd held up real good then, so this must be extraordinary. "Tell me." was all he said.

Officer Taylor explained that he and his partner had responded to the domestic dispute call and had determined that the recently immigrated daughter was deep into drugs and voodoo. Her mother spoke English but the daughter didn't. It seemed that the daughter was about to commit suicide when the mother had stopped her. Mom called 911 and that's how they ended up there.

After reaching the house and getting no answer at the open front door, they had entered the dwelling and heard loud voices coming from behind a closed bedroom door. Knocking on the door and announcing themselves as Police Officers caused the voices to stop for a minute. Then this really deep, ugly voice said "Leave, Now!" Well that wasn't standard procedure and the two policemen simply knocked again and demanded that the door be opened. What happened next was the cause of the call for Captain Hargrove.

Bill Taylor looked somewhat concerned that he would be considered unbalanced, but he stuck his chin out and went for it. "This.... hand reached through the door and grabbed me by the shirt front and then lifted me off my feet. It shook me violently, and the voice, still coming from behind the door, repeated the demand that we leave. The hand then dropped me and disappeared back through the door. But, the door was undamaged." The officer stood there daring his watch officer to doubt him.

Stan thought about it for a second. Bill Taylor was Detective material. He didn't drink (too much), and he didn't get crazy on the job. Therefore what he said must be true even if it didn't make sense at the moment. So he asked the younger man, "What did the hand look like?"

The cop shook his head, "That's another spooky thing, Captain. It was deep, deep red, and almost black, with really gnarled knuckles and black claws about three inches long. But the incredible power it had was like it was made of steel. It was that strong."

Stan considered what that meant. If what the officer had related was the unvarnished truth, then he had an idea what it probably meant, and that scared him. The woman he had been dating for the last three years was a born-again Christian who had talked to him for hours about the 'other' side. Which was the demonic side of the spiritual world, and that existed alongside our normal world.

Stan realized he was on thin ice here. First of all he had been dating a beautiful woman for over thirty months and he'd never gotten to first base with her in the bedroom department. Normally, the unmarried bachelor life he led was filled with much shorter involvements. But Debby was intelligent, fun, very strong in every aspect and exciting to be with, even if it didn't involve sex. He was puzzled about his attraction to her considering the nonsexual involvement. He truly enjoyed being with her and looked forward to their talks. Debby's references to the spiritual world were intriguing like an on-going novel, but up until now they had never had any reality to them.

Now he was apparently faced with an entity from this 'other' world who was threatening people in this world where he was sworn to defend them. Stan's mind spun quickly trying to remember what Debby had said about dealing with demons. He remembered her descriptions of encounters that she had gone through and what she had done to beat the enemy. He was about to see if this spiritual world she talked about was real. If it was, then he would need every memory of her conversations ready to remind him what to do.

Now that he thought about it, she had quietly been preparing him for this moment. It was like she knew he would run into this exact situation. He told the officer to return to the doorway of the bedroom while he made a call. Dialing Debbie's cell phone number he realized he was really nervous about not getting in touch with her. Then she answered.

Stan took a quick breath and organized his thoughts. "Debbie, this is Stan. How are you doing?"

"I'm doing fine Stan, how about you?"

"Great, just great, but I need your help, have you got a minute? Can you talk openly?"

There was a pause, then, she came back with, "I've got the time and I can talk Stan, what is the problem?" She could sense the nervousness and urgency behind his voice.

"You remember the conversations we've had concerning the "other" world?"

"Yes, clearly."

"Well", Stan started out carefully, trying to not exaggerate the situation, "I've got a problem here that sounds just like one of the bogies you described to me back a few weeks ago. It seems I need to address this situation and I'd like your advice on how to do it."

Stan then explained to her what the officer had said, and waited for a response.

Debbie came back with a quick set of instructions on how to handle the situation, but, she said, "You can't go up against a demon if you aren't protected. And Stan, you've never become a believer."

The officer at the door called to the Captain, "Come quick!"

Stan ended his call to Debbie with the words, "Well, I guess I'd better start believing right now. I've gotta go", Stan hesitated for a second. It seemed like he was going into all forms of strange territory today. Then he quietly said something he had never told her before, "I love you." With that he disconnected the call and walked to the bedroom door. He was aware that he may never see her again and he had suddenly realized for the first time that he really did love her.

There were at least three voices in the room and they were becoming violent in tone and content. Stan took a deep breath and said, "Jesus protect me." Raising his right foot he sent it crashing against the side of the door just below the handle.

The door splintered inward and flew open. All three of the men stared into the room with shock. In full, normal vision, a young woman knelt on the floor with a small handgun in her left hand. She was trying to bring the gun to her temple to shoot herself. Her mother had both hands on her left arm and was struggling to keep the gun away from her daughter's head. This was all Bobby Turick, the second beat cop saw. For Stan and Bill Taylor there was more. Superimposed over that scene was another scene in misty black and white. The scene it revealed was right out of Dante's Inferno for the two policemen. Where the back wall of the room should have been there was an indistinct blurry edge which surrounded a hole comprising the entire back wall. The hole revealed a vast distance of flame-shot darkness and chaotic movement and violence. There was an evil miasma coming from the hole that was felt in a person's soul. Extending into the room from the hole was an extremely ugly being with small, dark, leathery wings, fanged face, and clawed hands. His left hand was on the girl's arm, slowly pulling the gun up to her head so that she would finish her destruction with a bullet.

To Stan it was obvious that the demon could have easily pulled the girl's arm up and finished the thing. But it was equally obvious that the demon was enjoying drawing out the inevitable death as long as possible to generate more and more terror in the mother as she fought for her daughter's life. The girl's expression did not show any emotion. It was like she really didn't much care which way the drama ended.

Officer Bobby Turick hadn't been touched by this 'other' world nor was he tuned into it. All he saw was the girl with a gun and the ongoing struggle. He stepped past Stan and his fellow officer and went to aid the mother.

Stan saw the demon flick his free right hand and knock Bobby Turick into the wall next to the door. Bobby slid down the wall to the floor with the breath knocked out of him.

Stan stepped into the room and spoke to the demon. "In the name of Jesus Christ I command you to release this girl."

The demon did not let go of the girl's arm but instead turned his baleful stare on Stan. "Jesus I know, but you don't know him, and you never will." With that the demon thrust his right hand at Stan so fast it was there before Stan saw it start to move. The ghostly hand sank into his chest and it seemed that his heart stopped.

Stan felt intense pain and smelled the slimy, putrid odor of dead, rotting meat and knew that he was the one making the smell. He was consumed with grief and sadness because he knew he was dying. It was clear that he had stepped in where he wasn't capable of even saving himself. As his vision dimmed he looked at the girl and made one last plea, "Oh God., please save this young girl from this fiend." His life had been dedicated to protecting others and even as he was dying he did what he knew to be right.

Suddenly the motion in the room stopped and the grief, sadness, and pain that Stan felt killing him simply disappeared into peace. He heard a voice that he instinctively knew was the voice of God.

"The good shepherd lays down his life for the sheep". Stan felt the nearness of God almighty and His love for Stan. Stan was very aware of his unworthiness near a Holy God. But the Lord spoke again, "You were willing to give your life to save another and even in your agony you called on my Name to save her, so I will redeem her."

Several things happened in rapid fire sequence as Stan remembered it later. The demon's hand was slapped away from Stan. The demon screamed, "She's mine! I have a right to her. You will not take her from me!" The bolt of the purest white light struck the demon and seemed to shatter it into pieces and the hole in the wall slammed shut.

At the same time, the mother fell backwards and pulled the gun out of the girl's hand as she fell. The girl looked confused and started to cry. The mother threw the gun across the floor towards Bobby Turick and pulled her daughter into her arms.

Stan sat down heavily onto the floor and shook his head. He wasn't sure of what had happened, but he was sure that it did happen. He fumbled out his cell phone and pushed 'redial'.

Debbie's voice was scared when she answered the phone but filled with happiness when she heard his voice. Stan said, "Babe, you remember that Minister you wanted me to talk to? You need to see if you can make an appointment for me real soon."

Later, as he walked away from the mobile home towards his car, he remembered to humbly thank God for saving both him and the girl. Stan no longer had any doubts about the reality of Jesus, God, Satan, or demons or his capabilities concerning any of them. He was going to dedicate his life to Jesus and do it before the opposition took him out.

----------------------*****----------------------

As his memories returned to the present, Stan knew that he had been true to his word and had given his life to the Lord and learned to walk with God. He thought of the flashing gold and white figure in his dream. This latest development was something new and different. While he worked, he prayed and waited for a phone call.

CHAPTER SIXTEEN

Laura knelt in prayer with her God. Tears fell down her face as she petitioned the Lord for the life of her husband. Her intercessory prayer was the most profound she could remember. She knew that bad things happen to Christians as well as to the unsaved, but she wanted to change whatever had happened.

Her tears slowed and came to a halt as she entered deeper into communion with the Lord and a peace came over her. Her heart slowed from its desperate beating to a normal rhythm and her body posture relaxed from its rigid state. In her mind, she saw herself placing her requests on a golden platter and lifting them up to the Lord in supplication for Jack. In her mind's eye she imagined a glorious palace with marble columns and floors, all sparkling white with gold flecks in them.

As she knelt in the palace in her mind, the landscape beyond the open columns became more real and the beauty they showed was more breathtaking than anything Laura had ever seen. She felt a weight lift from her hands and the golden platter was no longer there. Instead, she saw a glow in the distance that approached and coalesced into the angel Rose. Rose was as beautiful and powerful as Laura remembered her.

The angel came close to Laura and reached out a glowing finger to touch her face where the tears had tracked down her cheeks. She smiled and spoke, "Laura, God wants you to know He has heard your plea and you will be reunited with your husband soon. It will take great faith and bravery on your part, but he knows you will be victorious." The angel darkened somewhat to a more golden hue and her smile disappeared. "Laura, go to the city you call Salt Lake and find a man named Stan. He works for the police department there. He will lead you to your husband. He will be expecting you." Rose started to float upward but checked her flight momentarily. "Use love to get Stan to help you." and then she was gone.

Laura's eyes flew open in her bedroom. She thought, "Use love?" Certainly she doesn't mean...! Laura stopped the flight of fantasy her mind was taking off on. "Not in the flesh, in the spirit." was the thought that came to mind. Laura realized that the angel meant Agape love or God's love, not the human physical kind of love, but the love of Christ for humanity. Pausing she thought, "Thank you Lord Yahshua, thank you Rose, and thank you Father God for your mercy." Getting to her feet she went out to the living area of the house and found Sarah using two phones and the internet on a laptop in an effort to track Jack after the call he'd made saying he was following some of the Master Prophet's men towards a restaurant in Denver some eight hours ago.

Laura sat down and waited until Sarah was finished talking to the person on the other end of the line. The Lord alone knew who she was talking to. With her contacts from her days at the Mossad and her new contacts with Mark's company it could have been anybody.

Sarah looked up with concern in her eyes. "Sorry Laura, I haven't been able to find out much about Jack as yet." Laura could see the tears in her eyes from across the distance. Jack had become very special to Sarah in the last couple of months and it pained her that all her expertise wasn't helping to track him down. The concern for Laura was evident in the tone of her voice. "I did locate his Cadillac on a side street near the restaurant. Mark went to get it with your keys, if that is all right with you?"

Laura smiled and said, "Sure, when he gets back I've got a lead and I need you and Mark to go with me."

Sarah choked back the smug superiority she still fell victim to from her days as a true spy about the abilities of these normal-seeming people. She had seen them walk with Yahshua and witnessed the miracles that happened in their walk. Having taken Yahshua as her Savior, and the Lord of her Life, Sarah now shared the power that Laura and Jack were given by God. Everything she had been taught and all her experiences didn't hold a candle to the things this 'housewife' had done in the last two months. She reminded herself that it wasn't her spy craft abilities that would win this battle against the dark powers, it was God's and Laura was very close to God. So, she brightened up and said, "What do you have?"

Laura repeated what the angel told her. Sarah didn't doubt for a second that what Laura said was the truth. She acted on it. Calling Mark on his cell phone she outlined a battle plan in three sentences. He said that he would arrange the flight and pick them up in about thirty minutes. He also suggested they pack light in the clothes department and put the 'other things', meaning the weapons, into the special pouch. He had top-level government approval to ship that package, unopened, on any commercial airliner in the U.S. Even so, this time they were going in style and the way he felt, just let anybody get in his way.

Hanging up, Sarah walked over to the closet their things were in and started putting together a traveling kit for Mark and herself, along with the 'special' pouch. Laura jumped up and ran to the bedroom to do the same for her and Jack. Sarah was surprised when Laura came out of her bedroom with a military M-4 Assault Rifle with a 40MM grenade launcher connected to it and a laser sight. Laura asked Sarah to include it in their special 'pouch' along with their rifles. Sarah mentally readjusted her thinking about Laura again. She remembered the golden armor and sword but it seems that there was a practical side to this woman too. She rather liked having a sister-in-arms.

An hour later the three of them were in a private jet, rolling down a runway on takeoff from Denver International Airport.

While they had waited for their plane to be made ready, Laura had called the Salt Lake Police and tracked down Stan Hargrove. It had seemed routine when she had asked for "Stan". The man at the switchboard hadn't even hesitated. "Yes ma'am, I'll connect you to Captain Hargrove's office."

Stan Hargrove had answered on the first ring. "Captain Hargrove, what can I do to help you?" Laura had explained that her husband had gone missing the day before and that she felt that there had been foul play in the disappearance and a mutual friend had suggested that Laura contact the Captain.

Captain Hargrove hesitated for a few seconds. When he started to speak it was a harder tone than before. "Ma'am, when did your husband disappear and where?"

Laura explained the time and place. The Captain's voice got even colder. "I'm sorry ma'am, but Denver is out of our jurisdiction. I suggest you contact the Denver Police on this."

Laura remembered Rose's last words. "Captain, I know you are busy, and I don't want to make your day more complicated, but I want to help you at the same time you help me find my husband. My friend Rose told me that you were the best person to reach out to for help. She also said that you'd be able to locate Jack. She was sure of it. In fact, she said that you would know that I was coming to you for this matter." Laura stopped talking and took a deep breath and held it.

The silence was lengthy. Finally the Captain spoke again. "Rose, huh? Does this have anything to do with the Omniscience Temple?"

Laura told him she was fairly sure that it did.

The Captain hemmed and hawed for a few seconds. "Did you meet 'Rose' anywhere special?"

Laura smiled and told him, "I met her while I was praying."

Stan Hargrove was relieved. He had thought that he was starting to lose his perspective, or his mind. He had been given a vision two nights before. The vision included an incredible person in the form of an angel named Rose. He had been given a mission by Rose. Part of it was to identify an evil in the Omniscience Temple. Stan knew just how powerful the Temple was in the west and really didn't want to tackle anything that could end his career in two hours. But then he had been praying for a chance to serve the God of the Universe. He figured that this must be that chance. One doesn't say "no" to God.

"Well then, when will you get here?"

Laura asked Mark and then told the Captain, "We'll be in your office within ninety minutes."

After his call with Laura was finished, the Captain reorganized his afternoon schedule and asked for the private file on the "OT". This was an unofficial file that most officers did not know existed. It detailed the research and investigations that weren't on the roster. Too many good men and women had been sacrificed when they found things that were not legal in the temple's dealings. Each of them had had a legal case but it just quietly disappeared, just before they retired, got thrown off the force, or mysteriously died.

The really galling thing was that the Omniscience Temple wasn't rooted anywhere in the State of Utah. Their closest "Temple" was in either Idaho or Colorado. The long-existant Mormon church and businesses had been able to prevent the

Omniscience Temple from getting a foothold anywhere in the State of Utah. But that hadn't stopped the OT from virtually taking over their Government, or at least in the law enforcement world and maybe the court system.

This file was an attempt by many good people to contain the "above the law" operations of the OT in their state. Even though this wasn't the first big group to try to run things in Utah. Stan knew that many people would know that he had asked for it and there would be notations made about the request. He also knew that he would be watched carefully to see that he didn't cause a problem for the department.

"The heck with that." he thought. Boy, since he had gotten saved four years ago his language had become extremely mild compared to before that. He would of laughed at any policeman that said 'heck'. But that was before he learned that your mouth speaks life and death. Bad language opens doors and Stan had seen what crawled through those doors. He wasn't going to open any doors if he could help it. That and his wife of two years, Debbie, would have his guts for garters if she heard him cussing.

Stan thought again about the defining point in his life. Where he changed from a hard-nosed, honest cop that didn't think that a righteous, loving God would have anything to do with the world he worked in, to the God-fearing, Bible reading, anything for Christ, Christian he was today.

CHAPTER SEVENTEEN

When Stan was told that there were three people to see him he knew enough not to mention the Omniscience Temple, the Master Prophets, or anything that related to them in the open. To his great relief the two women and man that had come to see him were smart enough not to bring up any names either.

After shaking hands all around Stan led them back to his office and shut the door. He still wasn't foolish enough to think that would prevent the subjects they were going to discuss from being general knowledge. He couldn't shut the blinds without causing people to suspect the wrong things and he was a good enough lip reader to know that there were others out there that do the same. So he kept it real general and no names.

All three of his visitors were young and in great shape. This bucked the trend that he had been seeing for the last two years in that most of the people he had to deal with were out of shape regardless of their age. The younger ones didn't really care about their condition and the older ones seemed resigned to their shape. He asked the usual questions regarding a missing person in their area and talked about getting a photo and putting out a MPB or missing person bulletin. He then suggested that they show him the area that the report was to be made on. They all filed out of the station and took the large rental they had to go across town. Once they were moving Stan felt he could relax.

"You guys were great back there." he said. "I doubt that anyone has any idea that we are nosing around in OT business."

Mark nodded, "Yeah, we could sense the strain and the suspicion when we walked in."

Sarah asked Stan a pointed question. "Were you able to get any useful information concerning where they would hold someone like Jack?'

Stan had to admire the business-like attitude of the group. No nonsense, no demands, just get after it. "Well, yes and no. It will depend on whether they want to drag him before the ruling temple council or if it is strictly MP business."

Mark thought for a second. "I'd guess that it would be MP business and that the main body and executive branch of the Omniscience Temple don't have a clue as to what is going on in this case."

Stan looked at the ex-SEAL with the obvious question plain on his face.

Mark continued, "This business with the Satanists is part and parcel of the Master Prophet's bag and that is who Jack was involved with when he disappeared. Also, he has something that the enemy knows about and wants really badly. Again, the Master Prophets seem to be the heavies here."

Stan thought about that as they continued to drive through Salt Lake City. He took out his cell phone and called the station. "Yeah, this is Stan. Let me talk to Assistant Chief Rogers. Thanks. Hello, Bud? Yeah, this is Stan. I've got the people here from Denver with their missing person case. I think I'm going to need to be out of sight for a couple of days to do this right. Can you cover for me? Okay, I owe you one. Bye."

He hung up and told Mark to drive to the interstate and head North.

After they were going North Mark's unasked question was answered. Stan said, "If things are as you say you won't find your friend in this state. My information is that the really doomed victims of the Master Prophets are shipped directly to their secret interrogation center in Boise, Idaho." That disclosure didn't sit well with Laura, "How do you mean, 'doomed'?

Stan turned around in the front seat to look directly at her. "In the regard that we haven't gotten a single returning survivor out of the place that we know of to date. They're taken there and then they're never seen again, ever. There are no grounds to allow us to interfere and every time we've tried to bring it up we get squashed by the politicians and our upper brass."

Laura knew that this wasn't the end for Jack because of what Rose had told her. The leading in her heart felt like he needed their help. "Okay then" she said, "We're going to break the old record."

Stan reached into the inner pocket of his suit jacket and produced some sheets of paper. "To do that, you're going to have to overcome some pretty stiff odds. Remember, this information is pretty much conjecture and just-plain guesses because we don't have any real solid data. But, it looks like the MPs keep their human guard dogs based at this location for training and protection. There are reportedly over thirty routine guards and a few dozen extras there for training or possibly punishment themselves. The word on the street is that none of these people are 'un-blooded' and they are the most unforgiving group of people you'll meet."

Stan got more serious, "I've run into some of them. Remember, these are the lower tier of the Master Prophets, 'The cannon fodder'. They were attempting to convince a group of punks to work for them. I had been staking the punks out before these MP stiffs showed up. Normally I wouldn't be used for this type of work but this particular group of punks had just killed twelve of their fellow gang types and a couple of concerned citizens. We knew they did it but didn't have any proof. They were on to every Narc and undercover type we had. So, I invited myself to help out with them. Well, it seems the gang thought too highly of themselves to work for the MPs. That apparently was the wrong answer. Even though these gang bangers were killers and really pretty tough, the MP group chewed them up and spit them out. I got the whole thing on tape and screamed for backup. I couldn't forget the way they took the leader out. They shot him so many times he fell apart." Stan didn't like the memory.

"Well, my backup rolls up and we brace the MP group. I mean I had them cold. I was an eye witness and I got it on video tape. They don't give us any problems and are processed. The next day they're released for a lack of evidence. To make a sorry story brief, I was told to forget whatever I saw and the tapes disappeared. After all, we got rid of the killer gang didn't we? And you know what galls me the worst? That group knew that they didn't have a thing to worry about when we arrested them. 'Arrogant twerps.' They killed fifteen kids and just walked away laughing."

Stan shook his head, "If you come on their turf, they'll harry you and hunt you until they catch you. Then they'll torture you until they're happy or until you're dead. The unofficial count is something more than forty people we think that they've taken to this place and probably executed in the center in the last two years."

Sarah reached up and tapped Mark on the shoulder. "Honey, that's maybe sixty tops, do we need any extra help?"

Mark thought for a minute. "No, I think we can handle that many. I'm sure we can if Stan and Laura want to join in."

Laura said, "I don't want to kill anyone but they are not going to keep Jack."

Stan shook his head. "You people still want to go onto their property when you have an idea of the violence and the military type of force these people can and will use on you?'

Sarah smiled a cold smile and answered him. "Oh, yeah, we have a really good idea of the type of people they are. The question is whether we'll have to destroy them or not."

Seeing the truth on Sarah's grim face and the solid confidence of all three people in the car with him told Stan volumes about them. They had been there before and they weren't afraid to walk into hell again for their friend. Then Stan wondered if the Master Prophets had any idea what they had stepped into.

Six hours later the car was parked at a motel four blocks away from the Master Prophet's center. They had rented three rooms just in case. They unloaded their gear and used the first room to plan and prepare for their invasion of the property.

As they inventoried an impressive amount of military weapons and other hardware Stan threw out the observation that they didn't really know if their friend was actually in the center and there could be a lot of people hurt defending the place for no reason if that was the case. Not to mention that the whole raid thing was totally illegal and might pit them against the Boise cops, Idaho State Troopers, the FBI, and who knew what else.

Mark finished loading an MP-5 submachine gun and laid it on the table. "Well Stan, here is how we look at it." He looked at the women and got their agreement. "Based on what we know, in the physical, this is the logical place for them to bring him to sweat him for whatever reason. Based on the supernatural, the angel Rose told us that you were going to lead us to Jack. Now with those two conclusions it's a no-brainer. He's here, they've got him, and they've had him for almost three days. Laura says he's still alive because God tells her that he is. Add to that the fact that we know the Master Prophets are up to some mysterious danger that is no good on a national scale and I think we're talking about terrorism in a major way. Now I have carte blanche authority directly from the White House, from the President himself, to deal with terroristic groups and individuals as I see fit to protect our country. Now, if you want to be a patriot and do both your civic duty and your sworn duty as an officer of the law, I can legally deputize you as a federal officer needed in this effort, your call."

Stan was more than intrigued by this. "You can do that?"

Mark nodded and showed Stan the federal badge the President demanded he carry while he worked for him. "In about three hours we are going to execute a federal terrorism raid based on our knowledge rather than a warrant since we feel that there is high corruption in the legal system that would run counter to our operational orders. We are there to look for a witness we feel is being held illegally and when we find him we will release him from any duress in which we presume he is being held. While we are in the process of determining if there are any violations of federal law we will respond with the necessary force to the people that get in our way in the process. Our normal rule of thumb is that we don't kill unless it is absolutely necessary. This process might not be pretty and it probably won't be quiet, but it will be effective, you in or out?"

Laughing, Stan said, "Count me in. I wouldn't miss this for the world, and, what the heck, being part of a federal task force will look good on my record."

Mark indicated the sketchy information they had. Since not much was known about the interior of the center the planning was only in the general not in detail. Go in, find Jack, and get him out. Successfully overcome anybody that says no. This would be a typically basic Mark Connelly-type operation. Sarah thought to herself, "Scorched earth again."

Three hours later the car was as close to the center as possible. That is without being seen from the building itself. There was nothing else to say so the four of them slipped out of the car dressed in black nylon body suits with various weapons, grenades, and gear hanging all over them. The communicators and night vision goggles were state-of-the-art and equal to anything the SEALs were fielding right then. This was natural because the equipment was all SEAL equipment loaned to Mark.

Stan had to admit it was an awesome looking group. He had a matching M-4/M203 combination assault rifle and grenade launcher to the one that Laura had. He was encouraged by the fact that they at least started out with smoke grenades rather than shotgun or high explosive rounds. Now to see how efficient they were. Talk is good but action was a better judge of capability.

At about the same time, Karl addressed the assembled troops in the large meeting hall of the Omniscience Temple center. It always gave him a feeling of importance to be standing tall in front of crack troops and giving them their marching orders, or, in this case, battle orders. Better yet.

"You men will be faced tonight with three veteran intruders. These people are friends of a man we have in custody and they want to break him out." At that there were snorts of disdain and general laughter that these people were that stupid. Karl nodded and agreed with his men. "Here is how we will trap these Christians." The angry buzz that moved through the crowd was the effect he had been looking for as he made that identification. These people hated the Christians. "Squads one, two, and three will stay behind those doors over there." He pointed to where the great hall began that ran the length of the building and led to the holding cells.

Karl turned and pointed to the other set of doors that led to the corridors around the great hall. "Squads four and five will secret yourselves behind the northern door. Squad six will do the same around the southern door. The intruders will come down the eastern corridor and enter this room through the middle door. When they are half-way across this room, I will signal and everyone surrounds them and keeps them covered with your rifles. I will demand their surrender and they will comply since we will have an overwhelming superiority of twenty guns against each of theirs."

At this point, Karl decided as a magnanimous leader he needed to provide some additional incentive to these crack troops. "We only need the blonde woman captive. The other two you can do what you want to with. In fact, I will personally give twenty thousand dollars to the man who kills either of the other two. If they resist, then I will give ten thousand dollars to each person that kills one of the

123

intruders." This was greeted with shouts and cheers. "I expect they will be here around the witching hour or somewhat later in the morning because they will expect us to all be in our beds asleep." That resulted in more hoots and laughter. "I want every man in their positions by ten o'clock tonight. Tomorrow we will celebrate our victory." More cheers and yells. He dismissed the men so that they could prepare.

As they left the assembly, one of the sixty men commented. "That twenty thou is going to be mine." Every other security guard knew better. It would be theirs.

Slightly after midnight, Mark led the team through some bushes and trees to the back of the structure and up to a fence surrounding the property. Checking the fence for voltage or sensors he wasn't able to detect anything. That bothered him. He had the other three wait while he went over the fence and did a survey of the property with his equipment. He came back in less than ten minutes. "Okay, here's what they've done. The fence is clear; it's just a physical barrier, probably to keep kids out. The more serious sensor stuff is close in to the building. They've got an infrared laser fence and ground trembler sensors as well as night vision closed-circuit TV cameras with an over-lapping rotation pattern. The doors and windows have breakage sensors and there is a roving set of guards on a twenty minute rotation perimeter search. In other words, this is just basic stuff."

Stan was more than concerned by all the security. "How in the world are we going to get past all that?"

Sarah said, "Just stick with me and do what I do. We do this all the time." Her history as a Mossad field agent gave her that confidence because she had gotten through much worse security in the past.

They simply climbed over the fence one at a time. Moving to within fifty feet of the building they went to ground again. In several minutes the two guards came from the opposite directions and met just ten feet from the raiders. Sarah and Mark each fired one round from their dart guns and the guards collapsed quietly into the grass. Reaching them the team used plastic riot cuffs and cloth gags to secure the sleeping men.

Using his infrared goggles, Mark found several major holes in the laser fence and they slipped through without a problem. Walking carefully by sliding their feet rather than walking defeated the trembler sensors and timing got them by the night vision cameras while they were rotated away and not looking in their direction. Mark slid over to the backup power generator and the incoming power lines from Idaho Power. He fastened two small packages on each unit and slowly slid back to the window. Two minutes with a jimmy and a probe and the entire team was in the building without their security being alerted.

Mark whispered into his microphone. "This is too easy. I smell a trap."

Sarah agreed, "I agree, I'm amazed they haven't left the doors unlocked."

Laura answered, "You're probably right, but what option do we have?"

There was no answer to that one. It was either proceed or abandon Jack to the Master Prophets. So, proceed it was.

After they moved through the outer lobby portion of the building and were about to enter a large room, Mark stopped them and gave them some direction. "We have only a few minutes before the outside guards are missed. If we are being set up, and this is a trap, just follow my lead and do whatever I tell you without question, okay?"

The other three agreed. Personally, Stan doubted that he would have to shoot anybody because he'd been a cop for twenty years and had only used his gun twice in that time.

Opening the door into the large, dimly-lit auditorium, they slipped in one by one. Although Mark felt like a turkey in a turkey shoot he kept moving. When they were almost at the middle of the room the lights came up and men with rifles started coming through the doors in front of them. There were lots of men. Sarah's voice came over the comm. link. "We've got a couple of dozen guards with rifles coming into the room behind us." Mark nodded as he thought, "Hook, line, and sinker. We've been had."

When the guards finished entering the room Karl's voice came over a speaker system. "Put down your weapons and surrender or we will be forced to shoot."

Mark looked around their little group and noticed that he and Laura were facing west and Sarah and Stan were facing east. He also noticed that all sixty four people in the room were pointing their weapons. He quietly spoke into his microphone, "When I say go, Laura, you and Stan fire your

M209s and Sarah and I will fire our MP-5s. But listen close, I don't care if you hit anybody or not. Just trigger your weapons and drop to the floor at the same time. Ready?"

Laura had discretely shifted her hand forward to the firing trigger of the grenade launcher hoping that Mark remembered that they only had smoke grenades loaded. The four members of the team tensed.

Karl spoke again. "Come, come, you don't have a chan...." The lights went out and all hell broke loose. As Mark said "Go!" he pushed the button that set off the charges on the power lines and triggered his MP-5 at the troops to the west. Laura fired her grenade and dropped to the ground forgetting to fire her rifle. Stan fired his grenade and fired a burst from his rifle as the lights went out. Sarah fired a burst at the troops to the east and dropped softly to the ground in the dark.

By now there were hundreds of bullets whipping through the air in both directions as the guards ran through their magazines on auto fire. Everyone wanted the bonus money as much as they wanted to kill the intruders. In response to the heavy incoming fire the troops fired back with everything they had.

Mark's voice came over the comm link, "Put on your NVGs now". All four of them put their night vision goggles on and started crawling quickly to the north side of the room and the heavy podium for shelter. The security guards continued to kill each other with as much effort as they could. Mark said, "This is what happens when people don't have actual battlefield experience. The adrenaline in their system overloads their common sense and they fire at anything firing at them."

Karl had been yelling into the dead microphone to stop shooting but the speaker system had died along with the lights. As stray rounds smashed into things around him, he abandoned his troops and fled in terror to his office.

Mark and the others were grateful when the firing tapered off. Mark scanned the two walls where the troops had been and saw many bodies. Only one or two were moving. Using their night vision gear the raiders slid among the dead and dying and exited the room. As they were going down the hall Mark found one young security man with several bullet wounds in the legs. The man was in a great deal of pain but had seen the team leaving the room. His bloody hands fumbled trying to pull the pin on a fragmentation grenade. Knocking the grenade away, Mark slammed the guy against the wall and gave him a chance to live. "Where is the detention area?"

Looking at the raiders with their smoking weapons and the pile of his recent acquaintances lying on the floor he decided the smart course was to cooperate. He said, "Straight back to the second to last corridor on the left." He moaned at the pain in his legs. Looking at Mark he sneered at him, "Too bad I didn't get all four of you. That would have been forty thousand dollars."

Mark made sure there were no weapons around or on the man. Opening his side flap pocket on his night suit, Mark took out several bandages to bind up the man's wounds when the wounds stopped bleeding Mark looked into the man's sightless eyes. He had lost too much blood.

The opposition had either all been eliminated or had withdrawn because there was no one around. Mark told everyone to stay alert and the four of them ran down the hall with Sarah watching their backs for more traps or strays.

Finding the security area they started checking each cell for Jack. Mark had just come out of one cell when he saw a security man sliding up behind Stan with a knife in his hand. Mark stepped forward and wrapped his arm around the guy's throat and knocked the knife out of his hand with the barrel of his submachine gun. Stan spun around and watched as the guard wilted into unconsciousness.

Mark dropped him and Laura used the riot cuffs to secure his hands and feet.

Mark unlocked the next door and seeing someone inside said, "Jack, are you in there?"

CHAPTER EIGHTEEN

The aches continued but none of them got worse. Jack stretched again and went through his exercise routine for the umpteenth time. The minimal food they provided him and the multiple sessions of exercise had honed his already lean body into excellent shape. He was glad of that fact because he wanted to be in top shape when he left the cell they had him in.

He had to admit that his prayer life had deepened considerably in his isolation from the rest of life. He had to laugh when it occurred to him that the Master Prophets were doing him a favor by eliminating all outside distractions. Still, he was getting very antsy at the lack of anything to do.

It had been two days since he had met with Karl and Jason and other than two meal deliveries a day; he had had no contact with anyone. But he had found great peace in his prayers concerning his wife and his friends. It seemed that God wasn't worried and therefore Jack resolved to listen for the Holy Spirit's instructions and be ready.

Slowly the day died into evening and then into darkness again. As Jack sat in his cell thinking about the situation, the lights went out in the cell and he felt the presence of the Lord. This time there was some urgency to the presence. Not worried urgency, but a pressure of oncoming events that would involve Jack. He was jarred by a series of heavy noises that might have been explosions. But there wasn't any reaction to the vibrations so he guessed that they were normal to this place.

Jack got up and paced his small room to get limber. He had been at this for about forty minutes when he heard footsteps approaching the door of his room. It wasn't time for a meal; therefore it would be something else. It would be several weeks before the suggested time to release him as inconsequential. Therefore it would probably be bad news. Well, this time he wasn't going to go quietly.

There was a noise at the door lock, a few seconds later the lock clicked open and the doorknob turned. The door opened into the room but nobody followed it. Then a voice spoke out quietly, "Jack. Are you in there?" Jack whispered back, "Yes", still not sure who was outside. When Mark Connelly walked into the room Jack felt a wave of gratitude crash over him. He stepped forward in the dim light from the hall and hugged his friend.

Mark hugged him back and stepped back to inspect the ex-prisoner. "Well, it looks like they left you intact."

Jack laughed quietly, "Mostly. Boy. I am glad to see your face. How is Laura? Where is she? How did you get in here? Where is Sarah? What are we going to do to get out of here?" It was about that time it registered on Jack the amount of weapons and gear hanging off of his friend. Also the smell about him was that of cordite and the gray powder on the end of the silencer meant use. "Did you have to fight your way in here?"

Mark shook his head. "Well, sort of. We'll talk about it later." He motioned for Jack to follow him as he turned and walked out of the room.

Jack walked out and had to step over the prone body on the floor, just up the hall from his room. He stopped and squatted down and checked the man. It was the man that had been bringing him his meals. Jack could tell from the pulse in his neck that he was still alive but unconscious. The marks on the throat told Jack how he had become that way. He could see Mark's muscular arm around the man's throat until he passed out. The man was thoroughly tied up and gagged.

Suddenly a form rushed at him and Jack went into a low defense stance. He stopped his motion as Laura jumped on him and hugged him tightly. He got them both up from the floor and put his arms around her and kissed her. "I've missed you so much", was all he said. She looked up through her tears and nodded "Me too".

Mark hissed and motioned them on down the hall. Jack and Laura hurried up and caught up to Mark just as they reached the door in the end of the hall. Once there Jack saw Sarah and a man he didn't know standing guard with weapons at the ready. Sarah looked at him and smiled. The stranger nodded at him and went back to watching the three halls that made up the rest of the intersection.

In his office, Karl was sweating through a very bad call to Prophet Roswell. "I am not sure how many troops they have but they've shot or blown up all of the security force, half the building, and destroyed the power lines and backup generator."

The ominous voice on the other end of the phone was very upset. "What about the prisoner and his wife? Do you have them?"

"No sir. I just told you that I am probably the only one alive here. I don't know if they've reached the cell where Mr. Malone is or not."

Roswell made it perfectly clear to Karl, "If you are the only one alive then you are the only one that can kill him. Do it NOW! If you fail in this, you will take his place. I will see to that!" The receiver went dead.

Karl was shaking but knew that there was only one thing he could do. He took the 9MM pistol out of the drawer and headed for the cell block.

In St. Louis, Missouri, Prophet Roswell smashed a large hole in the wall of the office he was sitting in. In his anger he wanted to destroy everything in sight. But, he restricted his outburst to that one punch. "Why." he thought, "Why do I have to work with such imbeciles?" He had trusted Karl to defend the center and to capture Ms. Malone. Instead the entire center was being destroyed and everyone in the Master Prophets service was being killed. That led to even darker thoughts about the powers ranged against him. Had they decided that he was no longer invincible? That he would start running away? They had a lot to learn.

As he sat there fuming he stared at the huge hole he'd made in the wall. His thoughts rambled "Reverend Thomas would be really upset by that hole in his wall." He looked at the twisted body near his feet. "That is if he were alive to care." That thought made him feel better. The Boise action was not a denial of his total success; it was only a minor setback. That was it! He would profit from the loss and come out even stronger, but, how? He continued to ponder the forces and intangibles of the overall situation. He had warned them, they had a much greater force than they expected the intruders to have. What went wrong?"

Back in Boise, Mark was about to step out into the hall when he heard a door close down the right hand hall around a corner and footsteps approaching. Careful not to make any noise, the five-man team made themselves as inconspicuous as possible. Jack peeked around the corner and saw Karl walking quickly down the hall towards them. This was the door that led to the cells. Karl had a frown on his face and was nervously looking around. The 9MM pistol in his right hand was up and looking for a target. Jack could figure that a bullet in that gun was his 'freedom' the man was bringing to him.

As Karl rounded the corner, Jack stepped out and snap kicked the man in the side of his head with his right foot. Jack had wanted to do something like that ever since he had met the man. Karl's lights went out like a switch had been thrown. The gun flew up into the air as he fell away from it. Jack reached out and caught the pistol before it hit the floor.

Mark and the stranger helped Jack to drag the man through the doorway into Jack's old cell. Mark went back into the hall and put the jailer into another cell and closed and locked the door with the jailor's keys. Just in case he woke up. This way he would not give them trouble.

Mark came back into the room and asked Jack, "The way you kicked this guy made it look like you two were acquainted. Is he anybody that would know anything?"

Jack nodded and looked at Karl, "Yes".

At a glance from Mark, Sarah undid the sleeve on Karl's right arm. Reaching into his side pocket on his black assault suit Mark withdrew a small package. Opening it up revealed a syringe and a vial. Estimating the man's weight, Mark loaded the syringe and carefully speared it into the man's arm at the elbow. Finding a vein, Mark slowly emptied the contents of the syringe. Withdrawing the empty syringe Mark snapped the needle off and threw the syringe into the corner of the cell. He then checked the man's pockets. Nothing of any importance, not even a wallet. Jack got up and checked the hall again. Finding everything quiet he walked back and asked Sarah, "How soon before the reserves get here?"

Sarah shook her head, "Not in this lifetime." She looked at Jack. "They weren't very hospitable so we let them kill each other. As she said this, she looked with pride at her husband. Jack said a mental prayer for forgiveness and thought "Yeah, they were stupid".

Jack reached between Laura and Sarah and held out his hand to the stranger. "Jack Malone. I want to thank you for helping my wife and friends get me out of here."

The slim man changed the rifle to his left hand and reached out and took Jack's hand and shook it. "Stan Hargrove and you're welcome. I'm a cop from Salt Lake City that just happened to be the one God used to help your friends find you."

Mark sat down next to Karl on the bench. Checking his watch in the dim light he caught Jack staring at him. "What?"

Jack motioned towards the recumbent man. "You forgot to sterilize the site before you injected him."

Mark laughed harshly. "You know, you're right. That will probably count against me as far as my becoming a doctor." Actually Mark didn't care if the man did get infected from an unclean injection; he probably deserved that and a lot more. After a few more minutes Mark began to gently slap the man's face back and forth until he got a reaction.

The man coughed and tried to sit up. Not succeeding, he fell back on the bench and moaned. But he was aware now and not unconscious.

Mark started interrogating Karl carefully. Mark had done this sort of thing quite a few times and knew how to get people to talk under the influence of Scopolamine. He began to get some facts after only a couple of minutes. He finally broached the subject of Jack and his kidnapping.

Mark asked quietly, "So why did we capture Mr. Malone then?"

The man on the bench implied that anyone that didn't understand that was a mental moron, "Because he has the nail and he was investigating us and you know we can't have anyone find out about Damocles at this time."

Mark looked at Jack. Speaking more conspiratorially he asked the man, "Do you think he found out anything about Damocles?"

Again with the attitude: "Of course not. He was just what he said he was a hick Christian who happened to be in the wrong place at the wrong time. He didn't even know about the circle or the purchases."

Mark thought for a few seconds. "But, didn't he have access to people who knew about the Damocles project and the purchases?"

The man thought about that for a few seconds. "Yes, yes he did. I was right to eliminate him tonight. If he could succeed in convincing anyone in the government about

Damocles we would have to move the schedule up, even if everything is not in place."

Mark toughened up his voice. "I thought everything was in place. You told me that it was all done.

Karl lost some of his color. "But, it is, almost, done. They have only the one casing to complete and it's probably done by now." He was almost in tears over this little delay in the Damocles project.

Mark kept after the subject. "Which casing is incomplete you moron? You know very well that they all have to be done on time!"

"I'm sorry Sir, the Kotzebue site." Mark looked at Jack with the question on his face. Jack thought for a moment and then whispered in Mark's ear, "I think Kotzebue is in the middle of Alaska, right on the Arctic Circle if I remember correctly."

Karl was continuing to attempt to placate his questioner. "They fell behind due to the bad weather and I don't know for sure that they have caught up yet." The fear the man showed implied an implacable boss. Karl was obviously in great fear of this person.

Mark took a shot in the dark. "Well at least tell me that Damocles will work properly when the installation is complete. And what is the schedule now?" He had to keep the man off his toes mentally.

"Yes, yes, Damocles will work exactly as Dr. Rostach designed it. All thirty-three sites will function in the proper sequence on the existing schedule if the government of the U.S. doesn't capitulate. But of course, they will."

Jack and Mark just stared at each other for several seconds. Each of them tried to understand what the man meant.

Mark went back somewhat. "Why isn't the Kotzebue site ready? Why have you jeopardized the entire operation? Do you know for sure that the other sites are ready?"

The man on the bench was sweating furiously, "Oh yes, they are all ready. I checked them this morning. They are all ready, honestly. We just need to cradle the system in Kotzebue and take it to the proper depth. Then it will be completely ready! I swear it!"

Mark shot back, "What was the last site prepared 'completely' before Kotzebue?"

The man seemed confused for a second and then answered, "Pangnirtuno of course. I personally oversaw the completion of that site and reported it to you at the time."

Mark looked puzzled. Jack leaned over and whispered to him again, "Pangnirtuno is on Baffin Island, Canada, at the Northwest extremity and it is also exactly on the Arctic Circle, could be what he meant by "the circle'?"

Mark whispered, "Possibly". He then returned to his patient "Then we will be ready for the demand by next week?"

Again the man seemed confused and somewhat angry. This time he didn't answer. His awareness had returned sufficiently to tell him he was a dead man no matter what happened. He began to cry softly.

Mark motioned to Jack and the others to leave the cell with him. Once outside he turned and shut the door and locked it. Testing the door to make sure it was locked, he said over his shoulder. "We're running out of time. I think the Master Prophets are about to do something drastic in the Arctic very soon."

Jack looked at the cell door. "Couldn't we get more information out of him?"

Mark shook his head. "No, he was already starting to overcome the truth serum. I could have given him another shot but there is a tolerance problem. It might work again or it could kill him. Either way we weren't going to be able to get anything more out of him or trust anything he would say from now on."

Laura shook her head, "Thirty-three 'systems' buried around the Arctic Circle as a threat? What do you think the 'systems' are?"

Mark's frown deepened considerably. "I'm not sure. But I've got a really bad feeling about this because of two reasons. First, I know who Dr. Rostach is. He's a renegade Russian nuclear scientist whose services are for sale to the highest bidder. He dropped out of sight a couple of years ago. Second, the President informed me that as of eighteen months ago two to three dozen two megaton nuclear warheads were stolen from a Russian arsenal in one of the breakaway republics."

Jack added those clues together. "Then what we're looking at is possibly thirty-three nuclear weapons buried underground around the world on the Arctic Circle. Why?"

Then he answered his own question. Jack shook his head. "Of course, it refers to The Arctic Ring of Fire.

Sarah asked, "I've heard of that. What exactly is this Arctic Ring of Fire?"

Jack thought back to his geography classes at Colorado University. "There are a large number of dormant volcanoes in the Arctic region. With the exception of a couple minor eruptions most of them haven't been active in mankind's recorded history. The problem here is that investigations into volcanic activity and plate tectonics have shown that the magma layer is only a couple of miles deep in a lot of these volcanoes."

Mark was following Jack's line of reasoning. "If the Master Prophets figured this out and have been able to buy, or steal thirty-three nuclear weapons and sink them to the proper depth in or around these volcanoes they might bring them all to eruption at the same time. Would that cause the polar ice cap to melt? While that would flood most of the lowlands in the rest of the world I don't see them threatening us with that. It might not even cause enough Greenhouse effect to melt everything."

Jack shook his head. "I don't think that is their plan at all. I believe they've studied the Ring of Fire very carefully with an eye to geological science. Remember that under truth serum Karl said "in the proper sequence?" Well, my guess is that they know about the myriad of fault lines that run close to the Arctic Circle. In that case, they could possibly threaten to fracture the Earth itself. Any fracture in the crust which would resonate through the entire planet and most likely result in the world tearing itself apart from rotational dynamics."

That was a sobering thought. As they got ready to leave, Stan indicated the cells that held the two men. "What if nobody finds them? They'll starve to death in a few days."

Mark smiled, "Now there's a thought." But he went back and quietly unlocked the two cell doors and set the keys on the floor.

As they carefully made their way out of the cell area again, Mark thought about the Master Prophet's plan and nodded his head. "This 'ring of fire' makes really solid sense as a trump card or a bluff. If you truly had sufficient explosive material, and could threaten to cause a major rift in the plate tectonics at that latitude, no one would dare refuse any demand you made. Also, once they have the threat in place, there will be no end to their demands on the entire world."

Jack got a determined look on his face, "We need to warn the President. What I want to know is how did the prophets transport that many nuclear weapons into various countries around the world and not be detected? And, why hasn't the intelligence community caught onto this threat?"

As they passed the middle of the building, Mark offered a theory to the group, "They may have shielded the weapons as much as possible and moved them to these sites as construction material. None of these sites are near significant population centers and are probably not inspected at any ports or airstrips. They may have landed off the coast and trucked them overland, thus avoiding all contact with people that look for things like this."

Jack agreed with that and answered his own question about the exposure of the plan to the intelligence groups. "The Master Prophet's partial control of the governments of the world could have prevented the intelligence apparatus from looking into their activities. In free countries it would be labeled 'religious persecution' and in Russia it was probably just power politics as usual. They would downplay any mention of this type of activity and ridiculed anyone who got near the concept."

As they exited the building they didn't see another person or even hear anything throughout the entire building. Jack eyed the massive destruction evident in the auditorium. "You made quite an entrance" he said. From the number of bullet holes in the walls, ceiling, and floor it was obvious that it hadn't been a cakewalk. Bodies piled at either end of the auditorium testified to the deadliness of their reception.

Sarah saw him staring at the corpses. "Hey, that was their handiwork. We were just trying to find you."

There was only an occasional emergency light working but it gave Jack, who was the only one without the night vision goggles, enough light to find his way out.

Checking outside first, they boldly opened a side door to the building and walked out. As they exited the building, Jack was a little surprised at the coldness of the temperature. Rubbing his hands together he turned to Laura, "Where are we?"

She looked confused for a second, "Oh, we're in Boise, Idaho."

Jack digested that and turned to look at the gaudy glass and chrome building they had just left. The sign with the hand reaching toward heaven wasn't lit up. Shaking his head at the rush of events, he hurried with the other four people across a well-manicured lawn and over a fence and some bushes. A dark luxury car sat there. After Mark checked the car for tampering they all put their large weapons and body armor into the trunk. Then they got in, grateful for the fast response of the heater and the heated seats. Jack got his hands on his spare cell phone that Laura had brought with her and quickly punched in a Washington number.

Stan's estimation of the group went up again when he heard what Jack was telling the assistant to the President of the United States.

After calling the President, Jack put his arm around Laura as Sarah drove out of the area of the Believer's Church on the Southeast side of town. He looked at Mark and reached over to squeeze his hand again. "You know that they knew you were coming don't you? They thought that they would capture Laura and use her to get me to turn over the treasure to them. Again, thanks for pulling me out of there." Jack looked at the two women and Stan, who were sitting in the back of the car. "Thank you all." He was just glad to be out of there. The three days of captivity had seemed like three weeks.

Laura asked Sarah, "What was Damocles? Wasn't that a Roman or Greek Mythology guy?

Sarah nodded her head, "Yes, in classical Greek mythology, Damocles was a courtier at the court of Dionysius I. He so persistently praised the power and happiness of Dionysius that the tyrant, in order to show the precariousness of rank and power, gave a banquet and had a sword suspended above the head of Damocles by a single hair. Hence the expression "the sword of Damocles" means an ever-present peril. An apt name for the type of threat the Master Prophets have manufactured."

CHAPTER NINETEEN

Certain that the Master Prophets would be mounting some type of retaliation for the raid and the freeing of Jack, the five members decided to change tactics and drove to the Boise airport rather than back to Salt Lake City. Jack was fairly sure that once the government started after the Master Prophets they would have their hands full and would have to forget about them.

They rented a private jet to take Stan back home to Salt Lake City and then run them to Denver. They had been airborne for only a few minutes when the cell phone in Jack's pocket beeped. Switching it on Jack answered and listened for several minutes. He then hung up the phone and sat there thinking for a while. He then looked at Mark. "What is the chance that Karl could have been lying? Or that he was only repeating something that he had heard?"

Mark thought for a few seconds. "I doubt that he could have beaten the truth serum and his answers were right from his life experiences so it wasn't second-hand information. What's the problem?"

Jack held up the phone. "That was Tom Kendric, the assistant to the President that I talked to before. He said that he told the President what I had given him and the President literally chewed him out. He said that the magic ring of atom bombs is an old rumor that was checked out thoroughly over a year ago and keeps resurfacing. There is no truth to the rumor and the President was not happy that we fell for such a phony story. Basically I was told not to bother the President again with fairy tales like this."

Sarah said, "Okay, then who is lying? Was it Karl, or the guy that told him the story, or, could it be this Tom Kendric?"

Laura listened to the debate and made a small statement. "I think we should ask the one in who there are no lies." The team settled down and started praying. They were quite serious about their prayers because it could have disastrous results if they were wrong.

While they were praying Jack felt a presence and the sense of the group and the plane fell away. He saw a pure white ground and light gray sky. Then a glow appeared and a figure approached him, floating above the ground. Jack tried the spirit and it responded with the name of The Lord Yahshua as its Lord and Master.

As the figure drew near Jack recognized Rose from Laura's description. She continued to draw closer until she was almost standing directly in front of him. The peace he felt reassured him that the angel was from God. She said, *"Your prayers have been heard in heaven. God wants you to know that you are walking the right path but cannot expect anyone else to champion this cause. This challenge is yours. Be brave and walk with God. He will fight those that oppose you and destroy those that try to destroy you. But, you must stand for Christ regardless of the effort or the danger."* She began to move up and away from him. *"Remember to honor your wife and her faith in the everlasting one for her role in this is critical."* She was gone and Jack opened his eyes.

Everyone started talking at once. Jack held up his hand and said, "Who got what?"

Stan said, "It was Rose again. She said that we were God's chosen ones for defeating the Master Prophets."

Laura added, "Yes, she told me to stand firm in my faith and see this through."

Mark laughed, "That was better than television. I got what Laura got, word for word."

Sarah just sat there smiling. Mark slapped her on the leg. "What did you get spy lady?" She tipped her head to the side and raised an eyebrow. "Watch who you're slapping sir, I happen to be the future mother of your children. And yes, she said that we will meet the enemy and prevail."

Laura clapped her hands and laughed at Sarah, "You too?"

Sarah smiled back and replied, "Yeah, me too. But, she cautioned me to follow your lead in this."

Sarah had thought some dark thoughts about that. She knew her capabilities and due to her extensive background and experience in combating the enemies of Israel she would have thought that God would have chosen her to lead. Then it dawned on her that God was not a man and knew far more about their situation than any man. It was a sign of pride that she felt that she was superior to Laura in this matter. God knew better. She humbly asked the Lord to forgive her sin of pride and empower her to follow as He directed. Sarah didn't have any problems doing what God said to do.

Mark looked at Sarah, "That future mother thing, you know something I don't?"

Sarah leaned over and whispered in his ear. His eyes got wider as he listened.

Jack said, "Okay, it only takes the confirmation of three witnesses and we've got five. So, is the assistant to the President a secret MP stooge or do we care at this point?"

Mark said, "It's pretty clear that we have the lead on this." With that he got up and went to the cockpit to talk to the pilot. In a few minutes the plane began to bank to the left and Mark returned. "Since God has conscripted you Stan, we are going to Denver and see if we can't get some assistance and maybe some military firepower to back us up."

Stan made a decision at that point. He got up and went to the cockpit and asked for a connection to a ground-based telephone system. Once he had a dial tone he made a call to his wife. Then he called his boss in the Salt Lake City police department. Once the operator at the station determined who was calling he hooked Stan directly to the Chief's desk.

Chief Vortees was basically an honest man but he was also a politician and he was worried about his job. He came on the phone with a bellow, "Hargrove, I want you in my office in no time flat. You'll be lucky if I don't bust you down to beat cop. If I find that you had anything to do with that Temple center attack in Boise I will see that you do big time in prison, you understand me Captain?"

Stan replied, "Yes sir, Chief Vortees, I understand you. And I don't want to besmirch the department. I can take care of all these problems with two words. I quit!" He then broke the connection and walked back to the others.

Jack looked up at Stan and saw that he looked happier than he had been since Jack met him in the prison wing of the Omniscience Temple. "What happened?"

Stan sat and rolled the new concept around in his mind for a minute. "Well, let's say I have just opted to work for God full time rather than the police force."

Mark smiled. "You noticed that our little firefight did not result in any response from the Boise police? As far as I know there hasn't been any news reported about it. But, I bet your boss has heard about the little set-to we had in Boise hasn't he?"

Stan laughed, "Don't know, I only got to talk to the Chief. He had certainly heard and put two and two together like he had an eye witness." He looked at Jack. "Listen, I haven't been a cop for all these years without developing a feel for people. I think you guys are real, real Christians, real people, and real friends. Before I called my station I called my wife. I told her to get out of town immediately and to come to Denver and call me on my cell phone. I'm pretty sure that someone will be going to my apartment pretty soon to get some leverage and I would not like it one bit if they got my wife in retaliation for our little "dustup" in Boise."

Laura got up and sat down next to Stan. "I'm afraid that your association with us isn't going to go well with the powers-that-be for a while. I got you into this and you can count on us to see you through it." Jack, Mark, and Sarah all agreed with Laura. Jack asked Stan, "Do you think your wife will be able to get away in time?"

Stan nodded. "Yeah, I told her to pack an overnight bag, the house pistol, which she is very good with, her Bible, and gas up the car before you guys ever showed up. She's been waiting for the word to go since then. She was on the road in her own car before I even called the station. By the time they think of her as a target she will be halfway across Wyoming."

Jack looked at Mark, "Hmm."

Mark got up and went into the cockpit again. The plane started banking to the left again.

Stan patted the younger woman's hand. "And, you didn't get me into this, God did, through Rose, remember?"

Mark sat down and told Stan. "You haven't been involved in the spy game before have you?" At the shake of Stan's head Mark continued. "It is a relatively easy thing to find out about your wife's car and to figure the few directions she could go. Your Chief could put a dragnet out that would get her inside of an hour. Of course, if he did that, then we would have to go get her back and he really, really doesn't want us to do that. So, to save him the embarrassment or possibly injury, I've rerouted the plane to Rock Springs, Wyoming and we will find your wife before they do."

Stan just sat there with a frown on his face. "I don't know how we'll find her on the highway. I told her to keep the phone off until she was in Denver. I know the car and the license plate number but we don't have the people to find her like the Highway Patrol does."

Sarah patted him on the leg. "Just stick with us and we'll get her before they do." Based on recent past performances Stan was greatly encouraged. He also was glad that Debbie was probably out of the State of Utah. He had a lot of friends on the force and after watching Mark, Sarah, and Laura in action he didn't want the team to go after Debbie if his own people picked her up.

CHAPTER TWENTY

The pilot called Mark up front to discuss the landing. "You know, the runway you want to land on is not rated for this class of jet? I can probably get us down, but I don't know if we can get enough running room to get off again. It would be a lot easier if we went into Laramie."

Mark looked at the map. "No, that's way too far East. We need to be on the west side of the state. Go on and land at Rock Springs. If we get stuck we'll pay for the extra efforts to get the plane out of there."

The pilot was used to eccentric requests and could live with a vacation while they got the plane out of the general aviation field. But he had another concern. "It's also against the FAA's rules for me to land there without authorization or an actual emergency."

Mark thought for a minute. Holding up his hand for the pilot to wait one, Mark got up and went back to the luggage and opened one of the compartments. Getting what he wanted he went back to the cockpit. Sitting down he took ten thousand dollars in hundred dollar bills and put them into the pilot's flight case. "That's an emergency, right?" The pilot smiled.

About ten minutes later the pilot called back on the intercom. "Folks, it seems our flight into Denver will have to wait. I'm having fluctuations in the right control surfaces and am diverting to a small general aviation field at Rock Springs, Wyoming. Please take your seats and buckle up. This could get a little hairy."

Mark looked out his window and decided that some prayer was in order. The field looked smaller and smaller rather than bigger as they approached.

The light jet flared out as it crossed the inner boundary of the field. Setting down lightly with the main gear, the pilot brought the front wheel down quickly and applied the engine retros and brakes. Being lightly loaded the plane bounced a lot but slowed rapidly. They ran out of runway but were able to stop within the mowed verge at the end of the runway. Mark got up and went to the front. When he looked out the windscreen and saw a farm yard with combines and tractors less than 500 feet in front of the stopped aircraft his rating of the pilot went up considerably. He might not be up to the level of USAF Major Mike White who had flown them in and out of Libya, but he was good.

They exited the aircraft with all their gear and headed towards the small building that served the air field. There was a staff of two people there who were both looking out the window at the stopped jet; an unknown sight on their little field.

While the pilot talked to them Jack called a rental company and got a car delivered to the airport for their use. The vehicle turned out to be a new Lincoln Navigator which easily held all five of them and their luggage. As they pulled out of the airport Sarah said, "What are the odds that this type of vehicle is for rent in this small town normally?"

Laura looked up from the literature that had come with the large SUV. "They are pretty good actually. There's a resort in the mountains here that is really exclusive and probably pulls a lot of high rollers needing luxury vehicles after flying into the flyspeck airport back there."

Mark added, "Did you see all those expensive twin-engine light aircraft parked back there? Good sign that there is money spent here."

Stan had been looking out the window at the mountain scenery. "Okay, we've solved the aberration concerning the local economy, what about Debbie?"

Mark nodded, "Good point." He took out his cell phone but couldn't get a signal. Borrowing Jack's satellite cell phone he called in some favors. He got a full description of Debbie's car from Stan while he waited for a connection. When he finally got the person he was seeking he talked rapidly. "This is a code Zeus Nine Able Twenty Omega. Do you concur?" He waited while the computers at the NSA complex ran his identity and priority for authorization. When the answer was received, Mark immediately got a senior analyst assigned to him. The clearance code was rated so high they didn't even have a category for it. Its authorization level was 'Just do it'.

The solid tenor voice came across with power and a clarity that just isn't there on most cell phone calls. "Your authorization is approved Alpha Omega, what can we do for you General Connelly?" Mark's smile turned up at the corners. He thought, "Wow, I'm a General". But it didn't show in his demeanor. "I have a high-priority search for a vehicle on Interstate 70 in the western area of Wyoming. This is an 'all birds comprehensive search', I repeat ABCS, with an Ultimate rating. The vehicle is a 2012 Mercury Cougar, white on white with a Utah plate, 964 LS. The target vehicle should be approximately thirty miles east of the Utah border. I need running coverage until I release it. The category is terrorism but the target is rated Victim. There is a SWF on board. Locate and tag, General Connelly out."

Stan was impressed all over again. "So the National Security Agency will jump to and even reroute a satellite on your say so?"

Mark shook his head. "Not mine, the cover of General and the security rating are the President's that he has authorized me to use as necessary."

Stan looked carefully at all four of them, "What exactly have you guys done that the President thinks so highly of you?"

Sarah shrugged, "Not much, saved his life, saved eighteen million Americans and eight million Israelis, ensured his re-election, prevented a national riot and eliminated various demons and bad guys." But then she turned serious. "But none of that will mean anything if we can't stop these nut cases from blowing the top of the world off."

Recognition dawned in Stan's eyes. The two images, one in white and one all in black and armed to the teeth merged for him. "You're the one that led the world-wide prayer for healing of the poisoned people, aren't you?" Sarah shrugged again, "It seemed like the right thing to do at the time."

Stan reached over from the third row seats and taking Sarah by the hand he told her that her prayers saved his brother's entire family. They had all been stricken with the poison that God removed from the world after the prayer session.

Sarah squeezed Stan's hand in return. "Thank you, but remember, it was Yahshua that saved everyone, not me. My part was only to focus the prayers of millions of people on Him. Like you, the rest of us here are just servants of the Most High God. We may do heroic things but it is because the Lord sends us here and there and empowers us to accomplish His will on Earth.

Jack's phone rang and drew everyone's attention. Mark answered it. "Yes?"

The same voice was on the phone from NSA. "General, we have your vehicle tagged and located. It is moving eastward at seventy miles per hour and according to our calculations it will be at your location in approximately seven minutes. Do you need assistance for an intercept?"

"No. Thank you for your assistance and I release the order at this time." Mark hung up. Jack had brought them to the eastbound entrance ramp of the interstate and they had a good view of the road to the west.

As Stan and Laura watched the oncoming road with Zeiss binoculars Stan asked Mark, "Okay General, how did NSA know where we are? You didn't tell them."

Mark liked Stan's police curiosity. "I didn't have to. As soon as Jack's cell phone got past the second level of the Agency they had a precise satellite fix on its position."

Realizing he had a lot to learn about the spy world Stan spoke up. "There she is, fourth car back in the right lane."

Jack timed out their entrance onto the highway so that they came on right behind Debbie's little Cougar. Pulling along side of the car, Stan powered down the right hand window and leaned over Mark's shoulder to put his head out of the car. Jack honked and Debbie looked over. Stan motioned for her to pull over.

She pulled over to the side and Stan got out and went over to the car. She jumped out and hugged and kissed him. He talked to her for a few seconds and then led her back to the SUV. Laura powered down her window and the cold mountain air flowed into front seat area of the vehicle. She told Stan to drive the two of them to the next exit and pull into a gas station or food place, anywhere there were cars.

Everyone kept a watch out for police highway cruisers for the next four miles until they were able to exit. Stan found an eatery that had six cars parked in the lot. He parked in the spot the farthest from the highway and out of sight behind the building. Taking Debbie's bags he loaded them into the SUV and they climbed into the third seats. Jack carefully drove out of there and back onto the road to the Interstate. Looking at Mark he asked, "What do we do now? Drive on to Denver?"

Mark shook his head and told Jack to head back west. Giving Mark a curious look, he did as asked. He was sure that Mark had a reason for going the other way.

In Boise, Alan Roswell listened as his new agent finished with his report on the thirty-three sites. Everything was in order. They could now contact the United States government and demand their surrender. He sourly thought that if the United Nations hadn't taken the terrorist's side and been done away with during the poisoning of the U.S. and Israel, he could have told all the countries at once. He looked at his new right hand man. "I'm pretty sure that Karl blabbed about our last Alaskan site to the invaders before he died. Send that group of mercenaries we hired to the Kotzebue site and tell them to mount a guard constantly until I tell them to stop. How many men do they have?"

His assistant looked at a chart. The response was; "One-hundred and twenty-five soldiers and four officers."

Roswell smiled at the number. "No doubt my prisoner will run to the President with his news. I expect Tom Kendric to prevent him from telling the President for the next thirty-six hours. After that it won't matter because I'll tell him myself and dare him to do anything about it.

CHAPTER TWENTY-ONE

Looking at the map as they rolled west on the interstate Mark looked at Jack and told him, "Head back to the airport at the next exit. Let's see if we can't get a flight out to Denver. That'll shave six or seven hours off the trip and even though we probably have two weeks until doomsday the clock is running and I think every hour is going to be precious."

While they were headed back to the airport, Stan introduced the rest of the team to Debbie. "Honey, up in front there we've got Jack and Laura Malone. He owns a manufacturing company in Denver. In the middle here we've got Mark and Sarah Connelly who have their own business in the security field. They're the ones that I was off helping the last twenty-four hours."

Debbie smiled, "I'm glad to meet all of you. I love Stan and he smells like gunpowder, But, Stan trusts you so I will do the same. I don't understand what is going on with everything but I'll try to stay out of the way." She then turned to Stan, "Honey, what will happen to my car?"

Stan bounced the question to Mark. Mark smiled back at Debbie, "When we get started on our way to Denver, I'll call the restaurant that you left it at." He reached into his pocket and pulled out a piece of paper. "I wrote down their name and number. I'll tell them that we're having a problem with it and that we will call a tow company to come get it if they could watch it for a few hours. I know a group that specializes in recovering vehicles that I sometimes have to leave all over the country. I'll have them take it to their lot until this is over and then bring it to Jack's house, if that's all right with him."

Jack nodded while decelerating on the off ramp with the beautiful Wyoming Mountains as a backdrop.

Debbie looked out the window and prayed that no one would find her secret compartment in the car.

Turning right Jack followed the winding road back to the airport. When they pulled in, the Jet Commander was still sitting off the end of the runway. They parked and walked into the small administration building. The same two men were there with the pilot. He looked up and waved when he saw them. "Found your lost lady, Huh?"

Mark nodded, "How are things going with the problem on the aircraft?"

The pilot looked concerned. "No problem but it's going to be later this afternoon before the FAA inspectors get here to examine the control surfaces and allow a mechanic to fix whatever is wrong. I called my company and they are going to bring out a neat little JATO (jet assisted take off) bottle to get me off the ground when the plane is approved for flight. But I doubt that it will be for the next couple of days though before I can fly you anywhere."

Mark was glad that the pilot wouldn't get in any trouble for the unauthorized landing, but just in case. He said, "Here's my card. If you have any problems with this, call me. Okay?"

The pilot took the card and shook Mark's hand.

Turning to the two administrators of the air park Mark made some inquiries. Five minutes later he came back to the team and explained, "I got hold of a private charter pilot that just brought two couples up here this morning. He is on call to take them back tomorrow but is willing to make some extra money on a quick round trip to Denver. He should be here in twenty minutes.

An hour later, after Mark took care of Debbie's car using the cell phone, the team grabbed a couple of hours sleep as the plane flew them back to the Denver International Airport and the SUV that Mark had left there on the way to Salt Lake City thirty hours before.

Almost everyone got some sleep. Stan reclined in his seat and tried to make sense of everything that had happened to him in the last two days. His mind tended to meander whenever he was near his wife so he wanted to put it all in order while she was asleep and not full of questions.

It seemed to him that his life had just taken a major turn. He didn't have any paycheck coming now but the money he'd been saving should see them through until he could find employment. Of course, if what Jack and Mark were saying was right, and he thought it probably was, there might be no reason to worry about money in the near future. Well, that tidied up things. He definitely had enough to last until the end of the month. He prayed that the Lord would keep all of them in the palm of His hand and let them win through to prevent the Prophets from finalizing their threat. From his history as a policeman he knew that a threat was only worth anything if you were willing to use it. He thought of Debbie and how much she meant to him. But he had come to the realization in the last two years that it wasn't his place to be the protector for her. It was his place as her 'covering' in the line of authority from Yahshua to pray for her protection. Only the Lord could keep her safe. And he knew that in the final draw that she had a wonderful place to go. On that thought he fell peacefully asleep. The bump and squeaking of the wheels on landing at DIA woke him up.

Finally arriving at their house they debated the best course of action and realized they didn't have any organized plan to attack the Master Prophets Damocles project. They had all been subconsciously counting on the U. S. military to take the point. The thought of them having to contend with this type of problem wasn't new to them. It was unfamiliar territory in that they would be operating on a much grander scale than ever before.

Jack reminded Mark that he had said that he thought he could get some military backup without going through the White House.

Mark nodded, "I think I can get us some backup and, like I said, firepower, but we've got to lay this thing out and execute it ourselves." He looked at the rest of the people and they looked pretty played out with only an hour or so worth of fitful sleep on the airplane flight to Denver. "Why don't we go grab a bed for the next few hours?" As everybody got going he told Sarah, "I'm going to mull this over for a while and then I'll join you, okay?"

Laura took Stan and Debbie to the second guest bedroom on the second floor and made sure they had what they needed. Sarah walked off stretching and looked back at Mark to make sure he was watching her. He smiled and waved her on to bed. Jack came over and sat next to Mark. "I got some sleep on the plane. Can I help you?"

Mark smiled, "Sure." They began to sketch out a plan to address the biggest problem they had ever tackled.

They had been at it for two hours when Stan wandered into the room. "Debbie finally got to sleep. I can't sleep thinking about the danger the world is in and we're the only ones that can do anything about it."

Mark indicated a chair and Stan sat down. He picked up a pencil and played with it for a few seconds and then looked at

Mark. "If you don't object, I told my wife I was working for your security company. She was really concerned about the fact that I quit my Captain's position with the Salt Lake police."

Mark sat back and thought for few minutes while he stared at Stan. Stan was starting to get uncomfortable and worried he had made a mistake.

Mark sat up and took a piece of paper and wrote a six-figure number on it and slid it over to Stan. "I think it is a great idea. I need someone with your experience rather badly. If that salary is satisfactory I'll call my people and have them draw up the papers."

Stan's eyebrows climbed upward as he looked at the number. "I'd have to work three years on the force to make this much money. You could have me for a lot less. Not that I don't appreciate it, but, I don't want to take more than I'm worth."

Mark laughed, "Stan, I'm a pretty good judge of people and some people call me a strategist. I think that is what you are worth to me and believe me, if you hang around this guy" Mark pointed at Jack. "You'll earn every cent of that money every year." Jack held both hands up and feigned a hurt expression, "Who, me?"

The three of them laughed together. Stan reached across the table and shook Mark's hand. "I guarantee you I'll work for every dollar you pay me."

Mark smiled, "Then it's a done deal. Now, let's get back to trying to save the world."

Four cups of coffee and three hours later they had a plausible plan and decided they would sleep on it. They left in three different directions. Five minutes later the lights dimmed in the kitchen and the burner under the coffee went off.

Alan Roswell stood in the shadows across the street from the sleeping household and fumed. He could walk through any physical barrier as he willed to. He knew about the NovaStar defense system and it couldn't stop him from his tasks. The people in there couldn't hurt him with their weapons as much as they were capable of in that area. None of that bothered him. What did bother him was the solid, impenetrable globe of shifting fire that surrounded the whole property. He was very familiar with that force and it was causing him pain even as far away as he was from it at the moment. He knew the reason it was paining him was because his desire was to get through it and acquire what he wanted so badly. The Holy Spirit's fire was an extension of God himself and it recognized intent as well as action.

Many nights he had stood here seeking a weakening of that protection. It had maintained its hedge of fire characteristics unabated for as long as he had attempted to enter that building. It was there in response to the prayers of the people in there as well as other intercessory prayers of other Christians. How he hated the followers of the Son of God. His plans in the world were coming to fruition and this tiny band of zealots was too active in their warfare against him.

"Well, we'll see about that tonight." he thought as he stood there. This insolent aggression against his people gave him ammunition against them and he was going to find a way to use their beliefs against them. After all they weren't opposed to killing other people were they? And they had certainly done that in Boise. He moved closer to the shifting wall seeking any gap or soft spot he could enter through. He became aware of another presence. He knew this one too. In the natural, the big dark man faced another man, slightly older and dressed in very casual clothes. They stood and faced each other.

In the reality of the spiritual world the sinister dark force stood against the bright white force which leaned on a large sword that gleamed with an inner fire. The dark force shifted slightly away from the sword. "Caleb, why are you here to disturb me?"

Caleb responded, "Because of their prayers. They have asked God for protection. Considering what you are attempting to do to His people He felt it was important enough to send me."

The archangel stared at the minion of the enemy and tried to understand what he was attempting to do. "Are you now foolish enough to dare to come against the Holy Spirit of God? Go back to the abyss where you came from and tell your Master to leave these people alone."

The dark force shifted back and forth looking for a weakness or a lapse of attention by Caleb. But the angel's focus was on him alone. He complained, "They are being used to defeat my efforts unfairly. God allows them to strike me but denies me the right to strike back. They are all sinners. Why do you defend them?"

Caleb distrusted anything this being said. "God is the judge of their sinfulness. All he sees is His Son in these that you are trying to destroy. He will not allow you to attack His Son again. You remember Christ don't you? You remember the cross?"

Visibly shaken by the name, and their defeat, the dark force retreated from the angel. "You didn't need to bring that up again did you? I remember." The dark force gathered its strength for an assault. Caleb's armor flared into incandescence and he raised his sword which was now giving off gleams of energy that made it look like it was on fire.

Daunted by the light, the dark force quailed, snarled his defiance, and fled. Caleb watched as it scurried back away. The archangel went back to waiting for the next event to transpire. He was concerned about the near future, not only for the group in the house, but for the entire human race in the face of this dark angel of Satan. Caleb could not see the future like God could and he could only obey and rely on God. Caleb's duties were to watch over and minister to the true church and the children of the most High God. When necessary, he would have to do battle with the dark forces of the enemy. While he was very good at his duties, he did his job gratefully and with humility as a servant of God, but he was concerned for them.

CHAPTER TWENTY-TWO

Jack woke to a delicious smell of eggs, bacon, toast, and coffee. He looked up to see Laura sitting on the bed with a tray with two breakfasts on it. He realized that he hadn't eaten since dinner in his cell the day before. He stretched and enjoyed the softness of the bed and the covers. Better yet, he enjoyed looking at his wife's smile. He reached out and took her hand. She let go and moved the breakfasts over to the desk and came back to the bed. She snuggled down next to him and kissed him. "It's really good to have you back. I didn't realize how much I could miss you until you were gone."

He held his wife and realized that he had never told them about anything that had happened to him since he'd left to stake out the Master Prophet's building five days ago.

He kissed her forehead and said, "You have got to hear about Caleb." He then told her about the day he was taken, the airplane, the jail, the drugs, the interrogation, and the information that the woman told him near the end of his captivity.

She had sat up while he was telling her about Caleb and listened to every word carefully. When he was done she expressed her thoughts. "I believe that we are in the very center of God's will on this Omniscience Temple thing." She then told him about the second visit from Rose that led them to Stan. "I really like Stan and Debbie. They're not only good Christians, they are good people."

Jack told her about Mark hiring him. She was glad that their involvement with the man who was now an ex-police Captain had worked out the best for him. Then she thought about what Jack had said, "Did you say the woman that told you we were coming was a tall blonde?"

Jack nodded and described her to Laura.

Laura got a little grim, "I think I saw her on our way out of their building. She didn't survive their gun battle. She told Jack about Mark's turning their being surrounded into an advantage due to the combat inexperience of the security guards. When we fired on them at both ends of the room, they each tried to get the reward for killing us. They saw us fire and then Mark killed the lights and we dropped to the floor below the line of fire and crawled away to the side. Each side thought the flashes they saw from the other side were us. Mark said that being under fire for the first time distorts your perceptions. Because this was the first time most of them had been in a firefight they were scared by the incoming bullets and used their rifles to defend themselves. Trying to kill us they died in the crossfire."

Jack explained about his thoughts of their not being too smart to "allow" the team to come after him. "It rather reminds me of someone with a butterfly net stalking a Bengal tiger. They got a lot more than they could handle. I wonder what the great prophet Alan Roswell thinks of that."

They ate their breakfasts and got cleaned up. Then they went out to find the others. Most everybody was in the kitchen again. Everyone thanked Laura for making breakfast for everybody. She just smiled. "Have you guys figured out what we are going to do?"

Mark, Jack, and Stan looked at each other. Mark replied, "Sort of. We've got a plan but it is going to take a lot of God to make it work."

Laura agreed and suggested they all pray for guidance and provision, which they did for most of the next thirty minutes. While no one had a vision or even a word, they all felt that they were on the right track and Rose had said that God would be with them and fight their enemies.

Mark outlined the points they had settled on. The plan required some military hardware and help. It also would need all five of them to pull it off.

Laura noticed Debbie sitting there quietly but with big eyes and a bit of a frown. She went over to the quiet woman and sat down next to her. "What's running through your mind right now?" Laura had been indoctrinated into the spy/combat world and knew it seemed impossible to someone not familiar with the action.

Debbie looked at her hands in her lap for a few minutes and then told Laura, "I know you think that because I'm new at this counter-terrorism stuff and don't understand a lot of it I should stay out of the way. But, I can contribute and I want to be a part of it too. I probably should be scared, but I'm excited to be so close to God and see His will being done like I

155

never have before. I've been praying and I know that the Lord wants me to be involved in this thing you're doing."

Laura was taken aback. She thought the woman was the quiet type that would have asked to go to her mother's until it was all over. Here she was volunteering to go in harm's way. Laura prayed in her mind. "Dear Yahshua, do You want Debbie to be involved in this struggle against the Omniscience Temple?" She got the impression that God was somehow amused but at the same time she got a confirmation in her spirit. She patted Debbie's hand and said, "Okay, the boss says you're in."

Stan didn't know if he should be happy or worried about that. He smiled at his wife, "You sure, honey?" She nodded. "Last night, while I was praying, the Lord told me I was going to fight by your side in this battle." She then looked at Mark. "What can I do?"

Mark absolutely believed Laura when she said that God had agreed that Stan's wife was to be a part of the action even though it seemed like he was always training another new person. "Oh well." He thought. "Stan said she was good with a pistol".

Mark smiled at her. "I don't know yet. But since God is in it, we'll find out as we go along. Just listen and if you have anything to contribute, jump in there. Don't worry about military backgrounds or previous experience. God uses who He wants to and we tend to go along with that. Welcome to God's First Team."

Jack stood up. "Okay then, here are today's actions. First, we have a little over two weeks until the end of the month which was their original date to detonate the weapons if the U.S. government doesn't capitulate. I'm pretty sure that they are going to demand that capitulation next week and give the government ten days to agree."

He walked around as he continued, "They might move their timetable up due to the raid on the center in Boise and the fact that we drugged and interrogated one of their senior people. But, we don't think they can crank it up much and still leave a reasonable time for the government to agree. Remember, their goal is to threaten, not actually detonate the nuclear weapons. They would not only lose their weapon but would become the most hunted people on what would be left of the world. That is, assuming that there would be people left afterward."

Stan asked, "What really is going to happen if they do set those things off?"

Mark answered that one, "We of course, don't know for sure. But it is possible that configuration and sequential detonations will knock the Earth for a loop. It could change the tilt of the planet significantly which would cause massive volcanic activity all around the globe, completely change the prevailing weather patterns, create a massive greenhouse effect, and generally mess up civilization as we know it today." He stopped talking and looked around the group. "That was the good news. The worst scenario is that they could fracture the crust so badly that the world would break apart, losing our atmosphere and turning the Earth into an asteroid belt between Mars and Venus. Needless to say that would result in a complete loss of all life on earth."

Stan stared at Mark. "Dear sweet Yahshua. Can that happen? I don't think that is the description in Daniel and Revelation about the last days in the Bible? I mean, God's word is true and it doesn't mention that total destruction of the world for another thousand years after Christ returns."

Sarah replied, "Maybe that is the tribulation period? But then that's supposed to last for three and a half years. Maybe they'll start something that will take three and a half years to reach a climax and the Lord will come back to stop it."

Jack jumped back into the conversation at that point. "We don't know for sure how this fits into the Biblical accounts. But remember that what Rose told each of us makes our efforts critical to this situation regardless of the outcome."

Jack sat down again. "Now that we know the probable timetable and the possible results if they are forced to set the bombs off, the next item is to locate all thirty-three of the sites. Then we have to verify that at least one of them has an actual bomb on location. At that point we will be able to prove our case and get all the help we need and nobody will be calling it a rumor."

Debbie asked, "How do you suggest that we, six citizens, find out where these bombs are hidden in time?"

Mark replied, "The nice thing about the spy/combat world is the friends that you make. If you both survive whatever you're into, they stay friends forever. Now, I have some friends that can help us locate the sites regardless of the preventions the Master Prophets have taken." He had everyone's attention then.

"A nuclear mass over a certain amount produces a lot of radiation. Most of the world knows that you can absorb most of this radiation with lead shielding, concrete, and lots of earth. What most people are not aware of is that there are two types of radiation generated by a nuclear mass that are not containable by anything. Beta waves and mu-mesons can go straight through the entire planet. They don't hurt people that we are aware of and are very hard to isolate the source because other things can also create them. Most people disregard them and consider these emissions as worthless. Fortunately the people in the U.S. intelligence community didn't think so twenty-five years ago. On every Keyhole satellite in orbit, and there are a lot of them up there, there are detectors that can pinpoint every active concentrated nuclear mass on, or around, planet Earth, regardless of how deep it is buried or what is covering it. These particles zip right through everything in a very orderly way. The amount of each type of radiation is different for different manufacturers. For example, a U.S. nuclear bomb has an entirely different third-wave signature than a Russian nuclear bomb or an American nuclear power plant. Third wave is the title they use for these emissions. I should be able to use my 'General Connelly' persona to get NSA to locate the bombs on the Arctic circle to within a few yards. I will get them to include the date of first discovery at the locations and we'll concentrate on ones near the Arctic Circle and two years old or less."

Sarah asked, "Wouldn't the NSA have detected the pattern of all these warheads as they were moved into place? And if we get a good enough pattern won't that be enough to get the President to act?"

Mark shook his head. "No, unfortunately there are a lot of miscellaneous nuclear masses scattered around the planet and a lot of them are Russian in origin. Also, there may be an innocuous cause for a pattern that can look like a bomb but isn't. Without direction from the CIA or the NSA itself I doubt that these patterns would have meant anything to the analyst watching for bombs coming into the United States. Unfortunately that means that we will need to go in and get physical evidence of an installation before we make a second try to get the President's attention."

Debbie spoke up, "I don't know the President but he is probably shown dozens of possible threats like this every month. I think Mark is right. We will have to get into a site and get the proof that they have a bomb there."

Mark picked up Jack's cell phone again and repeated his routine to get the cooperation of the NSA. It actually took less time to get a download from the NSA showing all emission sites at the top of the world than it had taken to find Debbie's car. Mark wrote several small software programs and turned them loose on the information they had received. In five minutes the software was finished eliminating the sources with other characteristics and they had a map marking what had to be the Master Prophet's sites. Each one was near the Arctic Circle, each one had a singular nuclear signature, and each one had stayed in a fixed position for less than two years. The clincher was that there were exactly thirty-three of them.

Jack asked Mark, "What is the distribution by country?"

Mark looked at the plot on his laptop. "Well, it looks like these Master Prophets are equal opportunity terrorists. There are two in the U. S. one near Kotzebue on the eastern edge of Alaska and one near Fort Yukon on the western edge. Canada has four about equally spaced across their country. There is one on Baffin Island near Pangnirtung, two on Greenland, one near Kagerlussuaq and one near nothing at all on the eastern side. There is one on Iceland at the northern tip of the country but near no town. There is one on Norway near Mo i rana. One is in Sweden, south of Maimberget. There is one in Finland near Movaniani and the remaining twenty are spread across the Russian Federation. There are none near sizable towns or cities in Russia but then there is a lot of space in which you can get lost in Russia, especially Siberia. They are not evenly spaced around the world but probably situated over high stress points near the magma or plate tectonic fracture points.

After plotting the locations on a map, the decision was made to go after the Kotzebue site because it was the latest to go on-line and it was on American soil.

Jack was about to go out and purchase all the Arctic gear he could when Mark stopped him. "I've got a better idea."

They put a call into Mark's commander when he had been in the U.S. Navy SEALs. Mark gave Colonel Simmons a cover story and explained what he needed. He gave the commander the authorization that the President had given them and his clearance level. The commander said he'd get back to Mark in a few minutes. While they waited, Mark got the sizes and dimensions for everybody so that when the commander called back he would be ready.

When Commander Simmons called back it was with a new respect for his former subordinate. He approved whatever Mark needed with his supply officer.

After researching the equipment needed, Captain Willingham told him that all the gear they wanted was available at a naval facility in Colorado Springs. That figured since the SEALs did a lot of their Arctic training in the mountains of the Rocky Mountain state.

Mark, Jack, and Stan took two vehicles down to the storage facility and got the gear. In the meantime Laura, Sarah, and Debbie worked the internet and the phones to get as much information on Kotzebue, Alaska, and the Arctic Circle as possible.

That afternoon Mark was able to reach Major Mike White of the Air Force. He personally knew Mike and trusted him enough to give him a brief idea of the problem. He got Mike's enthusiastic agreement to play a part in any action. Providing that his superiors agreed to let him and certain selected equipment be used in the project. Mark had Mike put him in contact with the Base Commander and 'General Connelly' secured the use of Mike and a very special helicopter for the duration. Mark wondered where the accountant was that was keeping a tab on the expenses he was running up as "General Connelly".

The team reconvened in the kitchen to sort out the information that the women had secured and firm up their schedule.

Sarah had done a good job of winnowing out the critical and useful information and everyone listened to the descriptions of life in the Arctic, warnings, and precautions against everything from frostbite to polar bear bite, and the location of any unidentified construction projects in and around the Kotzebue area that had been ongoing during the last two years. There wasn't a lot that could go on in complete secrecy but that didn't really help since there was almost no information on the area other than side notes in the general travel promotions.

Jack had talked to Major White again and they agreed to meet in Nome at the Nome Air Force Base in twenty-four hours. Mike needed the time to have the helicopter winterized and refitted for this specific mission.

Loading all the gear and personal items for six people on an Arctic mission almost overwhelmed Jack's SUV but they managed to squeeze it in. An hour later everything was loaded onto a private jet at DIA and the team headed northwest.

They had been airborne for two hours when the pilot called Mark up front. "Hi." The pilot said, reaching out to shake hands with Mark. I'm Pete Booth and I was an F-14 pilot on the Kitty Hawk when you were flying missions out of there. I doubt that you remember me my handle was "Cool Hand". I'll never forget the time you brought the Secretary and his family out of the jungles after their kidnapping."

Mark smiled and shook the pilot's hand, "It's good to see another swabbie doing well in the world."

Peter nodded, "Same here. The reason I called you up here is because I've been watching another aircraft on our six about four miles back that has matched our course changes for the last two hours."

Mark said, "Could it just be another flight to Alaska?"

Peter shook his head, "No sir, I took a couple of side tracks and changed my speed considerably and they matched everything I've done so far to the T."

Mark thought about the following plane. There wasn't a lot they could do about it and nobody he could call to check it out. Then he had a thought, "Cool Hand, how come this Jet Commander has rear facing radar?"

Pete moved his headphones to a better position. "I own this baby and I felt blind when I first got it. You know, after the avionics in a fourteen this was like looking out a porthole with no information. So I spent a lot of money and had some special gear included. I've got three-sixty scan, commercial ID notification, range gate rate and travel indicators, and even some minimal missile tracking electronics. It cost me almost a year's wages but I do feel a lot more comfortable now."

Mark slapped him on the shoulder as he got up from the right hand seat. "Keep an eye on our friend back there and let me know if anything changes. Who knows, maybe the bonus for this trip will help defray the cost of that gear."

As he got back to the team he got a questioning look from Sarah. "The pilot informed me that we have a tail a few miles back. Don't know who. It could be the Master Prophets or one of the alphabet agencies. I've been making so many contacts recently, just under their radar that they may have begun to wonder what I'm up to. The pilot will let us know if things change."

Stan quipped, "You mean like a strafing run?"

Mark frowned, "I hope not, the modern 'strafing run' is done from miles away with a 'fire-and-forget' missile that we couldn't escape with this plane."

But the rest of the run to Nome was uneventful and their pursuer broke off when they started to descend into the Nome airport.

CHAPTER TWENTY-THREE

The team settled into a large motel suite with three bedrooms to wait for Mike White to show up with their ride to Kotzebue. They studied the NSA plot and the maps they had acquired including a topological map of the area around Kotzebue. The site tagged by the NSA Keyhole satellite was roughly twenty miles southeast of Kotzebue. This was the only way you could go from the small town. That was because Kotzebue was situated on the very end of a peninsula running northwest to southeast. It turned out that the site was actually closer to Buckland than Kotzebue.

Six hours and two meals later there was a call from the Major. He had just landed at the Air Force Base and would be at the motel in less than thirty minutes. Jack used his laptop and called up the weather for the area. It was probably the best weather they were going to get for a while. There was a major storm front moving in from the Bearing Sea that should hit Buckland around noon the next day. They would want to be gone by then or expect to spend a week socked in there. That was a week they couldn't afford to lose. The conditions were balmy for the area. Minus two degrees Celsius with overcast skies and a gentle ten-to-twenty knot wind from the west. Colder weather after dark and it was a very short day. There was no indication of ice conditions or snowfall depth because it was all ice and the snow varied daily in height everywhere. The only constant was that there was always snow, except once in a while in the brief "summertime".

At the knock on the door, Mark checked it out with his pistol behind the door but aimed at whoever was out there. It was the Major and a Captain. Mark let them in. Major White introduced the Captain as John Travis, a fellow excitement junkie. He had actually been scheduled for a two week vacation at this time but jumped at the chance to accompany Mike on a "secret" mission with the possibility for some real "action". Mike needed the Captain's expertise which was weapons control from the super chopper he had managed to finagle out of his base commander after Mark's call. "Never know when you might need "Dead Eye John" here."

Everyone gathered around the maps as Mark laid out the strategy. He brought the two pilots up to speed on the actual purpose of the trip and got their input. Mike said that in the present configuration the chopper would only hold four people besides the pilots. He thought that he could put those four people down within a mile of the site, behind some hills where they probably couldn't be seen. He would then wait there unless they called for assistance or until they needed extraction. Mark turned to Laura and said, "I want you and Debbie to handle the communications again." He could see that she wanted to go but he wanted experience on the communications gear. "I know that you want to go but I need you to train Debbie so that next time you can go."

Laura wanted to have a fit, but she realized that Mark was probably right in taking Sarah, Jack, and Stan. They all had more combat experience and were probably more adept at wading through a mile of snow than she was.

Sarah mentioned that Rose had indicated Laura was crucial to the outcome of this mission. Jack concurred with his input being that he was supposed to follow her lead. Mark agreed but pointed out that the mission wasn't this one exploratory trip and that she could lead by staying in touch from Nome. "Anyway, I think you should expect a possible visit from the prophets while we are gone. So, if it's combat you're seeking you may find it right here in the comfort of your own motel suite."

That made sense to Laura who went over and picked up her M-4/M-209 combo and said, "Let 'em come." Mark had the stray thought that he might need to worry about what would be left of the motel.

The four team members headed for the site suited up in thermal underwear, a satin cover, Kevlar body armor with trauma plates, another satin cover layer, and then the outer wear in white camo. Picking up their hardware in duffle bags caused Stan to fall over backwards. Rolling around to push himself up he said, "How about a tank? A tank could carry all this stuff and not fall over." Jack and Sarah helped him up and got him loaded with his bag and stabilized so that he stayed upright.

After checking out the headset communicators they left the suite and headed for the short trip to the Air Base and the helicopter. The wind tore at them as they walked to the helicopter and Stan's comment was better this time. "Hey, I like this stuff. I don't feel the wind except for it trying to push me over." Everyone laughed at that.

The trip was roughly ninety miles and took less than thirty minutes for the quiet helicopter to reach their drop-off point even with flying nap-of-the-earth for the last four miles to stay out of radar sight of the construction site.

After disembarking, the team put on snowshoes and headed out, single file, for the Master Prophets' secret site. As they trudged along, getting used to the slide, step, slide of the snow shoes Jack asked Mark, "What type of reception do you think they'll have waiting for us?"

Mark peered through the blowing snow and shook his head. "I don't have a clue. They may think they are perfectly safe and just have routine patrols or they could be waiting for us with tanks and cannons. I don't have the pull even with the 'General Connelly' persona to request satellite imagery of the strike site. There just isn't any justification for that yet. We'll just have to handle whatever we run into."

Twenty minutes later Mark was rethinking his last statement. They had approached to within five hundred yards, which appeared to be a mine opening into the side of a mountain. As they walked into a quarter-mile round depression leading up the last ridges before the mine opening the proverbial doo-doo hit the spinning air agitator. Walking through a bunch of large rocks Mark saw something he didn't like, a reflection from the ridge between them and the mine, a glint off some kind of lens. Not good. Mark snapped "drop and cover' into his microphone as he dove behind a large boulder. Everyone copied his action as incoming rounds started whistling by and caroming off every rock in the area. The sheer volume of fire was staggering, with hundreds of rounds slamming into everything. Mark snuck a quick peek from behind the other side of the rock he'd gotten behind. The entire ridge, which was shaped like a "C" with them in the open end, was winking rifle fire at them. He pulled back in time to save his head. Every time one of them tried to take a shot, twenty or thirty rounds pounded the rock they were behind. Over the noise of the firing and the ricochets Jack yelled through his combat microphone at Mark, "What do we do?"

Mark yelled back, "Stay tight for a bit, there are over a hundred guns up there. The shooting will die down when they see that they haven't hit us yet, and then comes the fun part. They'll try to enfilade us. I mean that they will try to get around us and shoot us from the sides. If you see anyone trying that, shoot them."

But the volume of fire didn't completely cease which prevented them from returning fire even if someone was trying to get around them. Sneaking another peek Mark was about to call in the helicopter when he saw two people with Stinger missiles behind the shooters. Obviously they were aware of the helicopter.

Mark knew that their positions were not going to protect them for much longer. The enemy was bound to have a mortar or rifle-propelled grenades that would reach them. Shrapnel doesn't care about rocks in front of you. He thought through their options. Only one came to mind. He got on the comm net. "Listen, Sarah, you and Stan get ready to run back the way we came. Jack and I will try to keep their heads down as long as we can."

It was a long shot regardless, for two reasons. The first reason was, trying to get beyond the enemy's M-16 range. This was over 100 yards farther back than their position, would be hard. The second reason was, doing it on snowshoes, would be a gamble with ten enemy shooters on your own level. With over a hundred guns on an elevation the odds weren't worth calculating. But, it was all he could come up with in the killing field they were in. The Master Prophets had planned this trap carefully so that there could be no escape.

Mark was starting to count when the noise and volume of firing suddenly went to new heights. Crouching behind his rock he noticed that almost none of the rounds were striking around him. Sneaking another look, he saw their tormentors being knocked over and blown up on the whole ridge. He added his weapon to the unknown support as did the rest of the team when they realized that they might come out of this alive. The incoming rounds and explosions decimated the defenders with pinpoint accuracy and an overwhelming rate of fire. Besides their M-4s Mark heard M-16s, M-14 sniper rifles, and several M-60 and M-249 heavy and light machine guns blasting away from above and behind them.

The firefight dwindled down as the defenders of the site were eliminated. Finally there were only random shots and then silence. Mark walked out of the bowl back towards the support firing positions. He yelled, "Come on out Bill, I'd know that firing arrangement in my sleep."

A bunch of snow erupted and Captain William Carol stood up and waded through the deep snow over to Mark. Another hundred snow-covered troops arose and headed over to check the enemy shooters. Four snipers stayed in position to cover the approach. Mark and Bill hugged, which was difficult due to the amount of clothing they each had on. They hugged but were still a foot apart. Mark smiled, "Well, I owe you one for that. They had us in the barrel and were about to close it on us when you showed up. Want to tell me how you got authority to bring a whole platoon up here?"

Bill smiled, "Well, it seems our base commander, Colonel Williams, was very curious as to the requisition one "General Connelly" made of our supply depot in Colorado Springs. That curiosity led him to keep an eye on our U.S. Government property that we 'loaned' to you. In following you around it led us to Nome. A suspicious helicopter also requisitioned by "General Connelly" led him to believe that all four squads needed to have some Arctic training and, lo and behold, we ran across a firefight. Now if that isn't good timing then what is? General",

Mark had a grin on his face. "That's Mister General to you." Mark got serious then. "Well, you guys really pulled my bacon out of the fire and 'General Connelly' is going to see that a commendation is everyone's file for this 'unofficial' action."

Bill shook his head, "Thanks, but we weren't here. There won't be any records of this except in my report to Colonel Williams on how we were able to prevent severe puncturing of his loaned out equipment."

By then Sarah, Jack, and Stan had come up to where the two men were standing. Everybody ducked when one of the snipers fired a single round to stop a wounded defender from taking a shot.

Mark introduced everybody to Bill and told them that this was the last guy he trained to be a squad leader. "Now look at him, all grown up into a Captain and a platoon leader at that.

I'll bet a desk job isn't too far in the future for a bright, adventuresome lad like you."

Bill laughed, "No, you broke that mold. They learned from your departure. The leaders don't get a desk job unless they ask for it anymore." He pointed at the mine shaft. "Shall we go see what you've found?"

Jack had quieted Laura and Debbie down after the firefight and talked Mike into joining them near the entrance to the mine. The helicopter slid quietly into a resting position to the left of the opening to the admiring glances from a bunch of the Marines. Bill liked the armament on the bird, especially the twin Vulcan cannons in their chin mounts.

Two of his men reported that the mine shaft went back about eighty yards and then made a thirty-degree bend to the right. Beyond the bend was a ferroconcrete bunker with two entrenched heavy machine guns. It also looked like the mine shaft in front of the bunker was mined with Bouncing Bettys and Claymores.

Mark and the others conferred and decided that they couldn't just launch a couple of missiles in there because they could bring down the roof and that would make their job a waste of time.

Bill decided to give a concept of his a shot. A squad advanced down the shaft about halfway. There were two 'bullet-proof' Motorola closed-circuit cameras watching them. Two minutes later there were two piles of junk not watching anything in particular. The armor-piercing rounds fired by the M-249 paid absolutely no attention to the label on the housings.

The Marines had to hug the floor when the machine guns fired off sending ricochets back and forth down the tunnel.

Next, several smoke grenades were tossed into the area of the bunker and were followed by several fragmentation grenades. The frags took out all the Claymores and other mines by exploding them. When the debris had settled the troops advanced and a couple of anti-tank rockets removed most of the ferroconcrete bunker and the guards that were manning the machine guns.

The platoon split into three groups. One mounted a defense against a surprise attack from the outside. The other two filtered through the remainder of the installation hunting anyone still alive. Ten minutes later they brought out a timid-looking scientific type in a lab coat. One of the Marines that brought him out said, "We found him hiding in a coat locker. There was a rifle on the floor by him but he was smart enough not to try and use it."

Jack, Mark, and Sarah questioned the small man. Jack took the lead, "What is your name?"

"Adrian Pavel" came out in almost a whisper.

"What was your job here?"

"I maintain the system recording and electronics."

Jack looked at the others. Sarah took a mild tone with the man. "I'm sorry if we've disrupted your day but we need to know everything you can tell us about this facility."

Adrian looked up at her for a few seconds. "Okay. It looks like I'm out of a job anyway." He nervously took his John Lennon glasses off and wiped them with his smock. "This facility is a deep thermal experiment to determine the feasibility of geo-thermal energy generation. The system has a power-source that we lower down, to almost the magma level, and run tests with our sensors and recorders. If the project proves feasible then we can probably reduce, significantly, the use of oil for power in the U.S."

He delivered it openly and with no duplicity that anyone could detect.

The smell of cordite and explosive powder wafted over the group making Adrian cough. Mark asked the little man. "Does the fact that we've just had to fight our way through over 120 armed men and blow up the entire front end of your 'facility' seem slightly out of line for the type of 'experiment' you are running? Doesn't it strike you as a little strange that the U. S. Military has to fight its way in here?"

"Yeah, it does. That's why everyone grabbed a gun and ran out to defend the place."

Sarah said, "Everyone but you."

"Yeah, well, I was never into the physical stuff if you know what I mean. But they told me that it was a bunch of people trying to steal our secrets. But, why would the military want to do that?"

Jack asked Adrian, "What type of power source are you using down the shaft?"

Adrian replied, "Oh, it's nuclear. It has to be to survive the intense heat and still function. I'm sorry that we have to use Russian power sources but they are so much more affordable than the domestic ones. At least that's what the owners tell me."

Jack asked Adrian to show him the recorders and electronics he tended. He agreed and led them all through the interior of the installation to a work station near the actual shaft.

Bill had one of his men run out and come back with a Geiger counter and a rate meter. He started at the bunker location and started walking back towards the work area Adrian used.

Jack was busy checking the electronics and the wiring circuits for the 'power source'. He asked Adrian several technical questions and watched how he took his 'readings'.

Bill showed up and suggested they all go back to the bunker area because he had something to show them. Taking Adrian with them they went back to where Bill stopped them.

Jack put his hand on Adrian's shoulder and turned him around. "Adrian, I'm going to give this to you straight. I could sugar-coat if there was time, which there isn't."

Adrian paid his full attention to Jack.

Jack asked, "How long have you been 'monitoring' this power source?"

The little man thought and said, "About two weeks, why?"

Jack shook his head, "Because it isn't a power source to test geo-thermal energy release. It's a Russian nuclear weapon that is designed to crack the earth."

Adrian half smiled, "You're pulling my leg, aren't you?"

Bill chimed in with, "If you stayed down there another month and he pulled your leg it would fall off. Take a look at this reading. "He showed them the Geiger counter which was deep into the red zone."

Adrian shook his head, "We've got badges, and see?" He pointed to the standard RAD badge on his smock.

Sarah looked at it and took it off to examine it closer. "This film has been exposed before. It will never change because it's already exposed to maximum radiation. This means nothing." She threw it away.

Adrian was still not sure. Bill said, "Okay, you know how to handle one of these?" He was holding out the Geiger counter. Adrian nodded. Bill cleared the reading and handed it to him.

Adrian hit the test button and the meter jumped directly into the red. Unbelieving to the end, Adrian said, "It's broken, it only reads in the red."

Bill took the unit and cleared it again. He then sat it on a broken piece of concrete. He walked over and back and it read a slightly increased reading. Jack and Sarah did the same with slightly higher readings. Watching all of this carefully, Adrian then walked over to the meter and it started chattering and the meter started blinking red. He stood there for a few seconds and then started tearing his clothes off of himself. He stopped when he got to his underwear. The meter showed a half range reading of the almost nude Adrian. He turned to Bill with huge eyes and said, "I'm dead."

Sarah looked at the man's skinny frame and told him, "No, you're not dead, not yet. You've only worked there for a short time. You might have side effects but you'll live. That is as long as you don't go back there again."

By now Adrian was shivering so much in the fifteen degree tunnel he couldn't get many words out. But the one statement they did understand was "They tried to kill me!"

Bill had his men get some clothes together for Adrian and they used a stick to pick up his old ones and throw them as far back into the lab as they could.

Bill turned to Jack. "Can you shut this thing down?"

Jack shook his head. "I might, but then I might set it off too. We need to get some experts in here and quick."

Sarah added, "Yeah, smart ones, in lead suits, with self-contained air supplies."

Two large transport helicopters had joined the stealth copter outside the mine. Bill detailed two squads to keep anyone other than the experts from the government, which he would accompany, into the 'facility'.

Jack and Mark were talking to Sarah and Stan before leaving when Bill walked up.

Bill smiled, "Well, General Connelly, you and your merry men and women have been invited to the White House, without delay. They are sending a government jet to pick you up this afternoon."

Jack told him, "Thanks anyway, but we already have a jet and we want to be there more than he wants us there."

After returning the gear at the Air Base Mark told Mike White again why he wasn't invited to the dance due to the danger of the Stinger missiles. They then picked up Laura and Debbie and got Cool Hand to fly them to Washington. This ensured him of a healthy bonus and more than paid for his special radar gear.

CHAPTER TWENTY-FOUR

The new agent-in-charge stood undecided outside the door to Alan Roswell's office. He knew all about how Karl died at the hands of the Prophet and it was scaring him to death. He didn't want to ever make the Prophet mad at him. But now he had to give him some bad news. The voice from inside telling him to come in startled him but he did as he was told.

Alan looked up from the draft of the document he wanted to send to the President of the United States and glowered at the man. "What is it?"

Acting like he was opening the door to a blast furnace the aide replied, "Sir, I have..., I need to tell you..., there has been... We've lost contact with the Kotzebue site." He stood there waiting for a reaction.

Alan looked at the man and blinked. "Did you send the mercenaries as I asked?"

"Oh yes sir. They were there yesterday and ready to repel any invaders."

Alan sat back and wondered about the loss. "Could it just be a breakdown? Is it possible that it is just a malfunction?"

Not having been killed yet, the man became more articulate. "No sir, we have three completely independent systems of communications with the site. All of them are unresponsive."

Alan clicked on the computer next to his desk. Looking at several files he shook his head. "CNN doesn't mention any nuclear explosions in Alaska and there's no mention of any Alaskan action from the President's office or on any of the military schedules. Having to overcome a hundred mercenaries implies a large military effort. There is no sign of any such effort. Keep monitoring and send a helicopter from the Fort Yukon site to see what is going on. It's probably only a breakdown." Alan thought to himself, "Even if we have lost a site it doesn't make any difference. We really only need the right twenty-six bombs to work." He went back to his document.

The agent left and went straight to the men's room and threw up.

The flight to Washington was a good chance for the team to rest. Mark went up and spelled Pete several times for restroom breaks and just to let him relax. Mark wasn't a pilot but had handled the controls on a lot of different aircraft in his time. Peter tutored him on the fine points of aviation and let him handle the plane while they were both there. Mark appreciated the time behind the wheel and told Pete that his security service could use a good pilot in the future. They promised to continue talking.

The landing at National Airport was soft and sure. The aircraft was vectored to a CIA hanger and Pete put it inside before shutting it down. By the time he had the hatch/stairs extended the big hanger doors were closed and several Secret Service types were there with transportation to the White House. It was just after six a.m. in the Capital and the people were just beginning to move out onto the streets for another work day when the small convoy pulled into the secure lot and everyone took the tram to the White House proper. They had left all their weapons in their bags and got into the building without being strip searched or detained.

Waiting to see the President didn't take all that long. He was expecting them. As they filed in he came around his desk and shook hands with each one of the men. Sarah, Laura, and Debbie he gave a hug. Then it was on to business. The Man turned to Mark and asked, "What in blue blazes is going on?"

Jack volunteered, "We were attempting to secure proof for you that the "Ring of Fire" warning we gave you was not an unsubstantiated false rumor"

The President looked confused. "Why would it be a rumor? And furthermore, what warning? I never got a warning from you."

Mark bit his lip to stop from cursing. "Sir, could you have your Secret Service people pick up Tom Kendric and have him brought here?"

"Tom? Why? He's just an analysis I have filtering my incoming ca... oh no."

Jack looked at his watch. "Sir we called in critical information to you about a plot to blackmail the U.S. We told Tom Kendric this information three and a half days ago. He came back with a song and dance that you were mad at us for falling for an old fable and that we weren't to bother you again with sad stories like this."

The President buzzed an aide and in a moment the head of the Secret Service stepped into the office. The President told him, "Find Tom Kendric and bring him here, preferable alive, but at this point, I'm not picky. Understand?"

"Yes sir." The tall man left the office quickly.

The President then said, "Let me hear what I was supposed to hear three days ago and don't leave out any details."

The team laid it all out for the Man. By the time they were done he had broken his pen on his desk and thrown it into the waste basket. He turned around and looked out the window at the Rose Garden for a while.

Turning back he said, "I apologize for my culpability in letting Tom hoodwink me like that. I am beginning to think that there are more enemies than friends here in Wonderland. I also want to thank you ladies and gentlemen for carrying the flag when you had to, even though it meant risking your lives."

"I don't give a hoot about plausible deniability and you can rest assured that the Captain and his men will get commendations and more than that. That is, if I'm still in charge by then."

He sighed, "You know that the Congress will eventually cave into the demands if we don't have a solution in process when they get this ultimatum" The assembled group agreed silently. "Mark, you've been the closest to this problem. Is there a solution?"

"Mr. President. We have the location of all the sites. We have already captured one. I think we need to contact the governments of these other countries, especially the Russian Federation, and get them to sew up the ones in their countries. With our help if need be. Pull their fangs and they don't have a lever. Then find them and arrest them on terroristic charges."

The President sat there for a few minutes thinking Mark's proposal through. He looked older after his thinking than before. "I agree with you Mark but it won't happen. Let me tell you why it won't happen. As soon as we start for their sites, they'll know it. These Master Prophets apparently have spies everywhere, even one here in my own office, for goodness sake. As soon as we deploy they'll demand we step down or they'll drop the hammer on all of those sites. If we try to round them up they'll make the same demand. It's the only thing they can do. That's the problem of only having a single gun to threaten people with. You either use it or you lose. You can only threaten so long. I think the reason you were able to take that one site was because you people operated outside the normal chain of command and they weren't ready for you or actually for Colonel Williams' training' exercise. They won't be lax again."

Mark had been thinking as the President was talking. "Sir, how about this, you carry on like normal. Give me the job to take these things off-line without an official deployment. I think in the time left, that I can get enough coordination on my level in other countries as well as the U.S. for a coordinated strike. You've already given me enough authority and with this team here as coordinators we might be able to prepare a ground swell that won't be seen until it rises up and shuts these places down. I know that we might not be able to get them all, but if we shut enough down there is a good chance that the threat of a death knell for the world can be averted."

The tension in the room could have been cut with anything with a sharp edge. The President was examining the possibility from all angles. Everyone was wondering what the Holy Spirit would direct on this action.

President Bollen was trying to decide if it was the right thing to do. "There didn't seem to be any other option. If he moved against the Omniscience Temple there would be a huge outcry from people that had no idea what was going on. Not a clue. They were just against anything the government did to "religion". Others were just against anything the government did. And to top it all off, the Master Prophets would probably pull the trigger and kill the planet. But he was placing the entire world in this young man's hands. If he couldn't get the job done, or his buildup was discovered the results would be disastrous. Of course, any other course would be equally bad. Capitulation would be the worst form of slow death and anything less would be the reason for the enemy to blow up the world. So, what other choice was there? Okay, what can I do to make their job easier without giving the whole thing away?"

The President nodded. "Okay, you've got the ball. And the ball in this case is the entire planet. Fail and the human race is history, goof up and the future for all of us will be slavery, no less. Do you still want to do it?"

Mark looked at the other members of the Team. Everyone was nodding, giving him the chance to put all their heads on the chopping block except one.

Laura looked steadily at Mark and made a gesture. She pointed up with her forefinger.

Mark nodded, "Let's pray and see what God wants us to do." Mark spoke the prayer while everybody else including the President prayed. "Dear mighty Yahveh, you know our hearts and the terrible crossroads we've come to in this time. We all love and praise you as the living and eternal King of our lives and we ask you to give us a clear direction in our extremity." Mark went silent and everyone listened for God to speak. Mark registered brighter light on his eyelids and he opened them to see Laura's armor flaring up to an intensity he had never before seen. Laura rose and the sword appeared in her right hand, its blade reflecting the bright light so much it looked like it was on fire. Everyone's spirit surged up as Laura, using both hands, held the sword directly above her pointed up.

Jack heard that dulcet voice again. The first time he heard it coming out of his wife was when God healed a Mossad agent in Tel Aviv. This time it was a prayer language that was so powerful it caused waves in the air. Laura's voice said, "Koo Rumm Bi Shaleth, Koo Rumm Bi Shaleth, Your Will be done." As she said that she started to bring the flat of the sword down on Mark's right shoulder. Before she could touch him he slid out of the chair and kneeled on the floor. She then touched each of his shoulders and said, "God anoints you to go forth in battle and to slay the enemy."

Just as she finished saying that a door opened and the head of the Secret Service walked in with Tom Kendric. The look of astonishment on the agent's face was matched by the look of terror on the face of the assistant.

Laura's armor was so bright the light from the windows paled in comparison. She turned to the trembling assistant and said, "Kneel!"

The man dropped to his knees and placed his hands up and pled for his life. Laura looked at him for a second and said, "Confess your duplicity, now." This did not come as a request. Everyone in the room knew that the young man's life hung in the balance.

He bowed his head and said, "I have been a faithful servant of the Omniscience Temple and the Master Prophets. I have done as I have been told to keep our secrets safe from President Bollen and to guide any affairs of the temple to fruition. He gathered strength from his own testimony and stood up in defiance to Laura.

Laura's voice seemed imperious but at the same time gentle. "The Lord says, 'There is no truth in the Omniscience Temple and it is an abomination in the sight of God'. Repent and be saved."

The young man's face darkened, "I have not sinned and you shall not stand in our way." As he spoke, he jumped at the Secret Service agent and grabbed the gun from his holster before he could be stopped.

Laura's sword started moving.

Turning, Tom snap-aimed and fired the pistol point-blank at the President's chest. The golden sword in Laura's hand flashed twice, faster than thought. The first move deflected the bullet in its path and sent it into the ceiling. The back stroke ended the young man's life.

Everyone started to move when Laura said, "BE STILL!" This also was not a request. Everyone froze in position.

Laura raised her left arm and a mist, a sprinkling of light motes, something, fell from her outstretched hand and spread outward throughout the room. Everyone's vision was drawn to the twinkling dots of light. When the light motes quit twinkling, every sign of the assailant was gone. His body had vanished as if he had never existed. There was no sign that anything had happened except for the Secret Service Agent's gun laying on the floor. Even the bullet hole in the ceiling and the gun smoke had disappeared.

Her sword disappeared but her armor flashed brightly as she turned to the President. "God commends you for your stand. You will be sorely tested soon, but stay firm in your faith these last hours and remember, He is with you as you do His will." She turned to the team, "And with each of you." Then the armor faded and Laura walked slowly over to her seat and sat down and started quietly crying.

No one said anything for a minute and then the President cleared his throat and said, "Malcolm. Pick your gun up. And for my sake, don't lose it again."

The agent picked up his gun and holstered it. He stared at Laura for a moment and then nodded to the rest of the team. He then left the room and closed the door.

The President looked at Mark who was still on his knees. "I guess that settles that. I am going to do something here I need a witness for." He pressed the button and summoned the Chairman of the Joint Chiefs of Staff, a Five-Star Marine General who was waiting outside. The General came in and looked around as if he was looking for something strange. He didn't find it.

The President stood up, "General due to an extreme national emergency I need to make these six people general staff level officers in the Air Force, effective immediately, and I am going to do it with an Executive Order because we don't have the time to debate this in Congress. Can you facilitate their orders and ranks along with the appropriate documentation by noon?"

The Marine General wasn't at all pleased that civilians were going to have control of military personnel when they had probably not had any military training themselves. "Sir, I must protest!"

The President said, "Fine, then your resignation will be on my desk by noon. As Commander and Chief of the Armed Forces of the United States and as your commanding officer I hereby relieve you of duty, dismissed."

The General looked stricken but saluted and walked out the door not quite as ramrod straight as he walked in.

The President called the next officer in line after the Five-Star General. Four-Star General Howard Miles came in smartly dressed in his best dress uniform. Every crease on his clothes looked like they could cut your hand if you touched them. Not a hair was out of place. He had been the commander of all U.S. Army forces for the last two years and had a reputation as a very emphatic, no-nonsense, by-the-book type of officer.

The President said, General, I am hereby promoting you to Chairman of the Joint Chiefs of Staff. Since that is a five-star rank you are also promoted to that rank. This is effective immediately.

"General Miles, As your first command as CJCS, I want to make these six people General staff level officers in the Air Force, effective immediately, and since this is in response to an imminent and deeply grave national emergency, I am going to do it with an Executive Order. Can you facilitate their orders and ranks along with the appropriate documentation by noon?"

"Yes Sir!" He had a reputation as a no-nonsense, by-the-book, forceful officer, but he wasn't too full of himself to remember who his Commander-in-Chief was.

The President said that he wanted Mark to have a two-star General's rank and the rest were to be considered one-star Generals in the Air Force effective immediately. The General of the CJCS office took their names and asked that they stop for a photo after they left the President. Then the new CJCS left to attend to business.

After the General left, the President came around to the other side of the desk and sat down with the members of the team. Mark had jumped to his feet when the first General entered. He remembered General Miles from his time in the SEALs and regarded him as one of the best of the best, he had almost saluted him. He now sat down again.

The President said, "The reason I made you all Officers in the Air Force is so that you are legally covered if anyone wants to argue with you during this business. It also makes you accountable as an officer and gentleman, or woman of the service. Now, except for Mark I don't think any of you have had any service have you?

Stan spoke up, "Yes, Mr. President. I was a Marine Captain during the Gulf War. I left the service when Slick Willie started to ruin everything." The snide remark about Bill Clinton made the President chuckle.

Sarah added, "I was a squad leader in the IDF for two years.

"Okay, then you three can hold your own from your own knowledge." He looked at Jack. "Son, I've heard how you fight and how you handled a mix of military, FBI, and Texas Rangers. I'm not worried about you leading any troops." He turned to Laura, "Well, after what happened here today all I can say is that God's hand is on you and I pity the poor soul that makes that armor appear."

That left Debbie. The President looked at her and smiled. "Debbie, I think it is time you tell these people the truth." He looked at Stan directly, "Especially your husband."

Quiet little Debbie looked at Stan and said, "I'm sorry honey. I love you and I don't ever want to keep secrets from you. But this one I had sworn to never divulge unless the President told me to. And, I guess he just did. Remember when you met me at the Governor's ball six years ago?"

Stan just nodded, not sure he was going to like what he was about to hear.

"Well, I was on assignment then." She saw a stricken look come to his face, "Oh, no, no. It had nothing to do with you." He relaxed. "I ran into you as a completely unexpected bonus." She sort of ran out of words then.

The President gently said, "Go on".

Debbie took a big breath. "Stan, I was there at President Bollen's predecessor's bidding. I was tasked to prevent an assassination that evening. A rogue agent had decided to "terminate with prejudice" the new Governor of Utah for reasons too lengthy to go into here. I had been assigned to prevent an unstable CIA agent from harming the Governor. But, I wasn't a bodyguard. I was a highly-trained sniper. I had just found the rogue agent who was outside in the parking area with a rifle. I was able to terminate him with one silenced shot when a policeman spotted me with my rifle and used his radio to spread the alarm that a woman with a rifle was trying to kill the Governor. I couldn't explain my operation without breaking my cover. I disabled and left the rifle. Then, in my attempt to ex-filtrate the residence I was cut off by police officers who were collecting all single women looking for me. Since they did not know my mission, they would have shot me on sight to protect the Governor. As I walked across the crowded ballroom floor ahead of the sweep, I saw you. I knew who you were from the files I studied before the assignment. I liked what I saw. You were a decorated Marine officer, a police Lieutenant, and cute to boot." Stan smiled at that one.

She continued, "I doubted that I was going to make it through the evening so I decided that I wanted to get to know you, if only for a little while. You were so gracious and such a good dancer that I literally got swept off my feet and before I knew it we were out of the building and going to get something to eat. I know now that it was God's way of putting us together. I know that it probably looked like I attached myself to you to get out of there on your arm but God knows the truth and I really did fall for you that night."

Stan just smiled. "So you're a...what?"

Debbie looked at the President who nodded. "Stan, I'm an assassin-hunter/tracker for the CIA. I have been for twelve years. They've called on me twice since we've been married. Remember my trips to Arizona and Chicago? Then she allowed a far wiser look to show in her face as she looked at the rest of the team, "At the rate the Crossfire Team has been racking up the body count, my services may not be needed again for a long time."

There was a pause while everybody thought about these revelations and nobody said anything. Debbie added, "I'm real sorry if I had to mislead you guys but it was an oath, and I take all my oaths seriously."

Mark smiled and imitated Debbie's quiet little voice, "I don't have any idea of what's going on..." He laughed out loud and repeated his statement to her when she wanted to help, "Sure Debbie, if you have anything to add, just jump right in there." He took the sting out of his ironic talk by coming over and hugging her. "Now you are truly one of us."

Stan came over to his wife. She looked up at his eyes to see if there was hurt or humiliation there. All she saw was love and even some pride. "Well." He said, "It's good to know you have skills." They both laughed.

The President said that he had to get on with acting normal but in his heart he was now sure the Master Prophets were not going to beat this crowd. After all, that's what God said and if God says it, that's it.

As he ushered them out of the Oval Office he was mumbling something about having to take Malcolm out for a drink and help him sort out what happened. Maybe evangelize him at the same time. He thinks he's a Christian. Today was a wake-up call for both himself and Malcolm for sure.

CHAPTER TWENTY-FIVE

As they walked back to their tram for the return trip to the outside world, Jack kept his arm around Laura and steadied her as they walked. "Are you going to be all right honey?" She had stopped crying but wasn't acting like her normal self.

Laura hugged Jack and rested her head against his chest. She liked the warmth and closeness. She was still feeling drained of being the vehicle for God's presence in the Oval Office. She saw the look of anger and rebellion wiped off of Tom Kendrick's face as the sword in her hand executed him for rejecting God's offer of salvation. And that was exactly what it was. It had nothing to do with the current events. Tom was rebelling against the Lord and the Lord punished him for it. She was glad that the stroke was so quick he never had time to realize what was happening and to regret it. Of course, he's probably regretting everything about now.

The thing that still resonated through her mind and body was the ease at which she was able to destroy a life because it was necessary by God's laws. She couldn't bring that simple action in line with her normal approach in which she could only dispatch another human being in defense of her life or defense of other's lives. There was a psychic dissonance that she could not assimilate. She thought, "Oh my soul, God used me as an executioner!"

Jack stopped and said, "Let's pray about this, okay?" Laura nodded. The others stopped a short distance away and waited for them.

As they prayed that God would bring peace and understanding to Laura, she began to understand that the Lord was bringing her to a level of the warrior she absolutely had to be in the coming battles. Her experiential mores and morals were slightly out of line with what God commands. He was just rearranging her understanding and method of operation so that it matched His will, not hers. When she really understood that, peace came and she relaxed and praised the Lord. Then she nodded and stood back from Jack and announced that she was ready to go.

They joined the others near the terminus of the tram station.

Mark talked to Jack. "Man, I have seen some awesome things in this world but that was right up there at the top. Did you see that Laura blocked the path of the bullet he fired at the President?" He thought for a few seconds, "Does that armor appear often?"

Jack smiled and put his arm around his friend, "You mean like when we are at home cleaning house? No. Actually I have only seen it two times. I saw it today and that time in the den of the coven.

Mark was quiet for a few minutes. Then he asked, "Who killed that guy Jack? Was it Laura? Or was it an angel of God using Laura to extract God's justice?"

Jack sighed, "I'm not sure I can tell you the right answer to that question. It's probably a combination like your prayer language. Laura has to be completely submitted to the Lord to allow that type of interaction. If you want my opinion, and it's only my opinion, I think who we saw wielding that sword in the Oval Office was Rose working through Laura but Laura was completely in agreement with the actions. I wouldn't want to try to determine the difference in a court of law."

Mark agreed. They had been booked into a large pair of suites at one of the better hotels in Washington, D.C. They reached the place in government vehicles and were ready to go in while the valet picked up the luggage. Unfortunately the young man couldn't pick up the duffle bags with the weapons in them. Mark went back and lifted them both up and placed them on his luggage rack.

Retiring to their room they cleaned up and spent a while as couples. Mark called everyone into the main room in their suite. After everyone was seated he stood up.

Mark said, "Okay, looking at the layout of the sites we have eight countries to get support for a small military action that is all coordinated without using the command infrastructure in any of those countries. I will have a list of lower ranking officers in each country that we can contact to try to make this work. You are going to have to rely on the Holy Spirit to guide you in the selection of the right person because if you get the wrong one, we will blow the whole mission and with it, the world.

In the interest of time we are going to have to split up and each of us will tackle one or more countries if we're going to get this done in time. So, as a two-star General I made some decisions. Here are the countries and the assignments. I am going to give myself the Russian Federation because I know that Russia is going to be the hardest one to get any action on a sub-command level."

"Jack, I want you to tackle the U.S. and also Iceland, because they don't have any military. You shouldn't have any trouble with anyone due to your rank but I want you to work with Bill because you two have already met. I don't think Colonel Williams will give you any problems 'borrowing' some troops for a short time."

"Laura, I want you to tackle Canada and that will include the site on Baffin Island." He pointed out the island to her on the map.

"Debbie, I want you to take the two Greenland sites. The one on the east side is north of Tasiilaq. If you're not already aware of it, Greenland is a part of Denmark. The advantage here is that Denmark has an efficient military arm and is part of NATO."

Turning to his wife Mark pointed at the map again. "Sarah, I want you to tackle Norway and Sweden. There's one site in each nation. You've done work there for the Mossad and I think you can convince them to help rather quickly." She just smiled.

He turned to Stan. "I've saved the most fun for you Stan. I want you to tackle Finland. They have a small army but it is very tight-knit and it will be almost impossible to get anything going without the brass being in on it. But because that is where the Prophets will have their ears you have to avoid bringing the top people in on the action until it is over."

Mark got up and paced for a minute. "The key to make this whole thing work is that it has to be a simultaneous raid and disabling of the nuclear weapons before the Prophets can get up the nerve to push the button. I've talked to Bill again and he said that the team that took care of the site we control found a simple way to disable the firing circuits so that they can't be detonated by any outside signal. As soon as they can get that information to us we will take off for our assignments. Also, because a secret is only a secret for a short time, we have to have everybody ready to strike by Saturday at noon Greenwich Mean Time. That gives us only about thirty-six hours to accomplish our missions."

Mark handed out the assignment sheets. "We'll get airline tickets to each country along with your passports. We don't have time to arrange for military flights for this first leg. I've included the time for the simultaneous attack for each site on these papers. I realize that language could be a problem but you'll have to work around it or get a translator you can trust. I..." He was interrupted by a knocking at the room door. Going to the door with his pistol, he checked and saw that it was the military messenger. He opened the door and accepted a package which he opened on the way back to the team. Studying the contents he distributed them to each person.

"Okay, this gives the directions on how to disarm and permanently disable the weapons until they can be collected by the governments. It's in English so you might have to translate it for your group. For each one of us there is also the list of possibly cooperative personnel at the right military level in our assigned country.

Mark then led a prayer for their success and the protection of each and everyone in the team. They each took their assignment sheets and headed for the airport.

Each couple said goodbye as they got to the first of the flights.

CHAPTER TWENTY-SIX

Jack contacted Bill Carol and arranged a face-to-face meeting with him and his Base Commander, Marine Colonel Travis Williams. Bill set it up and they met in Florida at the Naval Air Station at which the SEALs were based.

Jack shook the Commander's hand and showed him his new military identification as a General which impressed the Commander.

"Colonel, I believe I know that you and Captain Carol are patriots and understand that there are times when extraordinary measures are required to defend this great country of ours." At a nod from the Colonel Jack continued. "There is a traitorous group in America that has mounted a nuclear threat to this country and others that can result in the slavery of this country, or possibly the entire world to their authority or the literal end of the world. I need two forces like the one you sent on a 'training mission' to Alaska and I need them in the next twenty six hours to be ready to simultaneously attack two more sites like the one near Buckland, one in Alaska and the other in Iceland. There could be casualties and the only superiors you can tell about this are the Commander-in-Chief or the CJCS."

The Colonel smiled, "After reading the report from Major Carol I don't have any problems assigning the assets I have command over to your service, General."

Bill hadn't missed the change in his status. "Thank you Sir. If it is the Colonel's wishes the Major would like to lead the Iceland sortie."

The Colonel opened his drawer and took out some oak leaf clusters and tossed them to the new Major. "I expected you to do that, and I expect that General Malone will want to accompany you as an observer. I will lead the other Fort Yukon attack personally" Jack nodded. They started making preparations for the simultaneous assaults.

Meantime Laura had arrived in Quebec and contacted the Major on her list and got a few minutes to talk to him. She checked with the Holy Spirit and got a confirmation in her spirit that he was a good person to talk to.

It was obvious that the Major found Laura pleasing and was interested in all the wrong things to start with. She straightened him out immediately by showing him her military id. He almost saluted but she stopped him.

"Major, I have a crisis that involves Canada and Baffin Island. I can't work through your superiors because there is the real possibility that the enemy involved has eyes and ears in the administration. I can assure you that the President of the United States and the Chairman of the Joint Chiefs of Staff are one-hundred percent behind this request and the need is such that if we don't do what we have to there won't be a Canada to worry about in the near future. Can you understand the urgency of this problem?"

The Major shook his head, "I hear your words but don't understand what the urgency is."

Laura laid out the plan of the Master Prophets and their nuclear blackmail sites of which there were five in Canadian Territories. When she finished the Major was hot enough to light matches off of. "How in the Bloody heck did they get the authority to place Russian nuclear weapons on Canadian soil in the first place?"

Laura assured him that they didn't believe in any countries eminent domain and that they had smuggled the bombs into Canada by taking advantage of the Canadian willingness to think the best of all people. By now the Major was ready to start WWIII by himself. She showed him the pictures of the site in Alaska they had taken. She didn't protect him; she showed him the pictures the troops had taken of the defenders spread all over the terrain, leaking blood into the snow and in all the different forms of death. She then showed him the pictures of the installation and the Geiger counter readings.

The Major sat there for a few minutes and then asked, "Where are these sites in Canada and on Baffin Island?"

She pulled out the map and showed him the locations. "We have to coordinate these attacks with the ones on the other sites at 12:00 noon GMT." He nodded.

He studied the map for several minutes and then called a Sergeant-Major over. "I want five platoons of men ready to do a coordinated live-fire training operation in the next six hours, full winter gear. I also want to talk to the second-in-command of the SAS immediately."

He looked at Laura. "I'll take care of this General. You can count on me."

Laura smiled at him. "I'm glad of that Major. But I am going with you, this is too important to not be involved." The Major nodded

Debbie, Sarah, and Stan fared similarly in the countries of Denmark, Norway, Sweden, and Finland.

Mark had finally reached Moscow and found the General he was aware was a true Russian patriot and an excellent armor officer who was on the rise in the new Russian Army.

Mark was pleased that General Serakov spoke English with almost no accent. He met with him at a Russian beerhouse in Moscow. Mark bought the drinks and bantered with the man for a few minutes. The Russian cut through the fog with a simple statement. "General Connelly, I am aware of an unspecified urgency with which you requested a meeting with me. Please be aware that I am not interested in working for your CIA or any other organization of the decadent west."

Mark smiled, "Do you think that is why I asked to talk to you?"

The General nodded.

Mark looked down for a few seconds. Then looking the General in the eye he said, "I came here today to plead for the future of the Russian Federation and all Russians in the world. I don't want your services for America, General; I want you to protect your great country in the finest tradition of the heroes of the past."

The General thought about this and said, "Continue."

Mark filled him in on the Master Prophet's plan and preparation for taking over the world. Mark then showed him the map and the pictures. He then informed him of the parallel efforts in ten other countries at the moment. "General, I won't minimize the effort needed to defend the Russian homeland. They have corrupted your great nation with an unprecedented twenty of their sites. They don't have the slightest concern about the Russian way of life or the traditions of this country. Their stated aim is the domination of all people or if that isn't possible, the destruction of the entire world."

The General smashed his fist on the table. "They will not succeed." He settled down for a few minutes and looked around. "You are right not to trust the government. There are traitors everywhere. We will have to be very careful and very quick to be ready at all these sites. They have the advantage of time, but they haven't counted on the true Russian soul. You will have your troops without anyone knowing. Where will you be?"

"Right with you General, I'm in this to the end. I'm proud to be an American, but I am also a citizen of the world and I'll be dead before I allow anyone to dictate terms to the rest of us through terroristic threats."

The General stood up, tossed his Vodka down and shook Mark's hand. "Then come my friend, we have a great many terrorists to kill."

CHAPTER TWENTY-SEVEN

Over the next twenty-four hours there were thirty-two training exercises scheduled in nine countries. These were unexpected live-fire exercises that involved a large number of troops but there was no press coverage because there were neither politicians nor military image makers involved. None of the families of the troops had any reason to see anything unusual in the normal training efforts because the troops were arranged and out in the field before they had any idea where they were going or what they were doing. If any journalist had been interested in these seemingly unconnected exercises they may have noted that they were all arranged in the northern latitudes in heavy snow country.

Through the team, United States satellite photos of the target areas kept the various troops up to date on the activities and arrangements of the sites and the personnel near them. In the last hours before the raids the troops had direct visual observation of their targets and arrangements were made to overcome any defensive bulwarks. The sites were very similar to the one that the team and the SEALs had overrun. Each one had a tunnel with a bend, usually to the right, a bunker with heavy machine guns and probably a mined entrance.

The team kept in touch by cell phone and messaging on their laptops. One of the most pressing questions no one had an answer to was; what were the Master Prophets doing? Another was; why hasn't any response to the battle and the loss of the Kotzebue site been seen?

When there were only thirty minutes before the synchronized attacks, Mark got a priority message from the White House. Answering his phone in the middle of a snowstorm on the steeps of the Siberian wilderness he heard the President's voice. "Mark. The other shoe has dropped. The Master Prophets have given us the ultimatum and something else. They said that if there is any type of organized raid on their sites they will push the button. I need to respond in the next fifty minutes. What do I tell them?"

Mark didn't hesitate, "Sir, at the deadline tell them that nothing is going to happen to any of their sites."

The President said, "You want me to *tell* them that nothing is being considered or planned for their sites, right?" The stress on the word 'tell' wasn't lost on Mark. "Absolutely Sir, in fifty minutes, you give them the assurance that we will do nothing because you need to study their ultimatum and discuss it with the other governments to decide what we should do."

There was a short silence and then the President commented, "Then that is what I will tell them. God protect us all." The connection was broken but the responsibility didn't go away. Mark thought to himself that this is the place where the ground usually falls out from underneath your feet. He hoped that the assurance that the President was going to give the prophets would cause them to feel less concerned. And it would be the truth. In twenty-five minutes there would be no attacks planned because they would already be in process."

Alan Roswell was pleased. The communique to the government of the U.S. had been delivered and it was too late for them to prevent it. He was congratulating himself when the phone rang. It was the security detail at the Baffin Island site. "Sir, we think we have intruders. You said to let you know if we saw anything out of place."

Alan frowned, "What have you seen?"

"Well sir, one of our men saw a blonde woman with an assault rifle at a distance from the site. He described Laura to the Prophet.

Alan thought, "The meddlers from God. This could be the chance I've waited for."

He told the man at the other end of the phone. "Don't hurt her. I will be there soon to take care of the situation." He hung up and got up from his desk. Locking his office door he disappeared from the room. He reappeared in the security office of the Baffin Island site much to the astonishment of the two people in the room. He wanted to talk to the security man that had seen the blonde woman immediately.

Deep in Siberia, Mark made a group call and was connected to the team and the leaders of the other raiders that didn't have a team member with them, mostly the other nineteen sites in the Russian Federation and the four sites in Canada where the SAS and Canadian Rangers were set to go. Mark had everybody synchronize their attack times at one minute to go and warned them that each raid had to be swift enough to get to the control rooms and disable the electronics before the obvious sank in on the Master Prophets. He also reminded them that if they weren't able to take the site in the first ten to twenty minutes that there would probably be no way that they could get far enough away to be safe. It really didn't need repeating, but he wanted everyone to be absolutely clear on the need to accomplish their missions.

The Russian Spetznaz forces that Mark was with were ready and much closer to the mine entrance than Mark and the SEALs had been the first time. Mark prayed for God's help and guidance as he watched the hour hand, minute hand, and sweep second hand on his watch all came together at 12 o'clock.

At a command from General Serakov, five rocket-propelled grenades flew into the tunnel. At the same time all communication frequencies were jammed and troops on top of the hillock that the mine shaft was in blew up the radio and satellite communications gear to take away any other form of communications for the people in the site. Mark knew that this was happening at all thirty-two of the active sites.

The RPGs were very effective in exploding the mines in the entrance and destroying the cameras, blinding the defenders to what was coming. In the dense smoke and debris caused by the RPGs the two heavy machine guns started rattling out bursts into the wall of the tunnel to ricochet them down and out the tunnel mouth. This had been planned for and a shoulder-launched anti-tank missile was fired into the tunnel and guided into the bunker. The twenty pound, shaped charge smashed into the ferroconcrete barrier and exploded sending superhot gases and shrapnel through the barrier. This effectively removed the barrier as well as the machine guns. The Spetznaz troopers charged down the tunnel and engaged the few remaining defenders in a short-lived gun battle. The overwhelming odds in favor of the attackers washed away the last of the defenders in less than four minutes.

The nuclear technicians, armed with the information provided by Mark raced to the control room. Mark and General Serakov ran with them. Mark was amazed by the identical layout of this Siberian site to the one in Alaska. It was like they had developed the layout and stamped out thirty-two more versions of it.

The technicians completed their work in four minutes and declared the weapon secure. To completely eliminate all possibility of a hidden control lead the technicians ordered everyone else out of the control room and started bringing the weapon up from its position more than two miles underground. Once it got to the surface they would completely dismantle the control mechanism and separate the nuclear warhead from any other device the Master Prophets had connected to it.

Mark had not agreed that this step was necessary because the bomb in the original site had been brought out and was simply a bomb. All the control electronics had been in the control room. But it wouldn't hurt anything and the things needed to be removed as soon as possible to prevent accidental triggering.

It was going to take several hours to get the thing back to the surface so Mark walked outside the tunnel and asked for a situation report or sitrep from the other team members and troop commanders. Some reports had come in and some were still under their jamming or too deep in the shafts to communicate. Sarah reported that the Norway and Swedish bombs had been nullified and they were being raised also. Stan had a similar report from Finland. Jack was able to report that the Icelandic site was neutralized but that there was heavy fighting at the Fort Yukon site in Alaska. Apparently the Master Prophets had re-enforced that site after the first Alaskan site was overrun.

The Canadian troops at the four continental sites reported success but there was no word from Laura on Baffin Island as yet. Debbie came on the net and sounded fatigued. There had been significant casualties for Denmark because of an unexpected configuration in the layout of that site. There were more booby traps after the barrier that went off as the troops advanced. They had thirty-six confirmed dead and twelve seriously injured. But that was the last gasp for the defenders and the remaining troops overran the few defenders. That battle had no survivors on the MP side. They had secured the site and defused the control for the bomb. They were also getting it out of the ground to ensure that there were no time circuits involved that would set it off after the control leads had been severed. Mark told Debbie to tell the Danes that if that were the case, it would have gone off right away to maximize the effectiveness at the position the Master Prophets wanted it at. He prayed for the healing and full recovery of the fallen.

The Russian attack teams had managed to gain complete control of all twenty sites spread across the huge expanse that made up the Russian Federation including their site in Siberia.

Twenty minutes later Major Bill Carol was able to report that the Ft. Yukon site was under control and disabled. That meant that thirty-two of the thirty-three sites were neutralized. The only unreported site was the one on Baffin Island. There still wasn't any word from Laura.

Mark called the President and reported their success so far. Even if the prophets detonated the bomb on Baffin Island, their plan of threatening to destroy the world was finished. Mark's God-directed gamble had paid off and it was time to start hunting prophets.

Finally a call from Baffin Island came in. Mark was encouraged just by the fact they were getting a call from the island because if the bomb had gone off cell phones tended to melt in a nuclear fireball. He answered, "General Connelly here."

The voice on the other end of the conversation was not the one he expected. "General Connelly, you and your armies have interfered with my plans and I expect full repayment of that debt."

Mark replied, "Who am I speaking with?"

"My name is Alan Roswell. I am the Supreme Master Prophet and I want to arrange a meeting with you and 'General' Jack Malone. I have something named "Laura". You have a nail I'm interested in. I want to trade with the two of you."

CHAPTER TWENTY-EIGHT

When the attack on Baffin Island had started, try as she might, Laura couldn't get the Canadian troops to let her be part of the attacking force. She had to wait back behind a curve in the mountain like a good 'woman' General, so that she wouldn't get hurt. She wondered if they had any idea of the devastation the nuclear weapon was going to unleash if they didn't get it neutralized before the Master Prophets set it off.

Since the jamming began there was no radio communications. So, dragging the two men ordered to stay with her, she crawled up to where she could watch the action with binoculars. The attack was well staged and finally she saw the Major in charge of the troops dispatch one his men in her direction. She started towards the mine as the man was only halfway to her. As she walked into the cave she felt a familiarity with it from all the descriptions she had heard from Jack and the others about the mine near Buckland.

There was a considerable amount of damage and several bodies lying about. She was glad to see that none of them had Canadian uniforms.

The technicians came out to report that they had spiked the controls like the information suggested and were going to hoist the weapon up from the hole to secure it.

The Major nodded and told the rest of the troops to keep a watch but that the battle was won. He told the radio man to discontinue the jamming.

Everybody relaxed and Laura decided to go outside and call Mark and let him know that this site was under control. She said another prayer for her husband and the others for a safe conclusion to their attacks. As she walked alone through the mine towards the entrance she heard her name called from behind her.

"Laura!"

She started to turn when she realized that the troops here didn't use her first name, they only knew her as General Malone. A man stood there much closer to her than she thought possible. She had just walked by there and there was no one there. He was a big man and he wasn't in uniform. Her spirit jerked within her as she saw him. About that time, the Major who had also been heading out saw the man and yelled, "Hey, You!"

The man stepped closer to Laura and grabbed her. She tried to resist but was seemingly paralyzed. She couldn't even speak.

The Major ran towards them and the man picked up Laura and pulled her through the wall of the mine shaft. She felt terribly confined and very airy at the same time. Suddenly they came out of the wall to the outside. The man staggered and set her down. He rested against the wall of the mountain where they had come out. He was obviously exhausted by their trip through the wall. As he tried to get his strength back her paralysis got lighter and she could move a little. Then he stood up and she was frozen again. He looked around and then carried her over to a small land vehicle and threw her into the back seat. He got in the front and started driving. Laura hoped that the troops around the mine would see them and rescue her. But they drove right by several sentry troops and none of the men even seemed to notice the dune buggy-like vehicle. It was like they didn't exist to the soldiers.

Laura was fully aware but still couldn't move a muscle or utter a sound. They drove for a quite while here and there through the snow and ice and then the man stopped the vehicle and got out and walked away. Laura kept praying that God would release her but all she got in response was a calming peace and the feeling that it would be all right.

The man came back and looked at her. "Mrs. Malone, my name is Alan Roswell and I am the Supreme Leader of the Master Prophets of the Omniscience Temple. I require your husband's secret treasure that he is keeping. Now that I have you, I believe that he will part with it." At that he reached in and touched Laura. She still couldn't move but could talk. She coughed a couple of times and finally got out, "I don't think you understand my husband's dedication."

Alan Roswell smiled an evil smile. "I understand your husband better than he understands himself. And, you have no idea about my dedication" He looked behind her. I need your assistance in getting him to bring me the nail. In trade for your assistance, I won't detonate all the bombs that are being raised at our sites around the world. Do we have a deal?"

Laura couldn't believe what the man was saying. "You spent two years and untold millions of dollars to build all these sites and threaten the entire world just so you could get the nail?"

Again the man made an evil smile. "You really don't have a clue as to the importance of that piece of metal do you? But, to answer to your question, no, I did this so that I could control the world or destroy it as I wanted to. To get to this point I started the Omniscience Temple. I'll let you guess who the angel was that gave me the Omniscience Bible in the first place? I started and built the Master Prophets and conceived all this," He waved his hand in the direction of the mine.

Anger seemed to strike at Laura on several levels. This person had the ability and the cold calculation to kill her without a qualm. She was quite sure he wanted to but was keeping her alive for his own purposes. That led to several dark paths she kept her mind from following. Right now he seemed very bitter, frustrated, and mad. He kept sugarcoating everything and was subtly lying through his teeth whenever it pleased him. On the surface he was very believable and even friendly. But on the spiritual level he was a seething mass of vileness and hatred.

"Did I do this simply to get you where I had the power to overcome you? I don't think so. Your little group destroyed years of my work, years that I've had to work with these simple, idiotic pawns. You see, Mrs. Malone, I pray too. And I get guidance also. This little side event was planned years before your husband came into possession of the nail."

His eyes became hard. "Now, will you help me or can I toast all your friends and soldiers?"

Laura had been praying for words. "I don't think you'll do that." Actually thought Laura, he can't do it now. Her mind made the connections that allowed her to see the truth behind his lies. He hadn't seen this. His guidance had not advised him about this turn of events.

Roswell lifted an eyebrow, "Oh, and why not?"

Laura said, "Because you'd also destroy the nail in a nuclear fireball. Your master wouldn't be pleased. He would probably add your soul to all the 'toasted' ones but mark you for special displeasure." Laura had no idea where that came from.

The man looked unsure for a few seconds. "You may be right in that. Oh well, I guess I will take what I can in the old fashioned way." With that he reached in and plucked Laura off of the back seat like a rag doll. He carried her over to a helicopter that had been sitting out of her eyesight. He ran his hands over her body which distressed her, but he wasn't interested in attacking her on the physical sexual level. That might probably come later and she quailed at the thought. He found her cell phone and punched in the preset number.

While he was talking to Mark, she tried again to get something to move. Nothing did and her prayers were still being answered with peace and a feeling that things were going the way God wanted them to go.

Laura prayed for Jack concerning this insane plan that Alan Roswell had to get the nail, a nail that had once been covered with Yahshua's blood.

He concluded his conversation with a location and advised Mark and Jack to be there alone if they ever wanted to see Laura alive again. The cell phone dissolved in a burst of flame in his hand and he threw the ashes away. He climbed into the helicopter and started the engine and then the rotors started whirling. As he pulled pitch and lifted the helicopter off the ground Laura knew one important factor about his power. Much of it was illusion. Why else did he need vehicles to travel in on the ground and the air? God would have thought it and they would have been wherever they were going in the blink of an eye.

As she lay on the back seat of the helicopter she prayed for God's intervention in this effort of Satan's to get the nail from Jack. She then laid still and waited to hear from the Lord.

Some indeterminate amount of time later she felt a tug at her spirit. She heard a strong but gentle voice repeat the words of Joshua 1:5, *"No man shall be able to stand before you all the days of your life; as I was with Moses, so I will be with you. I will not leave you nor forsake you."*

Laura relaxed as best she could. The knowledge that things were going God's way went a long way to make that possible.

CHAPTER TWENTY-NINE

Mark excused himself after congratulating General Serakov and promising that the American President would call his President and explain matters.

Heading back to his Russian helicopter that would take him to the closest air base for a flight to the U.S. he called Jack. After Jack answered Mark laid out the problem for him. "Jack, Baffin Island called in and everything went okay on the raid. They got the circuitry shut down and are in the process of retrieving the bomb from the bottom of the shaft. But there has been a hitch with Laura."

Jack sent a quick prayer to heaven for his wife and the news he was about to get.

The Major in charge of the Baffin Island raid said that he saw a man grab Laura and then he disappeared. It was like he walked through the solid stone wall of the tunnel carrying her."

Jack said, "I'll be there as quickly as I can."

Mark told him, "No. Don't come here. Alan Roswell called me on Laura's phone and arranged a trade for the nail. He wants us to meet him tonight at Midnight at the Omniscience Temple in Salem, Massachusetts."

Jack was quiet for a few seconds and Mark knew he was praying. "Okay, I will meet you in Salem at 10:00 p.m. if you can make it. You're a lot farther away than I am."

Mark simply said, "I'm sure he knows that but I'll still make it."

Jack hung up and started to call the other teams and have them stand down.

Mark hung up and called General Serakov and asked if he could arrange an emergency ride in a MIG-35. The General said, "We don't have a MIG-35 as yet."

Mark told him where there were three of them and that they had the ability to get him back to the U.S. in time to help save a person more important than the President at this time. The General thought for a minute, "What the heck, in for a kopeck in for a ruble." He told Mark to be at the tiny town of Zigansk in forty minutes and he would get his ride, but he had to promise that the plane and pilot would not be held in the U.S.

Mark assured him that he, General Mark Connelly would guarantee that the pilot would be refueled and on his way back before Mark left the airport.

"Das Vadanya Comrade" Replied the General, "Until we meet again, which I am sure we will."

Mark had the helicopter head for Zigansk.

On the way to Massachusetts, Jack stayed in continual prayer for the safety of his wife. He did not get a confirmation that Laura would come out of this alive and well, just that she was fulfilling God's will on Earth and she was in his hands.

Jack tried to imagine his life on Earth if he lost Laura. He decided at that point he would do whatever it took to keep her safe, even if it meant giving up the nail and his life to boot. The heat and anger started building and kept building each mile as he flew out of Canada toward the northeastern shore of the United States.

The Canadian F-22 landed at Logan International Airport a little after nine that night. Jack thanked the pilot and saluted him. The F-22 with the Maple Leaf insignia on the wings made the turnaround and lifted off from Boston's air field ten minutes later for a short flight home.

Jack had been carrying the treasure with him during the campaign because he had been led to do so by the Holy Spirit. He got a rental and drove to Salem which is like an oceanic suburb of Boston to the northeast. He was in the area of the Omniscience Temple's gaudy building by ten p.m. He stopped at a burger barn and had a sandwich while he waited for midnight.

About ten minutes after eleven he called Mark on his cell phone and they met at the burger shop. They compared notes and began praying for the power and ability to face this upper-level demonic personality. They prayed for cleansing and asked the Lord to show them any faults or defects that the enemy could use against them. They prayed and repented of everything that the Holy Spirit showed them. When they were done, Mark made the comment to Jack, "When am I going to get over this egotistical pride thing?"

Jack smiled, "About the same time I get over my superiority sins." They both looked at each other and shook their heads. "Okay" said Mark, "Its show time."

They got into Jack's car and drove to the Church building. Walking up to the front of the church they heard a car horn behind them. They stopped and looked back. In a minute Sarah, Stan, and Debbie ran up to them. "Where do you think you're going without us?" asked Sarah.

Mark grinned, "Obviously, nowhere." Jack said, "Roswell said that we had to be alone."

Sarah said, "God told us to be here."

The whole team turned and walked up to the massive front doors of the building and entered.

The lobby was huge. A thirty foot tall statue of Alan Roswell defending three 'poor', maligned witches from a rabid crowd filled the center of the lobby. Ignoring the symbolism there, the team made its way into the sanctuary. On the platform was Laura on her knees, completely unbound but also unmoving and, to her right, a large man that everyone assumed was Alan Roswell.

The Prophet looked at the group entering and said in a loud voice. "I didn't invite a crowd, just you Generals."

Sarah yelled back to him, "We're all Generals you twit." thereby setting the tone of the encounter.

Alan ignored her. He made a large sword appear in his hand and held it above Laura's neck. "It doesn't matter, but don't interfere unless you want to have her pretty neck in two pieces." Turning to Jack he spoke directly at him. "Did you bring the nail?"

Jack replied, "Yes, I did." He then held up the cloth covered spike.

The head of the Master Prophets lowered his brows and stared at the package. Jack could feel it vibrating in his hand.

Alan Roswell straightened up. "Bring it to me now." he demanded.

Jack shook his head. "Not until I get my wife back without harm."

Alan shook his head. "You don't have any say in this matter, child. I was here long before you were born. I make the rules and neither you nor your God is going to dictate to me what is to happen tonight."

Mark spoke up. "Aren't you going to rant and rave over losing your great threat to control the world?"

Alan turned his baleful glaze onto Mark, "You insignificant insect. I could have squashed you like a bug anytime I wanted to. I let you take those sites. I could have detonated those weapons at any time. You need to get on your knees and thank me for not incinerating you and the rest of the world."

Mark was hot at this point but he knew how to needle someone like this. He pointed his finger at him and replied, "I will never get on my knees to you. You are an evil slime and as such you are only worth the lesson we need to learn to prevent more like you from ever ascending to a position of power."

Mark got a word from the Lord, "You couldn't set those bombs off because you never knew we were coming. Your spies were in the wrong places. By the time you knew what was going on it was too late for you to do anything. You totally squandered the lives of your followers and the time and money you put into that stupid scheme. And I'll tell you one more thing, you bombastic bag of worm puke. You completely missed the boat on what the honest people of this world would do to your Omniscience Temples when they learn how you threatened to end their world. You and every one of your Master Prophets will be hunted down by every government in the world with the enthusiastic support of the public until they are all in jail or dead."

Alan laughed. "You idiot, do you think I care one whit about these people or this temple? It was a means to an end. Yes, I'll grant you that you stole an opportunity from me. But there will be other chances."

Responding to the urging of the Holy Spirit Jack knew what he was going to say was the truth. "You never planned to accept any agreement did you?" When the man on the platform didn't respond, Jack continued. "You always planned to detonate those bombs regardless of the agreement or rebellion of the world governments, didn't you?"

Alan chuckled, "You are starting to understand the real power in this world. It's not the useless human life forms that cram this planet. I wouldn't care if everyone on this miserable ball of mud is wiped out of existence in the next minute."

Sarah stepped forward. "Aw, are you and your Father still upset about the fact that God made humans higher than either of you in heaven?"

Obviously stung by this comment, the dark form on the platform screamed. It wasn't a desperate cry but angry denouncement of God's will that fueled it. "I am already higher than your God.

Mark drew his handgun and fired three rapid shots at the man on the platform. Roswell held up his hand and the bullets stopped in mid-air and fell to the floor. He then pointed at the team standing twenty feet away. All five of them were frozen into position. Mark's pistol was still pointed at Roswell but he couldn't make his finger pull the trigger again.

"Now," The form on the stage showed an evil grin. "Don't you go anywhere I'll be right along to collect that nail, but first I want to give you an example of my power." He smiled and raised the sword in his hands over his head and swung it down at Laura's bent neck. Jack's heart stopped beating. Laura was the world to him and this thing was taking that away from him. He was powerless to stop the sword as it fell towards the person he loved the most. In his mind he screamed, "Yahveh save her!"

What happened next was hard to describe. As the sword descended towards her, Laura moved, her golden armor flared into being and the flaming sword appeared in her right hand. She half rose and blocked the blade from the demonic being attacking her. Even though he had put tremendous effort in the stroke her sword stopped his as if he had hit the center of the Earth. Laura stood up and parried another slash of the enemy's sword without effort. Try as he would he couldn't break her defense.

Laura stood face to face with Alan Roswell and he looked smaller than she did. "Do you understand the fate that you have earned?" Jack was surprised that he didn't hear a dulcet voice this time.

The being that was represented by the form of Alan Roswell replied to the power of God. "I do, and I will never bow to You, I have the right to rule."

The golden sword flashed and even though he parried the blow the sword sundered his weapon and cut him in half. His body seemed to catch on fire and his scream was hideous for a second and then it faded away until the sound disappeared completely.

The power holding the team was gone and they ran to the platform where Laura was standing. Her armor faded out of sight and she looked at the five people standing below her and nodded. Then she smiled and turned to the stairs. As she came to the bottom of the stairs Jack enfolded her in his arms and cried on her neck. She just hugged him.

CHAPTER THIRTY

As the plane from Washington winged its way to Denver the team relaxed. Jack and Laura, sitting two rows in front of the others were talking quietly. He held her hand and told her of his feelings when he saw the prophet's sword coming down on her neck.

Laura could feel the emotional impact that scene had on him. She squeezed his hand. "I'm sorry that it happened the way that it did, with you having to watch. But I think I understand how God used us and the nail to make Roswell, or whatever its name really was, vulnerable within the spiritual rules that God has laid out."

Jack cocked his head and waited for the explanation.

She thought back to the Omniscience Temple in Salem. "He couldn't move on us because, at least in this circumstance, we were God's anointed and if he hurt us he would lose, well, everything. Roswell knew that. My abduction and the threat to kill me was a bluff to get you and the nail there. God was aware of your love for me and that you were willing to give up the nail or even die to save me. Your serious belief of his threat fit nicely into the plan the prophet had laid out. He didn't have to hurt God's anointed but by acting like he would, he could gain what he wanted. But the good Lord knows how feisty and irreverent that Mark and Sarah are to bullies. He was counting on them making the prophet so mad he would violate the rules and become subject to judgment. And, boy did they ever, I was frozen in position and couldn't speak. So when they went off on him I expected the worst."

Laura patted Jack's hand. "As he was raising his sword with murder in his heart against God's anointed, his power over me was broken and I felt the armor and the sword appear as I started to move. You saw the rest."

Jack leaned over and kissed her. "I was so happy I almost jumped for joy, but, being frozen helped to maintain my dignity."

She laughed, "I could feel your happiness all the way on the platform you know."

Jack thought for a few seconds as he relived that ultimate low and high in his life. "I didn't hear that extra voice-over when you were condemning the prophet on the platform."

Laura got serious, "I know. That was only me that time." She thought back over the other times she had been used by the Lord. "In Tel Aviv, when we prayed for David Zahavy after he'd been shot, that wasn't me at all. I think it was Rose that ran the show then. After I met her in my dream and was given the armor, I was half in charge in the coven and even more so in the Oval Office. That's why destroying Tom Kendric bothered me so much. I was being trained by Rose to handle God's judgments. In Salem it was like Rose did the fighting and I heard what the Lord wanted me to say to Alan Roswell and repeated it word for word. That last sword strike was my interpretation of what the Lord said to do. After that, I guess I graduated. Rose will now guide me but not rule in my place. No more dulcet voices."

Jack thought about the new level that Laura had attained and was both proud and glad for her. They went to sleep holding hands.

Four days later, there was a victory celebration at the Malone's house. Besides the team, Minister Throman, Sheryl Cantor and Jenny Samuels were there. Having stuffed themselves with a great meal and dessert they retired to the family room to tell each other what had transpired with each of them. After they had each related their stories. There were many questions. Laura led off with hers.

"Why was Alan Roswell on Baffin Island and able to catch me yet he couldn't tell that there was an attack coming?"

Jack had done much of the debriefing of the Baffin Island Canadian troops. He fielded that one. "I'm pretty sure that we caught the 'prophet' with his knickers down. He was so sure he had the stupid little humans figured out that he never checked beyond the spies he had near the heads of the government and the military. The new Chairman of the Joint Chiefs of Staff never let on to anyone what was going on, not even to the Joint Chiefs until the attacks were under way."

Jack held up his hand as everyone started to talk. "That's not all. The interrogation of one of the surviving staff for the Baffin Island site confirmed that one of their men spotted Laura in the field outside the site. It was a freak thing and he didn't remain long enough to see anyone else. It seems that the officer called Boise from the site and talked to the Prophet himself to inform him of her being there. The Prophet interpreted her presence as another attack of the six of us only. Two minutes later, the Prophet himself appears out of thin air in the control room. That's over three thousand miles in two minutes. Obviously he could transport himself anywhere he wanted to instantly."

Laura chimed in, "Why did he have to bring me back to the U.S. in a helicopter then?"

Jack smiled, "You had the answer all along. Remember you told me that after he got you through the wall he was exhausted? I think he could move his spiritual essence and the shell that was Alan Roswell without too much effort, but when it came to moving someone else the cost was much higher."

Minister Throman agreed. "It's a trait that they seem to have. I like to think that they are so full of hot air they can do anything with themselves but if they try to take on a human burden they are grounded."

Stan and Debbie had been talking between themselves and Stan threw in a question. "What is the latest on the Omniscience Temple and the Master Prophets?"

Mark took that one. "First, the Master Prophets have been branded as a terrorist organization by all of the world's powers. They are being hunted down and arrested for trial. The Omniscience Temple has been declared a racist organization and is being shut down everywhere by concerned citizens. It isn't meeting much resistance because they have had their representatives hounded from every level of government after the President's speech denouncing them and their hate tactics. Also, the membership in the 'church' has plummeted since Alan Roswell is no longer there. All the healings and miracles have been lost, reverted back to their natural state, which figures since they were only illusions and powered by the Alan Roswell being. When Laura terminated his stay on Earth his power ceased. This betrayal has made the temple believer's sore enough to hurt anyone trying to stop them from leaving. I hear that the Boise city council voted to bulldoze the Omniscience Temple's Center there and put in a park."

Sarah nodded, "That's about what it was worth to start with."

Sheryl added that all the kids from the school had recovered and were back at school again. The security on the property had been heightened to a point that even parents are worried about being strip searched before they could get in to see their own children. But, none of them are complaining. The school has made the crater with the back end of the bus in it a monument of sorts to act as a continual reminder."

Jenny added that the Satanists movement had gotten a black eye from their 'rioting' and had also earned the bad housekeeping seal of disapproval from the state government and got labeled properly as a hate group.

The entire group continued to discuss their plans for the future and relax after their efforts.

Rose smiled at Caleb and said, "They did well didn't they? Are they now allowed to enjoy a deserved rest?"

Caleb nodded, "But it's only for a short time. There is another event coming that will make all of them look back on this time as easy."

Rose's color darkened somewhat, "Do they have to stand against it?"

Caleb nodded, "Why do you think God has been training them? They have done well with little and now face much more in His service. Don't concern yourself about the challenge facing them, you and I will be there too, as we continue our battle with the minions of the evil one."

Rose looked at the happy group and whispered as she faded out of sight. "Enjoy yourselves while you can." Sitting with her husband and friends in her house in Denver, Laura cocked her head to one side slightly, and then smiled.

The Crossfire team will return in *"Spirit Crossfire"*.

If this story has awakened your spirit or moved you to seek the love of Christ and His power for your life, whether you've never accepted Jesus as your savior or you've fallen away, repeat the following prayer and begin a most wonderful journey into eternal life with Him today.

Father God in heaven, As You said in Your Holy Word, (Romans 10:9) that if we confess the Lord our God and believe in our hearts that God raised Jesus from the dead, we shall be saved.

(The prayer on the next page is a sample prayer when asking Jesus into your heart as your Savior. You can also pray this in your own words.)

Salvation Prayer

Dear God in heaven, I come to you in the name of Jesus. I confess to You that I am a sinner, and I am sorry for my sins and the life that I have lived; I need your forgiveness. I believe that your only begotten Son Jesus Christ shed His precious blood on the cross at Calvary and died for my sins, and I am now willing to turn from my sin.

Right now I confess Jesus as the Lord of my life and my soul. With all my heart, I truly believe that your Holy Spirit raised Jesus from the dead. Today I accept Jesus Christ as my personal Savior and according to Your Word, right now I am saved.

I thank you Jesus, for your unlimited grace which has saved me from my sins. I thank you Jesus that your grace that never leads to license, but rather it always leads to repentance. Therefore Lord Jesus, transform my life so that I may bring glory and honor to you alone and not to myself.

I thank you Lord Jesus, for dying for me at Calvary and giving me eternal life.

Amen.

If you just said this prayer and you meant it with all your heart, believe that you are now saved and have been born again.

You may ask, "Now that I am saved, what do I do next?" First of all you need to get into a spirit-filled, bible-based church that teaches the Scriptures, and you need to study God's Word.

Once you have found a church home, you will want to become water-baptized. By accepting Christ you are baptized in the spirit, but it is through water-baptism that you publically announce your obedience to the Lord Jesus. Water baptism is a symbol of your salvation from the dead. You were dead but now you live, for Jesus Christ has redeemed you for a price! The price was His atoning death on the cross. May God Bless You!

www.ingramcontent.com/pod-product-compliance
Lightning Source LLC
Chambersburg PA
CBHW071334250626
47159CB00004B/1597